D1562501

WRATH

WRATH

*The Tribulation has begun,
and the Church is still here!*

D. R. ROQUEMORE

WRATH

Copyright © 2017 by D. R. Roquemore

World Ahead Press is a division of WND Books. The views and opinions expressed in this book are those of the author and do not necessarily reflect the official policy of positions of WND Books.

Paperback ISBN: 978-1-94421-78-0
eBook ISBN: 978-1-944212-79-7

Printed in the United States of America
16 17 18 19 20 21 LSI 9 8 7 6 5 4 3 2 1

Edited by
Lee Titus Elliott & Taylor Haydon

Please send your comments, questions, or requests for speaking engagements to:
wrathbooks@gmail.com
For details on all of the books in the Wrath series, visit:
www.thewrathbooks.com

CONTENTS

1. Un Charter 99   7
2. The Discovery   19
3. The Pre-Wrath Rapture   26
4. It's True   39
5. Tolerance   48
6. Leaving the Bubble   59
7. The Watchers   66
8. The Epiphany   71
9. Bad-To-Worse   78
10. The Club of Ten   86
11. Geneva   94
12. The Antichrist   112
13. Day Two   129
14. Church   133
15. Final Planning   152
16. Saving Alyssa   162
17. Escape   171

18. The Cabin   182

19. The End Of America   199

20. The Starving Family   212

21. Our New Church   224

22. A Close Call   238

23. The Rescue   241

24. The Abomination   253

25. The Image   260

26. Rescued!   268

CHAPTER ONE

UN CHARTER 99

"Hey Chloe, what did you get on the last history test?" Taylor asks.

"The same as last time, a 98," I respond.

"You are so going to be some stuffy history professor with old-lady glasses one day!" Taylor says.

I have to deny it, even though it's probably true.

"Taylor, I've changed my college major three times this year, and I'm still in the 11th grade! I have no idea what I'm going to be! Besides, unless I get into an Ivy League school, which isn't going to happen, my parents won't pay for me to major in history. They say I'll never find a job. Its business, medicine, or law, remember?"

As usual, Taylor can't leave it alone. "Yeah right," she continues. "It will happen, Chloe! You're made for it!"

I try to change the subject. "Hey, why is Mr. Bradley late? He's never late. It will be chaos in here if he doesn't arrive soon." Mr. Bradley, the ever-punctual history / English teacher. More like a college professor than a high school teacher.

"I don't know," Taylor responds. "He definitely has not been himself lately. He seems distracted by something. Maybe it's all the rumors about how the Central Zone is not happy with Zone One."

Zone One. That's how we refer to ourselves. Canada, the United States, and Mexico became Zone One a few years ago. After Russia, Iran, and Israel got into a nuclear war, the UN came up with the bright idea to divide the whole world into ten Zones. The idea had been around for years. It even had its own name: UN Charter 99. Each Zone has its own president. I guess the world is supposed to be one big happy family now. As part of our education, they made us memorize the members of each Zone:

Zone One: Canada, the United States, and Mexico
Zone Two: Western Europe
Zone Three: Japan
Zone Four: Australia, New Zealand, South Africa
Zone Five: Eastern Europe, Pakistan, Afghanistan, Russia, and the former countries of the Soviet Union
Zone Six: Central America, South America, Cuba, the Caribbean Islands
Zone Seven: the Middle East and North Africa
Zone Eight: the rest of Africa, except South Africa
Zone Nine: South Asia and Southeast Asia, including India
Zone Ten: China

With the zoning in place, they then developed a majority voting system. If at least seven of the ten Zone presidents agree on a policy, all ten Zones must comply. Our Zone, Zone Three and Zone Four, always seem to be in the minority. The European Zone seems to be the most enthusiastic about this new world order stuff. At first, the Central Zone policies showed some level of respect for the constitutions in each Zone's countries, but not lately. The requirement to register your firearms with the Central Zone authorities didn't go over well here in the Lone Star State. Half of my friends said their parents ignored the requirement. Everyone is afraid that the next step will be confiscation. There would be an all-out war if they tried that here in Texas!

Our teacher, Mr. Bradley, had been talking a great deal lately about potential new Zone policies related to private schools. The UN and the Central Zone have always hated private schools and home schools. Recently there were rumors about a recent vote on this by the ten Zone Presidents. We never know what they are voting on and when. In the beginning, they were more transparent. The thought of moving to a public school puts knots in my stomach. I've been in private Christian schools since preschool. It would be a complete nightmare to lose all my friends my last year in high school.

The tension is heavy in and out of the classroom. Lately, the world seems more uncertain than ever before. Kids don't joke around like they used to. It's like they're all imagining the worst but are afraid to talk about it. Taylor doesn't even mess with me that much anymore. We hardly ever joke around. Most of us don't talk a lot about what might be coming. It's too upsetting. What seventeen-year-old wants to think about being thrown out of her school and forced to endure the official "Zone" curriculum?

My handful of friends who attend public school tell me that everything has changed at their schools within the last two years. The instructors are required to show films on the Russia / Iran / Israel nuclear war. The films were full of grotesque images of mangled, radiated bodies. It took seven months to remove all of the corpses from the battlefield. Because of the high radiation levels, the battlefield will be uninhabitable for a thousand years. In the films, they used the war as justification for the World Zones. The Zones are supposed to serve as a solution to everything—from wars to income inequality. I don't buy any of it! I hate the Zone system.

Taylor pokes me in the shoulder, bringing me back to reality.

"Hey Chloe, there's Mr. Bradley!"

I look out the window and see him walking toward our classroom. He had cleared the middle school library, so that meant we only had a couple of minutes to quiet down. That's a big task for a bunch of gossipy eleventh graders! It's 10:20 in the morning, and he's twenty minutes late. That has never happened before. We hold our breath as he walks in. It's unusually quiet until Grayson blurts out, "Hey, isn't there a fifteen-minute rule in high school?" Mr. Bradley says nothing. Now it's really quiet.

He sets a notepad he carried in with him on his desk. He doesn't look up at us until he is leaning on the front of his desk. My stomach is in knots. I feel like throwing up. Something bad is coming. I've never seen him so sad since I've known him.

"I know that some of you have heard the rumors about new Zone rules related to private schools," he begins. My head is spinning. I want to run out of the room, but I feel frozen, like in a dream. I want to move, but I can't.

"There was a recent vote on this issue," Mr. Bradley says. "As usual, the outcome was seven in favor, three opposed."

One, Three, and Four again, I'm sure. We never win. It makes me sick.

"They have decided," he continues, "to close all private, charter, and home schools effective at the end of the school year. Our Zone strongly disapproved, but there is nothing we can do. Seven Zones approved the change, so it's binding. There will be an official worldwide announcement today at seven p.m., our time."

I can hear Elizabeth starting to cry, softly at first, then more loudly. It's the only sound for what seems like an eternity. Katherine starts to cry as well. I can feel the tears welling up inside me, but I fight them back. I'm too angry to cry.

"How can they do this to us?" asks William. "We have a constitution! We are a sovereign nation! Why can't we just leave the system? They can't stop us!"

Other boys join in with similar comments.

My mind flashes back to that scene in *Gone with the Wind*, where the Southerners are longing for war, for independence from the Union. We all know how things ended for the South. Our struggle seems equally hopeless to me. One country against the entire Zone system? We could never win, even if Zones Three and Four joined us.

"I know how incredibly upsetting this must be for all of you," Mr. Bradley continues. "I can't even begin to tell you how upset I am. I am afraid for all of you. I am afraid for our country, and I fear what might come next. What other freedoms will they take from us? You are all just starting your lives. I've already lived most of mine. I never thought I'd see this happen in our country."

Elizabeth is completely sobbing now. I sense that Mr. Bradley is feeling remorse for his moment of candor, but he has always treated us like adults. He has always been completely honest with us. I find myself moving toward Elizabeth. As I do, several other girls do the same. A few of us begin to gather at her desk and wrap ourselves around her. Soon all twenty-one of us are in a circle at her desk, like some kind of football huddle. Mr. Bradley joins in, and I can hear others starting to cry. I'm still too angry to cry. My world has just turned upside down; there must be something I can do about it!

Our huddle is interrupted by the voice of our headmaster over the intercom. There will be an assembly for grades six through twelve in the Performing Arts Center at 10:45. It's immediately obvious to me why they've excluded the lower school kids. This change is too big, too emotional. I'm sure the administration will ask the lower school parents to break the news to the younger students at home tonight. I can't imagine how my younger sister Hannah will take the news. She'll be devastated. She's so outgoing and friendly. She's convinced that every kid in third grade is her best friend.

As soon as the announcement about the assembly comes across the intercom, my classmates start heading for the iPhone cubbies. Mr. Bradley doesn't object. Everyone is doing the same thing at once, texting their parents. From the responses around the room, it's clear that a few parents already heard the news. Some phones start ringing. Elizabeth calms down enough to call her mom but then starts crying again as soon as she hears her mom's voice.

We only have a few minutes until the assembly, so I have to decide very quickly whom to call. I call Dad.

"Hey, Chloe, what's up?"

He doesn't know. That makes sense. He would have called. There are so many conversations going on at once in the room that it's hard to think straight.

"The UN is closing our school, Dad! They are closing every private school in the world! They voted on it last night. Mr.

Bradley just told us. There's an assembly in a few minutes. Dad, I'm really scared! If they can do this, then what else is coming? Are they going to come after us because we're Christians?!" I'm sure he can sense the fear in my voice.

"Oh no! Honey, I am so sorry you're going through this. I had heard rumors, but I didn't think it would happen so soon. We'll get through this together. I love you, honey. Are they going to let you all go for the day after the assembly?"

I have no idea. "I don't know, Dad. Probably. I can't imagine anything productive happening the rest of the day. Or for the next two months."

Dad tries to calm me down. "I'll leave work by two thirty today and meet you at home. Does your mom know?" he asks.

"I have no idea. Can you call her, Dad? We have to go to the assembly now."

"I'll call her now" is all he has time to say before I hang up.

We all start to shuffle out of the classroom, and I deliberately hold back a little so I can talk to Mr. Bradley on the way to the Performing Arts Center. It's only a three-minute walk, so I know I'll need to focus my questions. He hardly acknowledges my blatant attempt to corner him as we exit the room.

"Mr. Bradley, I have to ask you where this is all headed. I mean, are they going to throw us to the lions eventually?" My voice breaks up as I say this. I'm determined not to cry. Joey and Katherine are eavesdropping, but I don't care.

"Let's not jump to any conclusions, Chloe," Mr. Bradley says. "After all, they've banned private schools and home schools in many parts of the world for decades. They aren't feeding Christians to lions in Madrid now, are they?"

I continue, "No, but this is America! We are supposed to be the most democratic and free nation on the planet. If they can do this here, over the objections of our Zone president, then what else can they do?"

Mr. Bradley doesn't respond. He's holding back, which is not normal for him. We run out of time, and we're in the Performing Arts Center before I can cross-examine him. I somehow manage to find one of my best friends, Jane, in all the chaos. She has the same concerned look on her face that I'm sure I have. She gestures toward a couple of empty seats about ten rows from the front, and we grab them. Normally, each grade has an assigned area to sit in, but no one seems to care. We don't normally have both the middle and upper school kids in the Performing Arts Center at the same time, so latecomers have to stand on the sides or in the back. I notice that a few parents have shown up. They must have gotten the news before us and headed straight to the school. A couple of them are sitting with their kids, but most are standing in the back.

Our headmaster, Mr. Morris, steps to the microphone and asks everyone to move to the middle seats so we can fit in more kids. I can see his administrative assistant at the edge of the stage behind him. Even from this distance, I can tell she has been crying. She's holding some papers in her hand.

"I need to ask everyone to finish their phone calls and texting. We need to get started here in about one minute," says Mr. Morris.

Gradually the room begins to quiet down. All eyes are now on Mr. Morris. I wonder if the middle school kids know what's happened. My guess is that the ones with siblings in the upper school already know.

"I know this is an unusual time for an assembly, and I want to thank all of you for your flexibility. I'll get right to the topic at hand. About two hours ago, we received word from the

Central Zone Administration site about a vote held last night. The results we not released until this morning around eight thirty, our time. We spent some time informing our teachers and administrators as soon as we received the news. The Zones voted on whether to allow for the continuing existence of private, charter, and home schools. By a vote of seven to three, they decided to require that all private, charter, and home schools be permanently closed, effective the end of this school year."

There is an audible gasp in the room. I can hear people saying, "No, no, no." I can hear some moms starting to cry in the back of the room.

Mr. Morris continues. "Unfortunately, there is no short-term appeal process for Zone decisions. As most of you know, if seven of the ten Zone Presidents agree on a policy, it is binding for all ten Zones. Once a vote on a particular topic is in place, it is not eligible for reconsideration for three years. I am so sorry, but we will be closing Addison Christian Academy, effective June 15, two weeks after the official end of the school year."

Jane starts to cry, but quietly. For the third time this morning I can feel myself fighting back tears. I'm still too angry to cry. I feel like if I cry, the Central Zone will have won. I can't let them win.

"Because this is all so sudden, I don't have additional details that I can share with you, but I'll try now to answer any questions you might have," Mr. Morris continues. In the haste to call the meeting, no one thought to bring in extra microphones for the audience.

Hands start to go up. Mr. Morris calls on a student, Emma Kate, near the front. Emma's a senior and an exceptional student.

"Can we just ignore their decision? This is Texas, and we are fiercely independent. Can't we just tell them to get lost?"

Clapping breaks out all over the room. Someone yells, "Screw the Zones." Probably not the most appropriate response from a Christian school student.

Mr. Morris motions with his hands to quiet the room. "As you know, the Central Zone Administration has established its own enforcement agency, and they have offices in every major city. They are not accountable to the local police authorities. They have the power to arrest and prosecute citizens in any Zone who violate Central Zone policies. So, while I agree with the sentiment, in reality, we don't stand much of a chance."

"So then let's get out of the Zones system!" someone shouts from the back of the room. More clapping and hollering.

This must be how revolutions or civil wars get started, is all I can think at that moment. History is my favorite subject, and I can recall with some detail the beginnings of several major world uprisings of the past three hundred years. I have to believe people all over our country feel the same way.

Mr. Morris motions again to quiet the crowd. "I think the right thing to do now is to pray. God is still on his throne, and he has allowed this to happen for a reason. Remember in the early church when great persecution arose after Stephen was stoned to death? The gospel spread to the entire known world as a result. Perhaps the biblical truth that you all possess will now be spread to all of the public schools in North Texas.

"We are going to end school at twelve noon today to allow you all to be home with your families. We will have after school care for the lower and middle school students until five o'clock today. I would ask that our middle school students head to their home rooms now and that the upper school students go to their fourth-period classes. While we were in this meeting an automated e-mail, text, and call were sent to all parents, letting them know about the noon closure. Please know that our teachers and administrators will be praying for all of you. You may now return to your classrooms."

With that, the assembly was over. There was nothing more to say. No amount of arguing or fighting words were going to undo what the Central Zone had just done to all of us. I stay in my chair with Jane as everyone moves toward the exits. I check my phone and see a text from my mom saying she would see me at home. Jane has a similar text from her mom. I want to find Mr. Bradley again, but I know he will have his hands full with fourth-period students. I have a strong sense that he knows more about what's coming than he let on in the hallway coming over here. I'm sure he wants to protect us in some way, but I need to know what he knows. I need to know what to expect. If we are now going to be actively targeted by the Central Zone, then I want to be prepared for it.

I turn to Jane, who is still working through her many texts.

"Jane, what do you think this means? What do you think is coming next?"

She hardly lifts her head, and when she does, her eyes are red.

"Chloe, I think we're in trouble, a lot of trouble. I don't just mean us Christians. I keep up with this Zone stuff, and the Central Zone leadership doesn't like Zones One, Three, and Four. We never vote with the majority. We are always protesting. Maybe if we still had control over our nukes. I'm sorry. I'm not trying to scare you. But look, we gave up that power two years ago. Everyone did except Israel. How could we possibly defend ourselves now? Even if 70 percent of us rebelled and said we want out of the Zones, they could just nuke us all!"

It's not something I had ever considered. Unlike Jane, I deliberately avoid news articles and rumors related to the Zones. I just want to be a seventeen-year-old kid and enjoy my childhood. I have that sick feeling in my stomach again, the kind I always get fifteen minutes before a basketball game, but much worse this time. It feels like someone kicked me in the gut. I feel like I'm going to panic. Jane sees my building anxiety.

"I'm sorry, Chloe. I don't want to freak you out. Maybe this will be the last bad thing they do to us. Remember what Mr. Morris just said. Everything happens for a reason. We'll get through it."

I turn so I'm looking directly at her.

"You've been a great friend, Jane," I say. "I am going to miss not finishing high school with you. We have to make every effort to stay connected starting this summer."

Jane is nodding her head, and her eyes are filling with tears. I finally give in, wrap my arms around her, and let myself cry.

After the early dismissal, I pick up my younger brother Jackson and my younger sister Hannah around noon, and we head home. Jackson, who is fifteen, was in the assembly with me, so he knows what has happened. Hannah, who is only eight, has no idea. I'm sure Mom and Dad will talk to Hannah separately once we are all home. Hannah makes a comment about how awesome it is to get out of school early.

"Yeah, pretty cool" is all I can say.

No one says another word on the drive home.

CHAPTER TWO

THE DISCOVERY

My dad gets home around three thirty, and he and Mom head into their room to talk. They keep their door closed, which under normal circumstances would be unusual, but today is anything but normal. Jackson is either in extreme denial, or he doesn't care, because he is in his room gaming five minutes after we get home. I go to my room and wait for the inevitable family meeting. I'm sure Mom and Dad will want to talk to Hannah separately before we all meet as a family. After about thirty minutes, I hear them call for her. I can hear her running down the stairs. Her world is about to change, and she has no idea what's coming. The rest of us had heard and understood the rumors. Although we didn't want to believe it, we knew this could happen. Hannah's world, by contrast, has been safe and protected, until now.

About twenty minutes later I hear someone coming up the stairs. There's a soft knock on my door, and I hear Dad's voice. "Chloe, we are ready for our family meeting now" is all he says. He doesn't come in. I hear him knock on Jackson's door a few seconds later. I try to compose myself. My stomach is still churning. I want to be a little girl again. I want all of this to go away. I have an overwhelming sense that this is just the beginning of some great darkness that is coming. I don't feel safe. I pull myself together and head down the stairs.

We all gather in the living room. As always, Jackson is the last one to join us. Hannah is sitting on the floor, pretending to play with her rainbow loom. It's rare for her to sit so still or so quiet. I glance at my mom and dad's faces. I can see their concerned expressions. I can tell that, just like me, they are thinking ahead to what is coming. I wonder how much they'll tell us.

"Mom and I want to talk to all of you about what has happened," Dad says. "Addison Christian and all other private schools will have to close at the end of the school year. You'll all be attending public schools in the fall. Chloe and Jackson, you'll be at Hebron High, and, Hannah, you'll be at Castle Hills Elementary. I think you know that the public schools are actually pretty good here in our community. That's one of the reasons we bought a home here. Having good public schools helps with resale values."

"What's a resale value?" asks Hannah.

Dad responds, "It means if you have to sell your house, you'll get a good price for it because people like to live where the schools are good."

Hannah jumps back in. "Are we going to sell our house?"

"No, Hannah. We don't have any plans right now to sell," Dad responds. I'm not so sure if he means it.

I don't know what the boundaries are since Hannah is part of the conversation, so I tread lightly at first.

"Dad, where do you think this is all headed?" I ask. "Do you think our Zone will try to get out of the system? If we can't get out, what else do you think is coming?"

Dad is quiet for a minute. I'm sure he will choose his words carefully.

"Ever since they put the Zones in place, things have gotten more difficult, not just for Christians but for everyone," he says. "The Central Zone seems to be peeling back our freedoms one by one. It has been gradual so far, but closing the schools was a big one. They don't want Americans, Canadians or Mexicans to think of themselves as citizens of one country. They want us all to think of ourselves as citizens of the world. With the ten Zone presidents, we are now very close to a One World Government. However, there is still hope because Zones One, Three, and Four are very strong economically, and it seems clear that we want out of this arrangement. At least the citizens of those countries want out. I'm not sure about the Zone presidents."

I continue: "So what could they do next? How bad could this get? I can't help but remember what we studied in the Bible about the ten kings. Remember from last summer? The book of Daniel. In the last days, these ten kings give their power over to the Antichrist. Then he defeats three of the kings."

I almost stop myself from saying my next thought because of Hannah, but I continue: "Dad, those three kings sound a lot like the Zone Presidents for Zones One, Three, and Four. And when they are taken out, 25 percent of the world's population dies. I didn't think we were supposed to be here when that happened! Isn't the Rapture supposed to happen before the Antichrist shows up? It seems like he could appear at any moment. I mean everything is lined up for him to show up. I don't want to be here when all this starts, and yet it's starting right now!"

I can see from Hannah's face that she isn't following the conversation, which is good.

"I don't think we'll be here, either, Chloe," Dad says reassuringly. "Quite honestly, I thought the Rapture would happen before they implemented the ten World Zones. I also thought we'd be out of here before the nuclear war between Russian, Iran, and Israel. I think we must be getting very close to the Rapture, because the Bible says God did not appoint Christians to suffer wrath. God will pull us out of here before he pours out his wrath on the Earth. We know this with 100 percent certainty, but there is a question in my mind about the level of persecution we will have to endure before he takes us out of here. The persecution of Christians in other countries has been happening for the past two thousand years. We've had it easy here in the United States, and here in North Texas, we live in a kind of Christian bubble. I don't think things will get as bad as in other places, like in the Middle East or North Korea, but they could get harder than we have previously imagined."

Jackson finally joins in: "Dad, I remember you have a friend that has come over for dinner a couple of times, Mr. Harmon. I remember that once the two of you had a long conversation about the Rapture. He believes the church will still be here during the first part of that time after the Antichrist shows up. The two of you had quite a debate about that. Why does he believe that? Could he be right?"

It's as if Dad was already thinking about that conversation with Mr. Harmon.

"Yes, I remember that conversation with him," Dad says. "It was last Fall. I hadn't thought much about it until now. He's a very smart guy. He used to believe like we do, that we'll be out of here before the Antichrist shows up. He read a book a couple of years ago. I think the title was *The Pre-Wrath Rapture,* or something like that. He suggested I get a copy and read it, but I never did. It sounded a little off to me. I mean, 90 percent of the Christians I know think we'll be gone before the last seven years begins. I'm going to see if he can come over this weekend for a couple of hours, and I'm going to try to find that book on Amazon. I don't think he's right, but given how things are going, I think it's worth checking out."

Jackson and I sense Dad's apprehension, which makes us all very uneasy. It's clear to both of us that Dad is starting to second-guess his thinking on the Rapture.

Jackson asks, "If Mr. Harmon is right, then what will happen to people like us?"

I can tell Dad knows the conversation is heading somewhere he doesn't want to go with Hannah in the room.

"Hannah, do you want to watch a movie upstairs?" Dad asks.

"Sure" is her quick response, and, within seconds, she is bounding up the stairs.

With Hannah safely away, Dad tries his best to answer: "Jackson, I'm not completely sure, because, to be honest, I didn't pay too much attention to the details of Mr. Harmon's argument. I guess I had made up my mind, so I didn't try to fully understand his position, knowing that I wasn't about to change my opinion. However, I think his main argument is that the first few years of the Tribulation are not God's wrath; they represent Satan's wrath or man's wrath. So, he believes we are here for that portion of the Tribulation; then God takes us out just before he pours out 'his' wrath. If he's right, then many Christians like us could be put to death for our faith. The ones who escape the Antichrist would be caught up in the Rapture."

I can see from Mom's face that she's starting to imagine the worst-case scenario. So am I. I think that Dad is on the fence, not sure what to think. I have a feeling that Mr. Harmon's phone is going to be ringing a lot this week. Dad tries to reassure us all.

"You all know that God is in control of whatever happens. Think about all of the miracles He has done in our family. After all, I wrote a book about that! Time and again, he has come to our rescue in difficult situations. I'm pretty sure God hasn't changed in the last twenty-four hours. He is the same yesterday, today, and forever. Even if things get tough, he will see us through this. I know I'm preaching to the choir here, but all things do work together for good; you all know that."

Mom finally breaks her silence: "It's a good reminder, and yes it's 100 percent true. God will not test us beyond what we can endure. Remember when I was sick that first time and I thought I might not make it. God came through for us. We just need to trust him. We need to faith out, not freak out."

I'm not sure Jackson is going there with her. He asks if Dad can call Mr. Harmon now and see if he can come by this weekend. Dad agrees, but first asks if we need to spend more time on this before he calls. We all agree we're okay for now, and Dad asks that we avoid talking about the more unpleasant possibilities around Hannah. She's just too young to process this. We agree. Dad reaches Mr. Harmon, and he agrees to come over right after church on Sunday. We always attend the second service at 11:15, so we'll all be back home by 1:45. It's only Wednesday, and Sunday seems like an eternity away. I retreat to my room and start replying to the dozens of texts from friends at school. Even Natalie, my best friend in California, sent me a note, asking if I'd heard. I spend the rest of the afternoon and evening responding to friends. By ten thirty, I'm exhausted, so I turn down the ringer on my phone and crash.

CHAPTER THREE

THE PRE-WRATH RAPTURE

The next two days at school are surreal. Everyone is quieter than usual, and we move through passing periods like zombies. I see lots of red eyes. In the bathroom, I can hear girls crying in the stalls. There is a lot of hugging with even the guys joining in. I ask Mr. Bradley if I can meet with him for thirty minutes after school on Friday, and he agrees. I want to ask him about this theory from my dad's friend and see if he's familiar with it. I arrive in his classroom by 1:35, and I am glad to see he's alone. I've always been his favorite student. It's an unspoken and unacknowledged truth. It's probably my love of history that has earned me this coveted position. I pull up a chair next to his desk and jump right in.

"Mr. Bradley, are you familiar with a theory about the timing of the Rapture called 'Pre-Wrath'? One of my dad's friends used to believe in a pre-Tribulation Rapture but completely changed his mind when he read a book about it a couple of years ago." To my surprise, Mr. Bradley has not heard of this before. He quickly Googles the words "Pre-Wrath Rapture" to see what he can find. He immediately finds a Pre-Wrath website and a book by Marvin Rosenthal titled *The Pre-Wrath Rapture of the Church*.

"I found something on it," he says. "Take a look."

He swings his monitor around so we could read it together. He then goes to Amazon.com and orders a copy. I am surprised when he selects "next day delivery," given that Mr. Bradley is one of the most frugal adults I've ever met. I can feel that knot coming back into my stomach.

"Let's do this," he says. "You go ahead and order a copy for yourself, and then once we've both read it, let's get together and compare notes."

"Sounds like a plan," I reply. I somehow feel encouraged, like we're going to solve a mystery together. At least I have something to keep my mind off the dreadful thought of losing my school, my friends, and my beloved Mr. Bradley.

"This friend of my dad is coming over to our house on Sunday after church," I continue. "I'll stay after class a few minutes next Monday and let you know what he says. But we will probably need at least an hour or more to discuss the book. Maybe we can do that in a couple of weeks." I know it won't be a couple of weeks. I have a feeling that the second that book arrives, we will both pull an all-nighter and read it in seven or eight hours.

"Sounds like a good plan, Chloe," Mr. Bradley says. "If we find anything interesting, we'll share it with both history and English sections. Have a restful weekend, Chloe, and try not to let all of this get you down."

"I'll try my best, Mr. Bradley," I say. "See you on Monday." To my surprise, I find myself hugging him goodbye. What's even more amazing is that he lets me.

Sunday can't come soon enough. I have to know what Mr. Harmon has to say about the closing of private schools and, more importantly, his thinking on the Rapture. We meet him in the foyer after church and decide to grab lunch before heading home. It feels like another delay, since I'm sure they won't discuss any of this during lunch, and I'm right. We finally arrive home around 2:45. Dad sends Hannah upstairs to watch a movie, and I am surprised to see Jackson give up his precious gaming and join the conversation. Dad skips the topic of the private school decision and instead asks Mr. Harmon to restate his conclusion on the timing of the Rapture. This time around, all of us, including my dad, are truly listening.

"So, as you know," Mr. Harmon begins, "about two years ago, my dad passed away. My mom had already died years earlier. I was at my dad's house for a couple of days just before he passed, so I decided to check out his library. Library is an overstatement. It was just a small collection of books, Christian books. He probably had fifty or sixty titles. I scanned through the collection, and one jumped out at me. It was titled *The Pre-Wrath Rapture of the Church*. I've always had an interest in the Rapture, so I pulled it off the shelf and read the back cover. I was immediately bothered, or maybe 'agitated' is a better word. It was clear to me that this book would argue that the pre-Tribulation Rapture, which I had firmly believed my entire adult life, was wrong. However, because I have always found this topic interesting, I walked to my dad's front porch, sat down, and started reading.

"I have to tell you that once I started reading it, I couldn't stop. The author is a true scholar and has a deep understanding of end-time prophecy. In his book, he systematically dismantled the arguments for a pre-Tribulation Rapture, in every instance using Scripture to prove his point. Chapter thirteen of his book would later be the clincher for me. He was able to demonstrate that two groups appear sequentially in Heaven in the second half of the Tribulation. The first group is souls under the altar who are martyred for their faith, and the second group is bodies in front of the altar. The second group is so large that it cannot be numbered and comes from every tongue, tribe, and nation. These two groups are completely separate, and the second one has to be the Raptured Church.

"I finished the book in about six hours, but I wasn't completely convinced. In fact, the very next thing I did was Google online rebuttals to the author's book. I only found a handful, and none of them used Scripture to refute the arguments in his book. All the rebuttals did was criticize his position and restate the same arguments for a pre-Tribulation Rapture. I was devastated. Over the course of the next few weeks, I did what the New Testament Bereans did. I searched and studied every Tribulation and Rapture passage in the Bible to see if I could refute his arguments. I could not. I came to understand and believe that the arguments for a pre-Tribulation Rapture are circumstantial and indirect, while the evidence for a pre-Wrath Rapture is overwhelming and direct. You don't need to contort some Scriptures and ignore others to believe the Rapture is pre-Wrath. It fits perfectly and unstrained with the Bible.

"For the next several months, I began to share my findings with Christian friends and family members. Not one was open to a detailed discussion of the merits of the pre-Wrath position. In fact, one of my aunts became so upset by just the suggestion that the church would be here for a portion of the Tribulation that I had to drop the subject altogether to keep the peace. In short, I couldn't find one 'Berean' among my family members or my close circle of Christian friends. At one point, I remembered a Christian friend, Greg, whom I had worked with years earlier. I remembered that when the *Left*

Behind book series came out, I offered him a copy of the first book. He politely declined, explaining he didn't believe in a pre-Tribulation Rapture. He went on to say that the church will still be here when the Antichrist is revealed and that he intended to fight against him.

"I didn't respond to his comment, but I remember feeling sorry for Greg. He was so misinformed about the end of times. At the time, I considered myself an 'expert' on the topic, but the truth was I hadn't done any real homework. I just believed what my pastors told me. Well, I decided I had to get back in touch with Greg for two reasons. One was to figure out how he knew the correct timing of the Rapture and two was to apologize for having those condescending thoughts about him. I was able to reconnect with him using LinkedIn. He said he figured out the timing of the Rapture just by reading the Bible, which made me feel like a complete loser. And he just laughed when I apologized for thinking he was a nut.

"So that's about it. I brought an extra copy of the book with me. I strongly encourage you all to read it with an open mind."

We are all bursting with questions.

Mom jumps in first. "So, based on what you know, roughly when will the church be Raptured?"

"That's a great question, Cathy," Mr. Harmon says. "In fact, it's the one people ask me the most. The answer is that no man knows the day or the hour. However, we can know the sequence. The Rapture will be sometime after the midpoint of the Tribulation, so more than three and a-half years into the Tribulation. As you know, the Antichrist goes into the Holy of Holies in the rebuilt temple in Jerusalem at exactly the three-and-one-half-year mark and declares that he is God and requires the whole world to worship him. It's at that point that the Great Tribulation begins. He goes after the Jews, of course, and also the Christians. Many Christians are martyred. Once the number of martyrs is complete, then God takes the rest of us home to Heaven. Immediately following the Rapture, God pours out his wrath on the Earth. You see, we're not appointed to wrath, God's wrath, but we will have to endure the wrath of Satan and the Antichrist."

My heart begins to sink, and I feel sick to my stomach like I could throw up. It is worse than I thought. If we're still alive after Zone One rebels against the Antichrist in the first three and a-half years, then we'll probably be executed by the Central Zone authorities at the beginning of the second three and a-half years. I suddenly realize that my many years of private college-prep education are all for nothing. How much have Mom and Dad spent on my schooling just since middle school? At least one hundred thousand dollars. And I might as well forget about college. That would be a total waste of time and money. I see a glimpse of my future, and it looks really ugly. Why couldn't I have been born a hundred years earlier? Why do I have to be alive now?

Everyone has so many questions to ask. I jump in next.

"How and when will we know if your theory is right?" I ask.

"Well, there are two key tests, Chloe," he responds. "The first test will be if we are still here when the Antichrist, whoever he ends up being, enforces a seven-year treaty between Israel and the Muslim world. The treaty will have to include the right of the Jews to rebuild their temple. It will have to, in some way, guarantee Israel's safety. The real clincher will be if some of the Jewish people believe that the Antichrist is their long-awaited

Messiah. In Israel today, if you ask a typical religious Jew how they will identify their Messiah when he arrives, they will tell you that it will be a man who finds a way for them to rebuild their temple.

"From the date of this signed treaty, there will be exactly seven years until the Second Coming of Christ. But they won't be 365-day years; they will be 360-day years. I'm not sure if the Antichrist will set up a new calendar system. It's possible, but if we are all here when the deal goes down, then my theory will have passed the first test. The second test will be if we are still here after the three-and-a-half-year mark. Again, this will be based on 360-day years. At the three-and-a-half-year mark, the Antichrist will go into the Holy of Holies in the rebuilt Temple in Jerusalem and declare that he is God. He will then require everyone to worship him. Those who don't will be put to death. That's the point where the worst persecution of true Christians will begin. If we are here at that point, then you can be 100 percent certain my theory is right."

I still have Mr. Harmon's attention, so I keep going. "So let's say you're right; we have two challenges then. The first will be if Zone One is one of the three Zones that rebels and is crushed by the Antichrist. If we are, would the resulting war happen in the first three and a-half years or the second three and a-half years?"

Mr. Harmon is quick to respond. "So you're referring to the ten kings in Daniel chapter seven, and it sounds like you have figured out the correlation between these kings and the ten world zones. I'm impressed, Chloe. I definitely think the war will occur in the first three and a-half years. When that happens, 25 percent of the world's population will die from war, famine, or disease. Throughout history, that is always the sequence, by the way. War always results in economic devastation, which causes shortages of food. Then people's immune systems are weakened by hunger, and they are more susceptible to various diseases. So the war itself won't kill 25 percent of the world's population, but the combination of these things will."

"We'll that's pretty depressing," I immediately respond. "Okay, so assuming, by some miracle, we survive the war, would our second challenge be to survive the persecution that starts right at the three-and-a-half-year mark? Or at least to survive it until the Rapture comes?"

"Yes, Chloe, that would be the second challenge," Mr. Harmon says, "And to be honest, I'm not sure which would be the bigger challenge, surviving the war or the worldwide persecution of Christians. I do know this, however, on the basis of Revelation chapter six, the group that is in the Rapture is substantially larger than the group that is martyred. The Apostle John said that the Rapture group was so large no man could number them, but he didn't say that about the group that the Antichrist puts to death. That tells me that only a small percentage of Christians, perhaps 10 percent, are put to death."

My dad rejoins the conversation: "So, again, if you're right, then all Christians have a critical decision to make at some point early in that first three and a-half years, fight or flight. Do they fight against the Antichrist in either the Zone rebellion or spiritually by trying to get the truth out, or do they head to some remote place and try to survive for four or more years? Since you obviously believe your own theory, have you thought this through? What's your plan?"

"As a matter of fact, I have given it a lot of thought in the past two years, but I've not made any firm decisions, Ray," Mr.

Harmon says. "And there is a third option: fight and flight. I've given a lot of thinking to that one. Under that scenario, we could wage a spiritual battle and try to get the truth to as many people as possible, then head for the hills when it looks like the Zone rebellions are getting started. I think we might have a decent idea of when the conflict is about to start. My hope would be for a least a few weeks of lead time. I wouldn't want to stick around for the physical fight since we all know that will be a losing battle. The Antichrist wins that one in all three Zones that are affected. Like you Chloe, I'm convinced our Zone will be one of the three that rebels.

"This strategy will require some fast planning from the date of the signed agreement by Israel and the Muslim countries. It's hard to say, but from day one of the seven-year period, I would think there should be peace for at least one year, maybe even two years. The Antichrist wins the complete trust and admiration of the ten Zones' presidents and the rest of the world through diplomacy, and diplomacy takes time. Also, my guess is that the Antichrist is not fully in charge at the beginning of the seven-year period. After the Israel deal, he will probably rack up several more wins around the world in less than one year, solving all kinds of lingering wars and conflicts. The Bible says that the ten Kings 'hand' their authority over to him. They are so amazed with this guy that they put him in charge of the entire Zone system and, by default, the whole world.

"If I'm close on the timing, then we would have at least one year to purchase a place to hide out and get it fully stocked—you know, food, water, and all that. This is where it starts to get a little crazy with underground bunkers, all the 'prepper' stuff. Do you want me to keep going?"

"Yes," comes out at the same time from all four of us: Mom, Dad, Jackson, and me.

"Okay, I'll keep going, but let's agree to keep this just between the five of us for now for several reasons. I don't want anyone to think I'm a 'prepper,' and if all this plays out the way I imagine it could, I don't want a lot of people knowing about my plans. Agreed?"

Of course, we all quickly agree. Mr. Harmon asks each of us individually to make sure. I can tell he's a little concerned about Jackson and me keeping quiet about this.

"So in terms of where to go, I don't think the lower forty-eight is a good choice," Mr. Harmon says. "As you know, the Central Zone has control of the nukes, and if 25 percent of the world's population is supposed to be wiped out in these Zone wars, then they will use the nukes. I have no idea where it would be safe in the lower forty-eight, and with wind patterns, you could be safe initially, then get hit with radiation carried east by the jet stream. Hawaii is out. Where could you possibly hide on an island? That leaves only one place, Alaska. I know you all have family up there and have been up there fishing several times."

"Five, to be exact," my dad volunteers. "The kids have been up twice."

"Great," Mr. Harmon continues. "Then you know how vast the forests are up there. I've researched land purchases in remote areas, and they're very affordable. You could easily get two hundred acres for less than one hundred thousand dollars. Also, you'd want to find a property with a house already on it. You wouldn't want to risk running out of time to build one."

This is starting to sound crazy and exciting at the same time. I absolutely love the outdoors, especially forests, and my two trips to Alaska were amazing. We fished for silver salmon on Price William Sound, outside of Valdez. It's a beautiful and rugged area with lots of wildlife. I am eager to hear more.

Mr. Harmon hardly takes a breath. I get the sense he has wanted to share his ideas with someone for a while, like it was all bottled up inside. "There are other things you'd want to consider when looking for land. You'd want to be near a stream for fresh water or find land where the water table was high enough so you could drill a well. The property should not only be in a very remote location, but it should back up to state or federal land. Here's why. As you know, in the second three and a-half years, it will be open season on Christians. We won't be able to buy or sell. Many people will be put to death for not worshiping the image of the Antichrist. The cabin's location in a remote area doesn't mean the Zone authorities won't come looking for you.

"My thinking is that we would build an illegal hideout underground within a fifteen-minute hike from the main house. This is where you get into the 'doomsday' bunker thing. One designed to hold enough food and water for a family of five would probably be around one hundred and fifty thousand dollars. However, my guess is that prices will go much higher once people like us start to develop survival plans. That's the tricky part. You'd want to wait until the agreement is signed to start, but before prices soar. If the Zone authorities come looking for you at your regular home, you'd need some type of early warning system so you could escape to your underground shelter. Because it would be on a large tract of government land, they wouldn't know where to look for you. My guess is they would stick to easier targets. However, it might be tough to get one of these bunker companies to put one on government land with no permits. By the way, I discovered that the largest bunker manufacturer in the United States is located right here in Texas. They're called Rising S. Anyway, that's my plan. It's not foolproof, so please punch some holes in it."

Dad is the first to respond: "Wow, that's quite a lot to take in. And for something that, for now, is still very hypothetical. My first thought is that the timing would be tight, trying to get all this done in twelve months. Just selling our house would take three months, unless we priced below market. I would think to get everything ready on the new property, including the bunker, would take at least six months. And you'd have to be sure you had enough money to last roughly five years after paying cash for everything in Alaska. I'm guessing we would have enough to cover it. It just seems like it could take a year or more to plan this out."

"I agree," says Mr. Harmon. "That's why I'm thinking this out now. I've done a lot of planning for myself. I've looked into property, and long-term food and water storage."

"Mr. Harmon," I interrupt, "it looks like you've chosen the flight option. Can you tell me why?"

"Actually, Chloe, I think I'll still be fighting up until the time I head for the mountains," Mr. Harmon responds. "My thinking is that Zone One will definitely be one of the three that gets crushed. It would be a little tough to keep fighting for the truth if you get nuked. I plan to fight as long as I can, then hopefully get out of town just before Zone One gets wiped out. I'd love to make it to the Rapture. I think it will be a huge challenge, but I'm always up for a challenge."

We spend the next hour digging into the details and risks associated with the fight-and-flight approach. Dad thinks large numbers of Christians will start losing their jobs in the first three and a-half years. We speculate about other forms of persecution that could happen. A lot of our discussion focuses on contingency plans. I feel slightly better because now my mind is focused on a plan of action rather than just on what the Central Zone is doing to us. I can't wait to get started on the Pre-Wrath book. As we're finishing up, I ask Dad if I can read it first. To my surprise, Jackson also wants to read it. Jackson has always hated reading books, even ones about topics he loves, like World War II. Mom seems very detached and doesn't chime in, so the three of us agree to a joint-custody arrangement. We will each read in two-hour shifts. By my estimation, Dad and I will finish in just under three shifts, and Jackson will still be reading it three days from now! As Mr. Harmon leaves, he agrees to meet with us all again in a few weeks.

CHAPTER FOUR

IT'S TRUE

D ad gives me the first shift, so I retreat to my room and set the timer on my phone for two hours. It's immediately clear that a lot of what I'm reading is way over my head. However, because I've been such an avid reader since elementary school, I'm able to pick up most of the key arguments. Since I've never done an in-depth study of end-time prophecy and the Rapture, I'm not sure how strong the arguments are that I'm reading. My gut tells me they are pretty close to airtight. Like Mr. Harmon, I'm hoping to find some fatal flaw in the Pre-Wrath argument, but with my limited knowledge, I couldn't spot one even if it jumped off the page. I really need Mr. Bradley's help with this. My time is up, and I pass the book off to Dad. He doesn't waste any time getting started.

I find Mom and tell her what I've read so far. The author faced the same resistance from his Christian friends and family members described by Mr. Harmon. I ask her why adults are so stuck in their ways. She explains that in this situation, it's not so much that people become stuck in their ways; it's that the Pre-Wrath argument is so upsetting that Christians don't want to think about it. They don't even want to entertain the possibility that it might be true. I mean, what parent wants to imagine that they will have to watch their children be put to death for simply believing in Jesus? It's a horrible thought. Here in the United States, we have had nearly complete freedom and liberty for almost 250 years. People here can't even imagine real persecution. They hear about Christians who are tortured and killed in far-away places like North Korea and the Middle East, but it's impersonal and distant. They can't imagine that anything like that would ever happen to them, so they ignore the possibility as fiction.

I can tell that Mom believes in her heart that she has been wrong about the timing of the Rapture, and like any mom who loves her children, she imagines the worst. If this plays out the way I think it will, then the next few years could look a lot like the mass killings of Christians I've read about during the first three hundred years of church history. How does a mother process this? I have no idea. I ask her if she's going to read the book.

"I will read it when you all have finished it," she says.

I can tell she's in no hurry. She knows it's true, so why rush into the details? I can see how sad she is and that makes me even more depressed. I keep having that same thought: why couldn't I have been born one hundred years ago? I just want this all to go away. I want to be a kid again.

My dad, Jackson, and I spend the rest of the day passing the book between each other every two hours. It's clear that none of us will finish tonight, but Dad and I are both about one-third of the way through the book by the time we all decide to call it a night around eleven o'clock. I can't wait for the end of the school day tomorrow, so I can find Mr. Bradley and start peppering him with questions. My guess is that he has probably read the entire book twice by now. I have to know his opinion. If he believes in this Pre-Wrath idea, then it's settled for me, and I can then start to grapple with the fight and/or flight idea. I can't move on until I know where he stands. My worst fear is that he'll say he's undecided. That would kill me.

I'm totally unprepared on Monday morning for an Algebra II quiz in first period, but I couldn't care less. Even our class president, William, seems unprepared and unconcerned. The focus of every conversation in every classroom and hallway is on either the closing of our school or what will happen next to Christians. You would think we would have at least some concern for our teachers and administrators. After all, in just over two months they will all be out of a job. I'm only thinking about myself, my immediate family, and Mr. Bradley. The school day drags until we are finally dismissed at 3:15. I head straight for Mr. Bradley's class. As I expected, he has a couple of students with him, asking for his opinion about this whole mess. I wait patiently until they finish up.

"Hi, Chloe," Mr. Bradley says. His face lights up just a little. I catch a brief glimpse of the former Mr. Bradley.

"Hi, Mr. Bradley," I say.

"How are you holding up, Chloe?" he asks. "I prayed for you this weekend."

This catches me off guard. He has never admitted to praying for me before. I can feel my emotions bubbling up, but I quickly push them back down. We'll never get anywhere with our analysis if I start crying. It stinks always having to fight off my emotions. I compose myself.

"I guess I'm doing as well as anyone around here, which isn't saying much," I say.

Mr. Bradly nods in agreement.

"I got about one-third of the way through the book," I say. "I couldn't finish it because of a joint-custody thing on the book with my dad and brother, and we didn't get started until around four o'clock yesterday. A lot of what I read was way over my head, but I think I understand the author's basic arguments. His approach seems to present each major argument for a Pre-Tribulation Rapture then to dismantle each of them using Scripture. Is that your take on it?"

"You're a very analytical reader, Chloe," Mr. Bradley says.

For a second, I forget the gravity of the topic and just enjoy his compliment. Mr. Bradley doesn't give them out easily, so any you receive are incredibly valuable. I remember he once told his fourth period honors history class that they were his "pretty" class. They were so flattered until they discovered weeks later that he referred to his other section of honors history as his "smart" class. That's classic Mr. Bradley: finding some improbable silver lining for a class that's not quite up to par intellectually.

"Thanks, Mr. Bradley," I say. "So do you agree that is the author's approach?"

"Yes, Chloe, rather that make his case directly, he makes it indirectly by systematically dismantling each Pre-Tribulation argument then immediately replacing them with his Pre-Wrath thinking. The author is very well versed on not just the Pre-Tribulation Rapture but on all of the various opinions related to the Rapture, including the thought that there won't be one at all. I was very impressed with the book."

I'm almost holding my breath as I contemplate the most important questions. Is the author right? Do you believe him? The implications of these questions are so profound that I'm almost too afraid to ask, but I can't help myself. My generation is not good at waiting for anything, much less an answer to a question this important.

I start with a more benign question: "So my guess is that you have read the book twice. Was I close?"

Mr. Bradley looks directly at me as he answers: "You're close. I read it three times, Chloe. It's sort of a record for me. I've read one other book three times but not in the same weekend. I read it the first time just to get a general sense of his arguments. I read it the second time more analytically, trying to find holes in any of his arguments. I then reread the various Bible passages related to the Tribulation and the Rapture. Then I reread just the chapters in his book that contain his primary arguments to see how they fit with Scripture. I took lots of detailed notes."

I can't wait any longer. I have to know. Mr. Bradley is the most intelligent person I have ever met, and he possesses an exceptional grasp of both history and Bible prophecy.

"Mr. Bradley, I want you to tell me honestly what you think," I say. "I know you've only had one weekend to analyze his arguments, but do you think he's right?"

He begins slowly: "Chloe, I spent a lot of time praying about this over the weekend. I asked the Holy Spirit to give me wisdom and understanding. This is such an important topic, given what is happening in the world. To be honest with you, I never thought that most of what has happened, the Zones, the war predicted in Ezekiel 38, would happen in my lifetime. I knew with certainty they would happen someday because they are in the Bible. It has been a little overwhelming for me to see all this playing out. I mean, we are clearly coming to the end of the game here on planet Earth. For the past two thousand years, the Tribulation was just a concept, a rumor, and now it's right at our doorstep."

I am a little stunned by how emotional this realization is for Mr. Bradley. I guess I somehow imagined someone so much older and wiser, so much more mature, would be able to synthesize all of this without much emotion. It's clear to me that Mr. Bradley is almost as shocked as I am by what's happening.

"I have to admit, Mr. Bradley, that I'm feeling a lot of anger about this" I say. "I'm angry that I might never get to attend college or have my own family. I might have to see my family and close friends put to death. I'm angry at the Central Zone. I'm angry that I have to be alive right now. All of this stinks. I'm sorry, I know I'm not behaving very scholarly right now, but it really does stink."

"You know, Chloe, you would think that since I've lived most of my life, this would be easier on me. It's not. I'm thrown off by this also. Everyone is. Well, Christians, anyway. The world doesn't have any idea what's coming. It will eventually be our job to tell them, regardless of the consequences of speaking up. You're smart enough to know there will be some very serious consequences. But before we go down that path of conversation, let me address the question that is at the top of your mind. The book. As I said, I read it three times over the weekend. I now believe that the Pre-Wrath Rapture is true, every word of it. I am completely convinced. Quite honestly, if I had stumbled upon this book ten years ago, before all of this Zone craziness, I still would have believed it. The arguments for a Pre-Wrath Rapture are biblical. They're airtight. They're all true."

I realize I have stopped breathing while he was talking, so I quickly exhale, and then take in another breath. I can tell that my face is flushing. So can Mr. Bradley, I'm sure. I don't say a word at first. I know that if he believes the arguments for a Pre-Wrath Rapture, I believe them. That settled it for me. The Pre-Wrath Rapture is going to happen, and definitely in the near future. Things will progress rapidly to the end. In that one moment, everything changes for me, from theory and speculation to reality. And the reality is that I will probably never make it to my twenty-fifth birthday.

I'm not exactly sure what to say next, so I ask the first few questions that pop into my head.

"So, what sold you on the idea?" I ask. "Was there a particular section of the book that convinced you? Was there an 'ah ha' moment?"

"I'm glad you asked, Chloe, because there was!" Mr. Bradley exclaims. "You see, the central issue in the timing of the Rapture is the time when God's wrath begins. I've always been taught, and I have always believed, that God's wrath begins right at the beginning of the seven-year period. Chapter twelve in Rosenthal's book provides irrefutable evidence for the timing of God's wrath. Let me read you the key verse from Revelation chapter six, verse seventeen: 'For the great day of his wrath is come; and who shall be able to stand?' This verse occurs after the opening of the sixth seal and just before the seventh seal. By this time in the text, we are already more than halfway through the seven-year period. The Four Horseman of the Apocalypse have already come, and Christians slain for their faith are in Heaven; that's the fifth seal."

Mr. Bradley goes on: "The sixth seal ushers in signs in the Heavens, which throughout the Old Testament are tied closely with God's wrath. Just before the seventh seal, God has angels put a seal on the 144,000 Jews for protection. You see, it makes perfect sense. The number of those killed for their faith from the fifth seal is complete, so the rest of us are taken up to Heaven in the Rapture. Now that we are gone, God can pour out his wrath but first he needs to seal the 144,000 Jews so that his wrath does not hurt them. If God's wrath had begun right at the beginning of the seven-year period, then God would have put the seal on them at that point!

"Also, prior to the seventh seal, there is no angelic involvement in what has happened on Earth. There is no mention of angels. However, beginning with the seventh seal, angels play a key part in what happens next, the trumpet and bowl judgments. The reason is simple. God is pouring out his wrath on the earth and is using his angels to accomplishment it. So, you see, to understand the timing of the Rapture, you have to understand when God's wrath begins, and it clearly begins between the sixth and seventh seals."

Mr. Bradley and I talk for more than an hour. I ask him dozens of questions. What were the other strong arguments in the book? What were the weakest ones? Why had he never considered this possibility before? He mentions a verse in the Old Testament book of Daniel that I vaguely remember. Something about "knowledge will increase" in the last days. His point is most Christians believe that verse is a reference to technical and scientific knowledge. Mr. Bradley thinks that the verse actually has a double meaning. He thinks that not only will scientific knowledge increase but also the knowledge of the end-time chronology. He talks about how, one hundred years ago, Christians would have been very confused about passages referring to a literal Israel. It wouldn't make sense to them because the Jews had not had a nation for almost two thousand years. Since 1948, those passages make complete sense to us.

Mr. Bradley doesn't make excuses for his lack of accuracy on the timing of the Rapture. He simply makes the point that our understanding has significantly increased since Israel became a nation in 1948. It is clear to me, however, that this new understanding is having a profound impact on him. I'm tempted to ask if he has been having the horrible thoughts that I have about what we will all have to endure. I sense that, like me, he needs some time to sort all this out. Now isn't the time to talk about "worst-case scenarios." I promise to meet with him again, once I have read the book a couple of times.

CHAPTER FIVE

TOLERANCE

The next few weeks at school are a blur. For the first time in my life, I allow myself to slip academically. However, it doesn't show up in my grades. I think that the entire teaching staff has decided to go easy on us for the last two months of the school year. Maybe it's their form of silent protest against the Central Zone. It doesn't matter anyway: our school is so challenging academically that probably 90 percent of us will coast through the rest of high school once we move to public schools. The thought of that change is so unsettling. I only know of eight other kids in my grade who will be going to my new high school, and I'm only close with one, Amanda. I have a feeling Amanda and I will be inseparable next school year, at least in the beginning. My hope is that we can arrange to have the same schedule, and hopefully a few of the same teachers.

I'm not just afraid of losing contact will most of my friends, I have a feeling these public high school kids will be quick to pop the Christian bubble I've lived in my whole life. I've never suffered anything close to persecution for my faith. How will I react when they insult me? What if they threaten me? I have no idea how bad it will be, and, as usual, I am imagining the worst. I keep coming back to what our headmaster, Mr. Morris, said at our meeting when he announced that our school would be closing. He described this as an opportunity for us all to be salt and light in our new public schools. I'm just not sure I'm up for the challenge. I won't have to wait long to find out.

My brother, Jackson, my dad, and I manage to finish the book on the Pre-Wrath Rapture. To my surprise, Jackson reads it twice. I doubt he has ever read a book twice, not even his favorites like *Diary of a Wimpy Kid*. Mom has still not gone near the book. We normally have a short family Bible study on Sunday nights, but instead Dad decides to use the next few Sundays to discuss the book.

It's a Saturday and finals are only one week away, but I can't focus at all. Knowing that our teachers are going to cut us some major slack doesn't help. I'm looking forward to our family time tomorrow night. We don't talk much about what's happened, and everyone is still dazed, except for Hannah. Would I really want to be her right now? Would I want to be eight years old given what might happen in the next few years? No, I'd rather be seventeen. At seventeen, I can put up a defense. I can fight! I can run away and hide if I need to. I spend most of the day Saturday on my iPad watching Netflix. My escape, I guess. It's an escape that won't last forever.

It's Sunday morning and we're running late for church, as usual. The service could start at two o'clock, and we would still be late. We've been attending our church for six years, since I was eleven, and I can count on one hand the number of times we have been early. This time, we're a little less late than usual. As we walk in, I'm surprised by how full the sanctuary is. We have to sit on the far left side in the back. My dad used to tell me that after 9/11, all of the churches across the country were so full that they had to bring in folding chairs. It didn't last very long. Within a few months, attendance was back to "normal," meaning most churches were barely more than half full on Sunday mornings. Ever the student of history, I find human nature to be so predictable.

Our pastor walks to the podium much earlier than usual, after just two songs. Something's up. My dad has connections with several of the pastors, but he hadn't mentioned anything special happening this Sunday. Even before our pastor begins to speak, that familiar panic starts to bubble up. I have that sinking feeling again.

"Today's service will be a bit unusual because we have some important things to discuss as a church body," Pastor Jon begins. "I'm not sure exactly how we'll spend the next hour. We'll need to just see where the Holy Spirit leads us this morning."

You can hear a pin drop. My stomach is churning. I look over at my dad, and he has a very concerned look on his face.

Pastor Jon continues: "As we all know, the world has changed a lot in the past few years, in ways that many of us could not have imagined. The Central Zone has begun to exert more substantial control over individual countries, especially those like the United States who have historically enjoyed the most freedoms. It has chipped away at many of our constitutional rights. Several of our board members have been monitoring new Central Zone initiatives related to religious expression."

Now I'm in a complete panic! First, they close my school. Are they now going to close my church?

"Before I get into those details," Pastor Jon continues, "I want to remind everyone that Christians are by far the most persecuted religious group on the planet. This has been consistently the case for the past two thousand years. Today, our brothers and sisters in many parts of the world are losing their very lives for their faith. In the Middle East, Islamic terrorists have converted livestock slaughterhouses into Christian slaughterhouses, and I mean that quite literally. We have seen nothing like that here, of course. For more than two hundred years, here in America, we have enjoyed religious freedom found nowhere else in the world. Our constitution has held evil at bay for two centuries.

"Even before the rise of the Central Zone, our religious freedoms began slipping away under the banner of tolerance and political correctness. This process accelerated even before the implementation of the Zones. Many Christian small business owners have lost their businesses for refusing to violate their deeply held religious beliefs. Some management employees in large corporations have lost their jobs or been demoted for refusing to sign tolerance commitments that contradict the teachings of the Bible. That particular form of religious persecution has grown exponentially in the last two years with the rise of the Central Zone.

"One question worth answering is 'why?' Why have Christians been singled out so specifically for persecution? The answer is simple: Truth. Christianity is the one true faith, and Jesus is the one and only hope for all people everywhere. Satan hates both people and the truth. Remember, he is a liar and the father of lies. Why would he waste time and resources persecuting those who are perpetuating lies, especially lies that he created? He is in what he considers a war with God, and he has always focused his most lethal resources on attacking the truth. One day, Jesus will return bodily, in person, and set things right. Until then, we will continue to suffer ever greater persecution. Jesus said, 'In this world, you will have tribulation, but be of good cheer, for I have overcome the world.' We know how the story ends. Jesus wins, Satan loses. But between now and then, we are told to persevere through tribulation.

"So let me switch gears and continue with my initial comments related to potential Central Zone Religious Tolerance initiatives that may be coming our way soon. Here's what we're hearing. A vote will occur sometime in the next thirty days related to religious institutions worldwide. While we don't have the specific language yet, what we're hearing is that every religious organization will need to adhere to specific guidelines. In the United States, the penalty for noncompliance would be the loss of our tax-exempt status. As you know, all religious organizations are exempt from federal taxes. That means that 100 percent of the $6 million you give each year goes to ministry. If we were to lose this exemption, roughly 30 percent, or $2 million, would have to be handed over to the Central Zone. I'm sure you can all imagine how the loss of those funds would impact our church.

"So back to the guidelines. What we're hearing is that the Central Zone authorities will prohibit any religious organization from declaring that any other belief system is untrue. For example, if we said that the Bible is the only religious book that contains the true Word of God, we would lose our tax exemption. If we said that Jesus is the one and only way to Heaven, we would lose our tax exemption. There are entire chapters in the Bible, like Romans, chapter one, that we could no longer teach. This is what is coming our way very soon.

"Our Elder Board met for several hours yesterday to discuss how we would respond to these new requirements, if and when they are enacted. The Board voted unanimously that we will never comply!"

At that, the entire congregation jumps to its feet and applauds for what seems like ten minutes. Pastor Jon begins to cry, as do many people in the audience. My mood changes from despair to excitement. I feel that same urge that I had felt when I found out the Central Zone was going to close my school, the urge to fight back, to confront this evil that is swallowing our world. At that moment, everything is settled for me. I am going to fight!

After everyone quiets down, Pastor Jon talks about the practical aspects of losing our tax exemption and how we could respond. In order to maintain all church ministries, our giving would have to increase by roughly 40 percent to offset the new tax liability. He encourages the roughly 50 percent of church members who never give to prayerfully consider making monetary gifts a priority. He reminds us that every extra dollar given before this change would be tax-exempt, so we might consider accelerating any giving we had planned for the following year.

At that moment, it becomes clear to me that the closing of my school and this attack on our church are just the beginning. Evil never retreats, it never gives ground. It pushes forward. Things will get worse and at an ever-increasing rate. Each new Central Zone initiative will probably be even more severe than the one before it. And it's only a matter of time until Zone One reaches a boiling point and rebels.

As Pastor Jon had suggested, roughly one month later, the Central Zone voted seven to three to approve the Religious Tolerance Initiative. Religious organizations around the world have thirty days to accept or decline the new guidelines. For those Christian churches in the United States that reject the new rules, their tax exemption will end on December 31. As we knew they would, our Church Elder Board votes eight to zero to reject the new guidelines.

The Religious Tolerance Initiative includes something incredibly sinister that clearly targets Christians. The Central Zone authorities call it "World Youth Day," and it will be implemented at some point next year. This part of the Initiative is not optional and requires that all children aged ten to seventeen attend a weekly youth day event sponsored and facilitated by the Central Zone authorities. World Youth Day sessions will occur every Sunday morning from nine in the morning to noon. After hearing about the way World Youth Day works, I remember something similar from twentieth-century European history. It doesn't take me long to find that similarity. I discover that when Adolf Hitler took over Austria, he required that all children attend a weekly youth day on Sunday mornings. The short-term goal was to keep children out of church. The longer-term goal was to turn the children into loyal supporters of the Nazi regime. The Nazis gradually turned the children against their parents. Now something similar was about to happen in my beloved America!

Something Mr. Bradley once told me also comes to mind. He said Satan never seems to have anything new in his arsenal. He has had several thousand years to study humans and perfect his evil strategies. Century after century, he simply redeploys the same strategies over and over again. Clearly, that was the case here with redeploying an old Nazi technique. I decide to dig a little deeper into what else had happened in Austria in the late 1930s and early 1940s, and I found many more parallels. Early on in Austria, the Nazis had banned the ownership of personal firearms. The Central Zone has already required the registration of all personal firearms. I now have no doubt that the next Central Zone decision would be an outright ban, just like in Austria. My guess is that will be the action that triggers the Zone One rebellion.

I'm so discouraged by the news at church that I give up on studying for my finals. It feels like my country is about to reach a boiling point, and I can't think of anything else. I keep remembering what Mr. Harmon said about "fight then flight." What if we fight too long and we're caught here when the war comes? Alaska is a long way from Texas. What if the Central Zone authorities begin to restrict travel before we can get our plans in place? I have to talk to Dad about this at our family Bible study tonight. I need some reassurance that he is working on a plan.

My dad gets us together a little earlier than usual for our study. Given what we learned in church this morning, we have a lot to discuss. My dad starts with what is on all of our minds, the new requirement to attend World Youth Day.

"Your mom and I spent some time this afternoon talking about World Youth Day," Dad begins. "It is clear that the Central Zone will use this to keep you out of church on Sunday mornings and to turn you into loyal Zone citizens. I'm sure our church will respond by moving the morning services to the evening so families can still attend church together. The good news is that the requirement to attend World Youth Day won't go into effect until sometime next year."

Remembering what I had discovered about Austria, I jump into the conversation: "Dad, you won't believe what I found. When Adolf Hitler took over Austria just before World War II, one of the first things he did was require the registration of all firearms. He then moved to confiscation, making it illegal to own a gun. That's not all. He also implemented a weekly youth day on Sundays, and attendance was mandatory. Dad, it's just like what the Central Zone is doing now."

"Wow, that's really interesting and concerning, Chloe," Dad says. "Was there much resistance from the Austrians?"

"Very little from what I could find," I reply. "They seemed too afraid of the Nazis to put up much of a resistance."

Dad continues, "Well, it will be very different here in the United States, and especially in Texas. If the Central Zone authorities try to confiscate our guns, it will get pretty ugly. I would guess that only 20 percent of Texans would comply. The authorities have already begun to restrict the purchase of ammunition, but people in the United States have been purchasing large quantities for more than a year, so there's a lot of ammo on the black market. Some people have begun making their own, which I understand will be illegal soon. We don't own any guns, at least not yet. I might need to rethink that whole issue."

I glance over at my mom, and she looks so incredibly sad. What kind of a conversation is this for a normal, patriotic, middle-class family to have? The world Mom and Dad knew for most of their lives is slipping away. Evil is right at the door, and they are powerless to stop it. My dad changes the topic.

"Let's spend some time this evening on the Pre-Wrath Rapture book," Dad says. "Chloe and I have both finished it. Jackson, did you get through it?"

"Yeah" is all he says.

"Well, Chloe, I know you talked to Mr. Bradley, and he's convinced it's true," Dad says. "I would say I'm about 70 percent certain that it's true. Chloe, where are you in your thinking?"

"One hundred percent that it's true," I say, without looking up.

"Jackson, what do you think?" asks Dad.

"I'm not sure," Jackson says. "It's pretty complicated. I didn't follow much of what I read. It seems like you'd have to be a pastor or someone like that to understand the author's arguments, so I guess I don't really know at this point."

Dad continues: "Well, I'd say there is enough of a chance that it's true that we should do some initial planning."

"You mean the Alaska thing?" I ask.

"Yes. I'll talk to Mr. Harmon again and ask how he did his research on properties," Dad says. "I'll see if he just used an online tool like Zillow or if he used a real estate agent. It might make sense to try to see what's available in the same area where he is thinking about buying property. He seems way ahead of everyone else on this. We could all benefit from collaborating with him. If we decide to do this, we would need to sell our house first in order to have enough money to pay for something in cash. So we would need to be close to 100 percent certain that it's the right thing to do. This won't be easy."

Mom seems really sad now. She raised us all in this house, and I know she's very attached to it. It won't be easy for her to let it go. If we sell, we'll probably have to get rid of almost all of our furniture. This is going to be really hard for Mom.

"Mom, what do you think about all of this?" I ask.

There is a long pause before she answers.

"I have conflicting thoughts," she replies. "One part of me just wants to ignore all of this and hope it goes away or at least doesn't get any worse. I want to see you go off to college in a year, Chloe. I want to see you start your career and have your own family. I want the same for Jackson and Hannah. But all of that seems to be unlikely now. Part of me wants to stay and fight to the bitter end. Another part of me feels we should just get out to the woods and try to survive until the Rapture. So I guess you could say I'm unsure of what to do, so I'll need to pray and ask God to give me wisdom."

Hannah hasn't said a word during our conversation, which is unusual for her. I know my parents want to include her in the conversation, but I'm sure it's painful for them. Painful to watch their youngest child robbed of her youth. How do you process this when you're eight years old? I'm struggling at seventeen. I feel so sad for her. I remember how fun and carefree I was at eight. She is going to have to grow up fast. Will she even be allowed to grow up at all? I'm sure Mom and Dad will talk to her separately later this evening.

Dad closes our meeting by reminding Jackson and me that it's finals week. I think he knows that we don't plan on spending much time studying this evening, but I suppose it's hard-wired in him to encourage us to do well in school, even in these insane circumstances. Dad promises to provide regular updates as he begins looking into property in Alaska.

CHAPTER SIX

LEAVING THE BUBBLE

I can hardly believe that this is my last week at Addison Christian Academy and that I'll be spending my senior year at Hebron High. Addison Christian was established in 1970, and now the Central Zone has destroyed it. It's destruction still seems impossible to me. Where will all of this end? How close are we to the end? How close are we to the beginning of the Tribulation? Will it start this year or even this summer? I have a hundred questions, and the only person I truly trust with the answers is Mr. Bradley. I am determined to spend at least an hour with him this week before the school year, and the school itself, ends.

The last days of school fly by because it's finals week. Before I know it, it's Friday, and I'm heading for Mr. Bradley's room. Some of the teachers have already begun to take down personal items in their rooms. It's so incredibly sad. Many of them have been here longer than I've been alive. For some, this is the only job they have had since college. I've heard that a community college might purchase the campus and that the school will then divide up the money from the sale among the administrators and teachers. At least they'll have something to carry them over until they can find another job.

I've seen more crying and more hugging this week than I've seen in my entire life. Many of my classmates have been here since kindergarten. Some of their parents even attended Addison Christian. In a few hours, the academy will just be a memory. The school is planning a special farewell ceremony for all sixteen hundred students and their parents this weekend at a local church. I know I need to go, but it will be so painful to say good-bye to everyone officially. I know I'm not supposed to hate anyone, but I can feel my hatred for the Central Zone growing stronger every day. And it makes me sick that they are going to win, that they will destroy Zone One just like they destroyed my school. I do hate them, but maybe it's right to hate them. We are supposed to hate evil, and that's exactly what they are.

My mind is racing as I approach Mr. Bradley's room. To my surprise, he's alone, even though the last class of the school year ended just ten minutes ago. I knock gently on the door. He looks up slowly, and his face brightens. There is a recognition as our eyes meet. I'm his favorite student, as he's my favorite teacher. We don't have to acknowledge it. We both know it's true. How can we possibly say good-bye to each other? As I always do, I suppress my emotions and give him a long hug.

"I had a feeling I'd see you today," he begins. "You have been an exceptional student, and I expect great things of you in the future."

He can see from my expression what I'm thinking. What future? We are all marked because we're Christians. It's just a matter of time until it is open season on all of us.

"Thank you for a fantastic year, Mr. Bradley," I say. "I learned so much from you this year. You really stretched me. You stretched all of us. I'll always carry that with me. I can't imagine that I'll ever find a better history or English teacher. I'm going to miss you."

My eyes are watery now, and so are his. Mr. Bradley rescues us both with a change of subject.

"Chloe, tell me your thoughts about the Pre-Wrath Rapture book," Mr. Bradley says. "I'm sure by now you've read it at least twice. What more have you gleaned from it? Are you still a pre-wrath-er?"

I laugh a little, which helps me to compose my thoughts. "Well, you're close," I begin. "I've read it about two and a half-times so far. Even though I've read mountains of classical literature, including books like *The Scarlet Letter*, this one is still difficult for me. I think the reason is it's a new genre for me. I found myself rereading the more complex chapters multiple times. That's why I say I've read it two and a-half times. There are some chapters I've read four or five times. Rosenthal is truly amazing. I love his argumentation style. He clearly articulates both sides of this argument, unlike his opponents."

"I agree that he is very systematic and thorough," Mr. Bradley says. "He doesn't avoid any of the difficult questions or opposing positions. He effectively dismantles them all. It's kind of an intellectual blitzkrieg. The pre-Tribulation arguments are left looking sophomoric, almost silly. I found myself thinking, 'Why didn't I figure this out on my own?' The Holy Spirit confirmed the truth of the Pre-Wrath Rapture by giving me other insights not found in Rosenthal's book. One has to do with Satan. Do you remember, Chloe, what he does day and night?"

I think for a second, then respond, "He accuses us, right?"

"That's exactly right, Chloe," Mr. Bradley replies. "And remember where he is when he's accusing us. He's in Heaven.

God doesn't kick him out of Heaven until the midpoint of the Tribulation. So think about it; if the Rapture happens at the beginning of the seven-year period and we're all in Heaven, why is Satan still up there in Heaven accusing us? It's simple, of course. He's still up there accusing us because we're all still here on Earth! He would stay in Heaven past the midpoint of the Tribulation, but God kicks him out. He then makes war against both the Jews and the Christians."

I suddenly remember my dad's friend and say to Mr. Bradley, "My dad had a friend named Greg he used to work with in California. He apparently figured this all out just from reading the Bible! My dad said he felt somewhat humiliated that his friend solved it so easily, and it took this scholarly analysis by Rosenthal for my dad to find the truth."

"Maybe my problem, and your dad's as well," says Mr. Bradley, "was we weren't willing to consider the possibility we could be wrong. Also, I think you know it's so much more comforting to believe that we won't be here. Your mind is saying there's more to this, but your emotions pull you away from digging any deeper, for fear of what you might discover. So back to my initial question: are you still in the pre-wrath club?"

"Absolutely," I say with complete confidence.

"I am, too, Chloe," he says.

We pause for a moment, both recognizing the implications of our understanding. The gravity of what's ahead is hanging in the air. Do we imagine the same things? Are we both imagining the violent deaths of our friends and family members? I know I am. I think Mr. Bradley senses where my thoughts are headed and skillfully redirects the conversation once again.

"You know there are no coincidences for Christians, Chloe," he says. "We are both here, right now, because God has a part for both of us to play in what's coming. Our job is to find out what that part is."

"I agree, Mr. Bradley," I say. "In fact, I've been giving that a lot of thought these past few weeks. In fact, our entire family has been discussing this very thing. The question we're considering is fight, flight, or both."

"I'm intrigued, Chloe. Tell me more," says Mr. Bradley.

"Well," I say, "we all agree that Zone One will be one of the three Zones that eventually rebels against the Antichrist. And, of course, we know that the Antichrist will destroy the three Zones, or kings, that rebel. So our decision is related to how long we would stay here in Texas and fight against his lies before we head for the woods. Please don't say anything about this, Mr. Bradley; my dad wants to keep it quiet. But we're looking into property in Alaska. My dad and a friend of his think that might be the one place where we could survive in Zone One. If 25 percent of the world's population dies during the Zone rebellions, then it will have to be a nuclear war. The lower forty-eight won't be safe, and Hawaii is out. Nowhere to hide there.

"So our thinking is to fight the Central Zone's lies and propaganda, then head north just as the Zone rebellions are getting started. That's the 'fight-then-flight' scenario. We know that the seven years will begin with the signing or enforcement of a seven-year treaty between Israel and its enemies and that the treaty will include the right for the Jews to rebuild their temple. At that point, we would probably purchase some remote property in Alaska. The Book of Revelation seems to suggest that there will be an initial period of peace, so we should have time to get something in place up north."

"Well, that's not a bad idea. What do you think of it?" he asks.

"Well, I came up with an even crazier idea! We know that two-thirds of the Jews will be killed by the Anti-Christ right at the three-and-a-half-year mark. The remaining one-third will flee to the city of Petra in southern Jordan, where God will protect them for the final three and a-half years of the Tribulation. So my idea is for all of us to fly to Jordan a couple of weeks before the three-and-a-half-year mark, and head to Petra! Think about it. That's the only place on planet Earth that will be 100 percent safe for those final three and a-half years. We would then be raptured right from Petra just before God pours out his wrath on the Earth. What do you think?"

"Well, Chloe," Mr. Bradley says, "I think that's great thinking on your part! If you could get to Petra, I agree that you would be safe. The only challenge would be the Zone rebellions. They will most likely occur in the first three and a-half years, so getting a flight from Zone One to Jordan at that point might be impossible. Canada, the United States, and Mexico might be one big ash heap by the middle of the Tribulation, but it could be a good Plan B."

"Mr. Bradley, I'm sure you've given this some thought as well," I say. "What are you planning to do? Where will you go?"

I sense some hesitation from him.

"Well, I have thought about it," Mr. Bradley says. "You know I'm well past my prime, Chloe, at least physically. Most of my life is behind me. In a 'normal' world, I'd probably have only twenty or twenty-five years ahead of me. Of course, normal is no longer an option for any of us. There won't be any 'flight' for this old bird, but I still have some 'fight' left in me! I will stay and fight! I will proclaim God's truth as long as I have breath in my lungs. My guess is I won't have to worry about any mushroom clouds. The Central Zone will likely send me to Heaven long before that day arrives."

I hadn't wanted to go there in this conversation. I didn't want to come to terms with the inevitable. My beloved Mr. Bradley will suffer a martyr's death. He will be arrested, tortured, and killed for his faith. The thought is more than I can take. My emotions get the best of me, and my eyes fill with tears. All I can do is wrap my arms around him and cry. I leave his office, knowing that I might not see him again until we meet in Heaven.

CHAPTER SEVEN

THE WATCHERS

My summer is anything but a vacation. My parents decide not to spend any money on a family vacation since we will likely need every penny for our eventual escape. I don't know what to expect in public school. I'll have a handful of friends from Addison Christian there with me. I'm sure that will help ease the transition, but I've heard so many negative things about what the Zones have done in the last few years to public schools. Apparently, most of the Christian teachers were forced out for not signing tolerance pledges. These pledges would have forced them to teach things that completely contradict the Bible, so most left rather than signing.

I am amazed at how oblivious I was to all of this. I was willfully ignorant. I wanted to stay in my bubble and just be a kid as long as I could. I would hear rumors here and there over the years of how difficult things were getting for Christians. I just filtered them out. As a result, my reality has changed so violently, so suddenly. Would it have been easier if I had paid more attention? Maybe.

The week before school starts I make a concerted effort to connect with all of my former Addison Christian classmates who will be attending Hebron High School. I thought there were only eight, but it turns out there are twelve of us. We are from four different cliques, but those barriers seem to have evaporated, at least for now. Two of the girls are from the popular clique at Addison Christian, but they treat me like an insider now. I hope this will last, but I fear it won't.

At least I have one long-term friend who will be at Hebron with me, Amanda. We have been friends since sixth grade. Although she has floated in and out of my group of friends over the years, she has never completely abandoned me. With the new normal, I can tell she is really afraid, so this past summer we were as tight as we were in sixth grade. We engineered our electives in the hope of having at least two classes together, and it worked. We decide to drive to and from school together the first week.

The first day arrives so quickly. Amanda picks me up around seven. I tell her my stomach hurts, and she admits to having knots in her stomach, as well. My stomach cramps are so strong that I feel like throwing up, but I don't tell her. I have always been the stronger one emotionally in our relationship, and I feel somehow obligated to maintain that status quo. Neither of us could tolerate a change in our relationship at this point.

The campus is huge. My old high school had around five hundred students. I've heard that Hebron has more than three thousand. I'm amazed at the ethnic diversity. Addison Christian was mostly white kids. The dress code at Hebron seems pretty lax. I see lots of midriffs. I can tell we stand out because we dress more conservatively. We can't help it. We've both been in uniforms since kindergarten. Amanda and I part ways and agree to meet for lunch. My first four periods are mostly uneventful. I can tell the curriculum will be ten times easier than what I'm used to. None of my teachers even acknowledge that I'm new to the school. Maybe they don't know. Maybe they don't care. None of them seem very friendly.

The lunch bell finally rings, and it takes me ten minutes to find Amanda. We grab some lunch and find a table as far from the chaos as possible. We compare notes on our classes. The two classes we share are both after lunch. A few minutes into our lunch, our conversation is interrupted by a familiar voice. It's Brittney! She left Addison Christian after the eighth grade. I only heard rumors, but the word was she was struggling academically and was asked to leave.

"Amanda, Chloe!" Brittney exclaims.

"Hey, Brittney!" I respond, and we take turns with hugs.

"I didn't know you were here," I continue. "I thought you lived in Plano."

"I did," says Brittney, "but with the money my parents saved on private school tuition, we were able to move to your area two years ago. This is my third year at Hebron. I can't believe I spotted you two. What are the odds? This place is so big that you can go for weeks without seeing people you know unless you have a class together. I'm sorry about your school closing. It was a big surprise. So I guess even if I had stayed, I would have ended up here anyhow. It's not too bad. You just have to watch your back."

"What do you mean?" asks Amanda. "Are there gangs here or stuff like that?"

Brittney laughs.

"No, nothing like that," says Brittney.

She looks around carefully, and then lowers her voice a little.

"It's the 'watchers' you have to avoid," she says.

"What's a watcher?" I ask.

Brittney looks around again. Her demeanor changes. My stomach is hurting again. I have a feeling I'm not going to like what she has to say.

"Well," she continues, "please don't tell anyone I told you this. The Central Zone has a big influence now in public schools. They keep an eye on things. They pay some students to watch for things. It's mostly students, but also some teachers."

"What kind of things are they watching for?" I ask. In my mind, it's a rhetorical question. I already know the answer. They're looking for subversives like me.

"So they keep an eye out for the anti-Zone types," Brittney says. "You know, people who still believe that the U.S. Constitution is more important than the Central Zone policies. People who complain about the Central Zone a lot. They keep lists. They pass along names. You have to be careful what you say. Be cautious about any random kid who seems to know you're new here. In a place this big, they shouldn't know that. If they do, it means they were assigned to you, to feel you out, see where you stand. Be careful what you tell them. Keep a safe distance."

I feel sick to my stomach. I'm not safe. I'm being watched. I'm so angry! How did this happen in my country? How did evil get this far this fast? This is like something out of Stalinist Russia. I'm almost too upset and shocked to ask my next question, but I continue, "So what do they do with the lists? What happens to kids who say negative things about the Central Zone?"

Brittney looks at her watch, probably to see if she has time for a detailed answer. She doesn't. There are only about five minutes left in our lunch break.

"Well, we don't have time right now for a lot of detail," Brittney says, "and it's mostly rumors, but I know of one kid from last year. He was one of those 'don't-tread-on-Texas' types. You know, live free or die, secede, kick the Central Zone's butt. Well, his dad got fired from his job, and the family moved away. I don't know where. No one has been able to connect with him on Facebook. I know this sounds crazy and scary. I'm sorry to dump this on you as it's your first day here. Let's meet in this same spot tomorrow, and I'll give you more details."

The bell rings, and Amanda and I head to fifth period together. We don't say a word. We are both in shock. We are being watched by these 'watchers.' Great. As disgusting as it all is, I'm thankful I found out about the 'watchers' on the first day before some random kid baited me into saying something that would get my dad fired from his job. This is all insane. It's like a bad dream that just gets worse. How can I 'fight' if it will wreck our family financially? Maybe the only thing we can do is run away and hide.

CHAPTER EIGHT

THE EPIPHANY

I get home before Dad and can't wait to tell him what Brittney said. I consider texting him at work, but after what she said, I decide not to. My guess is that the Central Zone authorities are monitoring e-mails and texts also. I had no idea things had gotten this bad. I was tucked away in my little Christian bubble. I bet Mom and Dad knew about this kind of thing but just didn't say anything. I hear the garage door opening downstairs, so I run down to see if it's Mom or Dad. It's Mom.

"Hey Chloe, how was your first day of school?" Mom asks. "How do you think you will adjust to it?"

"It's a huge place, Mom," I say. "There are thousands of kids. The teachers don't seem very friendly or personable. It's like they keep their distance from the students. But I wanted to tell you about something that happened today. Do you have a few minutes?"

"Of course, Chloe," Mom replies. "Let me change into some home clothes first."

I wonder if the 'watchers' will be a surprise to her. I wonder if they have them at her work. I have a feeling she and Dad know more than they're telling us three kids. I need to get as much out of her as I possibly can. We settle into the couch in the living room. Hannah's in the media room, and

Jackson's in his room, so we have some privacy. Even still, I talk quietly.

"So, Mom, do you remember that girl named Brittney that left Addison Christian after the eighth grade?" I ask.

"Sure" Mom replies. "She's the bubbly, gossipy one, right?"

It's always interesting to me how parents characterize us teenagers. They always see us much differently than we see ourselves. I'm not sure who's right. I guess it's just a matter of perspective.

"Yeah, she's pretty outgoing, I guess," I say. "Well, Amanda and I were having lunch today, and she spotted us. I thought she was attending West Plano, but Brittney and her family moved to our area a couple of years ago. So seeing her was quite a surprise. It was kind of cool at first to run into someone from Addison Christian who could give us the scoop on Hebron High. Well, she gave us the scoop all right! The first thing she talked about, more like warned us about, was the watchers. She said that the Central Zone pays kids to make friends with other kids and then report their names if they say anything negative about the Central Zone! She talked about one kid last year who was super anti-Zone, and his dad lost his job. Mom, did you know about this kind of stuff?"

"Not as it relates to schools, Chloe," Mom says, "but at most large companies, Christians and even non-Christians have to be careful about what they say. We generally avoid any casual conversations about the Central Zone, unless we're talking to someone we've known for a long time. I don't know if there are these 'watchers' at companies, but you do have to be careful, especially with e-mails and texts."

"Why didn't you ever tell me about this, Mom?" I ask.

Mom pauses for a minute before she responds: "Chloe, I would have told you after you finished college and were starting your career. I didn't want to stress you out. You would have worried that Dad or I would lose our jobs, and that could have impacted your performance in school. You have enough stress as it is."

What we both know but leave unsaid is that our stress level will be a hundred times greater in the coming months and years. We are on the front end of the worst period of time in human history. When the Antichrist takes over, we'll have a short period of peace, and then all hell will break lose. There's no point in reminding each other of the obvious.

"Well, Mom," I say, "I'm just glad I found out about the 'watchers' on the first day of school before I said something that would get you or Dad fired. I'm going to be extremely careful with what I say. And I'm going to be very selective on whom I become friends with. From what Brittney said, if another kid tries hard to be friends with me, then that's a red flag. They probably work for the Central Zone. So basically, I have to be the one to initiate a friendship; otherwise I won't know if it's real or a trap. Maybe I'll just stick with Amanda. I don't know. It's too much to think about right now."

"I'm sorry, Chloe," Mom says. "I'm sorry you have to finish high school under these conditions. It stinks. When you were little, I never imagined things would end up like this. This was not how I pictured your high school years. This isn't how I imagined your life, our lives."

I can hear the resignation, the sadness, in Mom's voice. I know she doesn't like to talk about this.

I try to change the subject slightly: "Mom, I tried to warn Jackson about this on the way home, but he just blew the whole thing off. He remembered Brittney and said she's a big gossip-chick. He said she's imagining the whole thing just to get attention. I'm worried Jackson's going to say something stupid and get us in trouble."

"Have you ever heard him say anything negative about the Zones, Chloe?" Mom asks. The way she says this sounds more like an indictment than a question. I suddenly realize what she is implying in that one brief question.

"Well, no," I reply. "He seems pretty disinterested in the whole thing. He didn't even seem to care that much that Addison Christian closed down. All he cares about is eating and gaming. School is pretty far down the list for him."

I can tell that I'm trying to dismiss his actions as indifference. But I know deep down inside Mom is on to something.

"Mom," I ask, "do you really think he is supportive of the Zones, that he somehow thinks they're a good thing? I can't believe he would think that!"

Mom avoids eye contact. She looks away and says, "Well, why don't you ask him what he thinks?"

Mom ends the conversation abruptly by starting dinner. Mom is always trying to escape from all of this, but there is no escape.

I am stunned by what Mom is suggesting. If Jackson is for the Zones, then he will one day have to choose between them and us. If he chooses them, then he will turn us all in. It doesn't seem possible that my own brother could ever do this, betray his family. It's insane. How could that possibly happen? Just the thought of it seems impossible. I want to talk to him about this, but I'm afraid. I am afraid he might confirm my fears. I definitely need to talk to Dad about this first. I need to see if he has the same suspicions.

Dad gets home an hour later, and I corner him at the garage door.

"Dad, can we talk for a few minutes?" I ask.

I'm sure he can hear the concern in my voice. There seems to be concern in everyone's voices these days. I guess this is the new normal.

"Sure, Chloe," Dad says. "Give me a minute or two to change. How was day one at Hebron?"

"Not good," I respond. "I'll give you the full story after you change."

We meet in our home office a few minutes later. I close the double doors to give us some privacy.

"So, Dad, I gave Mom the scoop on this about an hour ago," I say. "Well, to make a long story short, I found out that the Central Zone hires kids to spy on other kids at school! They look for kids who say negative things about the Central Zone, then pass along names. At least one kid disappeared last year after both his parents lost their jobs. No one has been able to reconnect with him on Facebook. He just vanished!"

Dad looks upset but not surprised. Did he know this already and not tell me? What else is he hiding from me? I'm almost an adult now!

"Who told you about this Chloe?" Dad asks.

I doubt he remembers Brittney.

"It was a girl who left Addison Christian after eighth grade," I reply. "We played basketball together."

"I think I remember her," Dad says. "Was she the tall girl with puffy red hair?"

"Yep, that's her," I say. "She has been at Hebron since ninth grade. She ran into Amanda and me during lunch and warned us to be careful what we say and whom we make friends with. Dad, did you know this was going on?"

"So here's the scoop, Chloe," Dad says. "This kind of thing has been happening at large companies for a couple of years now. Mom and I avoid discussing the Zones at work. A couple of times, I felt like someone was trying to 'bait' me into saying what I really thought, but I stopped myself. I've seen people who were too vocal get laid off, but no one has disappeared the way you described what happened to the kid at school. Mom and I have speculated that this might be going on in public schools. I'm sorry. I was going to say something before your first day of school but got distracted and forgot. As you know, we have all had a lot of distractions lately."

I almost apologize to Dad for overreacting, but I quickly realize I'm not overreacting. All of this is very real and very serious. I give Dad a hug and say I'm sorry for what is happening to us. Then I remember something I've wanted to tell him. It's kind of an epiphany.

"Dad," I begin, "do you remember that song by The Band Perry called 'If I die young'?"

"No, not really. How does it go?" he asks.

I quote the main lyrics for him: "If I die young, bury me in satin, lay me down in a bed of roses. Sink me in a river at dawn. Send me away with the words of a love song."

"Okay, now I remember it," he says. "That's a really touching song. It's kind of sad."

"Well, Dad, I had an epiphany this week when I was listening to it," I say. "The song talks about 'the sharp knife of a short life.' I was thinking how this is the song for my generation. All of us will suffer from the sharp knife of a short life. Those who choose Jesus will die in the coming Zones wars, be killed for our faith, or be taken up in the Rapture. Those who choose the Antichrist will be killed in the Zone wars, die when God pours out his wrath, or if they make it to the end of the seven years, be thrown into the Lake of Fire. Do you see it? My generation will all die young. We'll all suffer the sharp knife of a short life. Dad, I've come to terms with this. Whatever time I have will be 'enough' time. I don't want even one extra day. I'm good with this."

Dad is unusually quiet. I know he agrees with me but can't bring himself to say it.

"Chloe, do you have your phone on you? Can you play the whole song for me?" he finally says.

"Sure Dad," I say. I sit in his lap in the office, and I play the song on my iPhone. When the song ends, I say, "Dad, if I go first, will you play this song at my funeral?"

His eyes fill with tears as he nods his head. We sit together for a long time with the words of this beautiful, sad song playing over and over again in our minds.

CHAPTER NINE

BAD-TO-WORSE

In the next few weeks, Amanda and I warn the other ten students who came from Addison Christian about the watchers. We are careful to do this in person and not use texting or social media. I'm not sure they all believe us, but we have to try. A few weeks into the school year, a girl named Alyssa in my pre-calculus class starts up a conversation with me. Alyssa would not normally be in my clique at Addison Christian, so I am cautious. She asks me what colleges I plan on applying to. I give her the standard answers for a Texas high school senior: Texas A&M, UT Austin and Baylor. Alyssa says she is shooting for the McCombs School of Business at UT Austin. She had read that it was rated a top-ten business school.

In the next few class sessions, we continue some small talk, and I get a friend invitation from her on Facebook, which I accept. She seems curious about what school was like at Addison Christian. I let her know that it was much more difficult academically, but I avoid sharing my feelings about the Central Zone's closing of all Christian schools. I continue to keep my guard up, and I have a feeling she can sense this from me.

In September, the college application process kicks into high gear. It all seems a bit pointless to me. Even if I finish college before the Tribulation starts, what kind of work future would I have, given my faith and my feelings about the Zones? I had heard that some large companies were starting to implement questionnaires for job candidates that ask political and religious questions. These types of questions were illegal prior to the Zones, but not anymore. If I answered those questions truthfully, my guess is that no large company would hire me.

I compare notes with Jackson on his experience at Hebron High School. He seems to have adjusted quickly to this new secular environment, maybe too quickly. He added three 'gamer' friends to his core group of five from Addison Christian. His Addison Christian gamer friends always seemed to be bashing Addison Christian. I decide I have to know where he stands regarding the Zones. I am afraid of what I might discover, but curiosity gets the better of me.

One Friday on the short drive home from school, I began with a fairly benign question. "Hey, Jackson, what do your friends think about the Central Zone?"

He is quiet for a moment as if he is deciding whether this is a casual conversation or an interrogation.

"They don't really care much either way," Jackson says. "Like everything else from the government, there are some good things and some not-so-good things. They have certainly brought more stability to the world in the last two years. That's a good thing."

I'm not exactly sure where to go next, so I throw out the whole watcher thing: "Have you heard that the Zones pay some kids and teachers to spy on students?"

This time, he doesn't hesitate. "Oh, yeah, and I'm sure the Illuminati are behind the whole thing!" he says in his most mocking voice. "I've heard those dumb watcher rumors, and it's all a bunch of right-wing conspiracy crap. None of it's true. Name one person who disappeared from our school because they criticized the Zones."

My response is just as quick and sharp. "Well, given that I've been at Hebron for a whole seven weeks and that I know maybe twenty-five kids there personally, I would say it's a little early for me to answer that question!"

"Whatever" is his only reply.

We end it there and endure an awkward silence the rest of the drive home. I now know that, at best, Jackson is indifferent about the Zones, and, at worst, he supports them. This was what I expected, but the reality of it is hard to swallow. How could the two of us attend the same churches and Christian schools, and end up with such radically different beliefs? It doesn't make any sense to me. I have to talk to Dad about Jackson. We need to be careful now around him in terms of what we say. The thought that this Zone evil could potentially impact my immediate family makes me so angry. I'm not even safe at home!

That weekend I decide to ask Dad if just the two of us could go to a local donut shop in our neighborhood to talk. Dad has been taking me there ever since sixth grade. It always felt special that he would take the time to hang out there with just me and talk. So many of my friends have like a zero relationship with their dads, but we have always been super close.

"Hey, Dad, can we run over to Escape and grab a couple of donuts?" I ask. "We haven't been there in a while."

"Sure, Chloe," he says. "Give me ten minutes to finish checking my e-mail; then we'll go."

We make small talk on the four-minute drive to Escape. As soon as we have our donuts, I jump right in. "Dad, I have the feeling, more than a feeling, that Jackson is a Zone supporter. We talked yesterday on the way home from school, and he pretty much said that I was crazy for thinking they are up to no good."

Dad pauses before answering, clearly giving careful thought to his response. "You're right to be concerned about him, Chloe. A few months ago, he told your mom and me that he is an atheist. It was quite a shock to us. I mean, he has been exposed to the truth of God's Word since he was old enough to talk. He has been given more biblical truth, at school, home, and church than probably 95 percent of kids in this country, and yet he has rejected the truth."

I am stunned. Why didn't I know this? Why didn't I see this coming? We grew up together. Every 'first' thing we ever did— parasailing, snorkeling, surfing—we did together. How could we both hear the same facts and come to radically different conclusions?

Dad must sense what I'm thinking and says, "Chloe, I know it sounds crazy. We were going to tell you eventually, but not Hannah. It's a tough topic to bring up. I mean, what are we going to say? 'Hey, Jackson, can you bless the meal tonight? Oh, that's right, you're an atheist. Never mind.' It's very painful for your mom and me, especially given where we are on the prophetic calendar. You know what could happen. During the Great Tribulation, children will turn in their parents and have them put to death.

"What we don't know is if his rejection of Christianity is just a passing form of teenage rebellion or a permanent decision. There is no way for us to know this. As a result, Mom and I have decided not to include him in future conversations related to our 'fight-then-flight' planning. We won't be having any future meetings with Mr. Harmon at our house. Since Mr. Harmon is single, we will meet at his house. We would like you to join us?"

"Of course," is all I can say at first, given my shock concerning Jackson.

"How did this happen, Dad, I mean Jackson and his atheism?" I ask. "You and Mom have been such amazing parents to all three of us. I don't mean to brag on you two, but I've had seventeen years to compare the two of you to my friends' parents, and you two are rock stars by comparison."

It feels weird to say this, but it's the truth. Mom and Dad have made incredible financial sacrifices to send us to private school. And it's not just the money stuff; it's the personal time they have invested in all three of us.

"Thanks for the five-star rating," Dad says with a smile. "We have done the best we knew how. Regarding Jackson, I agree it doesn't make any sense. I've had a few months to think about this, and my conclusion is that atheists are born, not made. What I mean by this is that some people's hearts are so rebellious, so full of pride that no matter 'who' raises them, they end up rejecting the truth. I want to be careful to say that as long as Jackson is still alive and he hasn't taken the mark of the Antichrist, there is still hope for him. You probably remember our pastor from our church in California, Pastor Raul. Well, one of his three sons ended up on drugs and totally rejected God in his early twenties. He eventually came around to the truth and now teaches a Sunday night Bible study at the church. Do you see, Chloe, that as long as someone is still breathing, there is hope? We shouldn't give up hope for Jackson, but we will need to be cautious about what we tell him."

"I get it, Dad," I say. "I'll leave this whole 'fight-or-flight' topic off the table in my conversations with him going forward. And I'll be careful not to mention anything about our ongoing planning. He's really smart, though, Dad, so he's going to get suspicious and wonder what we're up to if all of the sudden we stop talking about it. How will we handle that?"

"Good question, Chloe," Dad says. "Let your mom and I figure that one out. If he asks you, just say that you haven't talked to us in a while about it. Say something like our work has kept us so busy that we must not have had time to do any additional planning. If he pushes for more, just tell him to ask Mom or me. Sound good?"

"Sure, Dad," I say.

"Chloe, while we are here in our 'secure' location," Dad says, "I want to bring you up to date on something else."

That's Dad, always trying to make me laugh. It works.

"Chloe," he says, "I've heard some rumors about negotiations in Geneva between Israel and several Muslim nations. I know this is not surprising. They are always 'talking.' I remember one former Israeli prime minister quoted as saying privately, 'I love the peace *process*. I hope it continues for a thousand years.' The idea behind his comment is ingenious. The Arab nations always break every agreement they make with Israel, so why cut a deal? However, it's politically expedient for the Jews to have an ongoing peace *process*. At any rate, there is talk that secret negotiations are taking place now. I don't know if this will be the real thing, you know, the seven-year agreement that starts the clock ticking, but it could be."

My heart sinks. This is not what I wanted to hear. It means we could be close to the beginning of the end. But it also means we could have a chance very soon to fight back. And given how much anger I have toward the Central Zone, I'm ready for a fight!

My dad is already reading my thoughts and continues before I can respond: "Chloe, I know this is not what you wanted to hear. It's incredibly stressful to think it could all start soon. Even Mom and I have difficulty talking about this. But God has put us here, in this place and at this time, for a reason. He has a specific work for us to do. Think about it. For almost two thousand years, believers have been waiting for Jesus to return, to set up his kingdom for one thousand years here on Earth. We are the generation that will see this fulfilled! It's amazing if you think about it."

"Well, that's sort of true Dad," I say. "We just have to avoid getting nuked or having our heads chopped off. Other than that, yeah it's pretty cool."

We both laugh.

"So, Dad, how reliable are these sources?" I ask. "I know there are lots of those Christian conspiracy websites that are always saying things about the end of America and all that."

Dad laughs and says, "I'm reading it on both the 'crazy' Christian websites and on traditional secular sites, as well. That's why I think there is some truth to the rumors. Given this, I've scheduled another meeting with Mr. Harmon for next weekend. As I mentioned, given the Jackson thing, we will be meeting at Mr. Harmon's house. Mom and I would like you to come with us. We've arranged a sleepover for Hannah with Ivy. Are you in?"

"Of course I'm in dad!" I say. "I wouldn't miss a conversation about the end of the world for anything, except the end of the world, of course!"

Dad laughs again, and the irony sets in. Here we are at our neighborhood donut shop, enjoying a play on words and laughing about the end of the world. What else can we do? It's going to happen. Why not inject a little humor as we tumble headlong into the end of days?

"Great," Dad says. "We'll plan on being at his house next Saturday around six o'clock, so we'll leave at five-thirty. We'll have dinner there. I'll order a pizza for Jackson before we leave. If he asks where we're going, I'll make up some reason."

CHAPTER TEN

THE CLUB OF TEN

At school the next week, my new 'almost' friend Alyssa asks me to join her for lunch off campus on Wednesday. It will just be the two of us. I agree, but I know she can sense my apprehension. She hasn't brought up any controversial topics with me, just typical girl stuff. It's amazing to me that we could be at the doorstep of the worst period in human history when more than half of the world's population will die, and I'm still engaging in high school girl talk. It's bizarre. I need to keep up some semblance of normalcy, however, if for no other reason than to keep the 'watchers' at bay, but I fear Alyssa might be one of them.

Alyssa offers to drive since she invited me. We head to a local mom-and-pop Italian place just a few minutes from school. I've seen it but never eaten there before. It's fancier than the typical high school lunch hangout. The place is only half-full, and I get the sense that Alyssa picked this place to avoid running into other students. The hostess offers us a table next to the other diners, but Alyssa asks for a booth away from everyone else. I have a really bad feeling. I was hungry when we left school, but now my appetite evaporates. I can feel a knot in my stomach. We both order sweet tea and look at the menu. Alyssa must come here often because she clearly knows what she wants to order. I take longer than needed to review the menu, trying to stall for time. I have the feeling she is going to steer the conversation to the Zones.

Alyssa breaks the silence. "So what are you getting, Chloe?"

"The meatball sandwich sounds pretty good. Have you had it?" I ask.

"Yes, several times," Alyssa says. "You'll like it."

Our server returns, and we place our orders.

Alyssa looks at me for a moment before she begins to speak, almost like she is sizing me up. "So, Chloe, we've known each other for a few weeks now. We have some things in common. I haven't mentioned this yet to you, but I'm a Christian. I'm guessing you are as well since you went to Addison Christian." There is an expectant pause as I consider how to answer.

"Sure, yes, I'm a Christian," I say.

"Great," Alyssa continues. "Given the times we're living in, it's not exactly safe to be out there with your faith. You might not know this, but it can negatively affect your grades. Like if you challenge one of our teachers on evolution, you'll never get an 'A' in that class."

I didn't know this. There have been a few opportunities to challenge my teachers so far this year, but it was mostly around Zone stuff, and I had kept quiet after hearing about the watchers.

"Really," I respond. "Has this happened to you?"

"Yes," she says. "My freshman year was really tough. That was the year most of the Christian teachers left. They had to sign a teaching contract with language that totally contradicted the Bible, and if they didn't sign it, they were forced to resign. Most left. A few stayed. I was pretty vocal my freshman year and paid the price. I only got one 'A' that year, and I'm typically all 'As' and maybe one 'B.' Anyway, I'm glad you are a Christian. Not all Christian school kids are Christians you know."

I want to mention how much I knew this to be true from my own family, but I decide to play it safe and just agree with her in a general sense.

Alyssa continues: "You have to be sort of careful who you confide in around here. That's why I waited a few weeks before I asked you to lunch. I get a sense that you are safe. So here's the deal. There are a few of us who get together at school to talk about our faith and what's happening in the world. We don't meet in a classroom. It's not safe. There are some tables out near the softball field where we meet. Do you know the ones I'm talking about?"

"Yes," I respond.

Alyssa continues: "We meet every Thursday during the lunch hour. I'd like you to join our group. There are ten of us, not including you."

My first thought is the ten Zones. I can't help but say it: "So do each of you represent one of the ten Zones?"

We both laugh.

"Nice one," Alyssa says. "It's not a bad idea. The ten of us could take turns criticizing each of the Zones. That would be lots of fun!"

A warning light goes off in my head. Is Alyssa for real? Is she actually a watcher who is now baiting me into saying something negative about the Zones? My demeanor changes. I try to hide it, but I'm terrible at this. I would make an awful poker player. Alyssa senses my apprehension and says, "Look, Chloe; you have only known me for a few weeks, and it's healthy to be paranoid these days. Trust me; I know. I was 'baited' my sophomore year by a kid I suspect was working for the Zones.

He was really cute and outgoing—you know, a football clique guy. I almost let my guard down because he was so charming. I was right to be suspicious. When I didn't take the bait, he moved on and never talked to me again. It was a setup."

I can't help but ask the obvious: "So, Alyssa, how do I know this isn't a setup? Let's be honest; at my last school we would have been in totally different cliques. There's no overlap between your clique and mine. It's a red flag to me."

I think Alyssa must have anticipated my concern.

"I get it, Chloe," she says. "Here's my offer. Join us tomorrow during the lunch break. Don't feel compelled to share any of your opinions. Just listen to what the ten of us have to say. Draw your own conclusions. If you think it's a setup, then simply walk away. No worries."

I agree just as our lunch is served. I know I need to do two things before tomorrow: pray a lot about this and talk to Dad.

I talk to Dad that night about the Alyssa lunch. He thinks I should go but stick with my plan of keeping quiet. He suggests that if I get a good feeling about the group, then I should continue to attend but hold off on sharing my opinions for at least a month. Dad reminds me that we have a dinner on Saturday with Mr. Harmon. He's already let Jackson know that the three of us will be out for a few hours. Dad told him we were meeting with some friends who have kids at UT Austin. Dad played it off as another college planning meeting.

It bothers me that Dad has lied to Jackson. I begin to wonder how many times I'll have to lie in the coming years to stay alive. Is it wrong to lie in this situation? I'm not sure.

Dad also provides an update on the rumors about the peace negotiations happening in Geneva. Apparently, once word began to leak out about the meetings, the Central Zone authorities put some type of gag order in place. As a result, no new details have emerged. People aren't even sure if the meetings are continuing. The whole thing went silent, which makes Dad think that these negotiations are more serious than what he has seen in the past.

The next day, I'm so nervous about the meeting with Alyssa and her lunch group that I skip breakfast. I have a hard time focusing in my first four classes. When my fourth-period class bell rings, I almost change my mind and don't go. Something inside me says it's safe, so I head toward the softball field. Seeing the field brings back memories. Softball was the last sport I played at Addison Christian. I had previously played volleyball and basketball and loved both. But when I stopped growing in seventh grade, I had to give them up. I just didn't have the height to be competitive. Leaving Addison Christian was so upsetting that I had decided not to play any sports my senior year at Hebron High. Deep down inside, I really miss them, though. I miss the camaraderie and winning games.

As I approach the benches near the softball field, Alyssa spots me and waves me over with a big smile. She looks a little surprised that I came. The other nine girls are all there and have started eating their lunches. One by one, she makes introductions. I recognize just one of the girls, Meagan, from my pre-calculus class in period five. The other eight are all new faces to me. It hits me immediately that these ten girls must be from at least four different social groups on campus. I think to myself that this could be a red flag. However, if they are 'truly' Christians, then it makes sense. At my last school, there were so many kids who I'm convinced were not saved. They always rejected any kids from a lower clique. However, the true Christians would hang out with everyone. They weren't hard-wired to any one clique. It suddenly occurs to me that there might be more true Christians at Hebron High than at Addison Christian.

One of the girls asks if I had played softball at Addison Christian. I'm a little surprised and concerned that she would know this.

"Yes, I played my sophomore and junior year," I say. "I played basketball my freshman year."

I don't ask her how she knows this. Maybe she has become friends with Amanda. But then why hadn't Amanda been invited to join their little collective?

"What position did you play in basketball?" she continues.

"I played point guard," I say, and I can see she's a little surprised, given my height. What I lacked in height I made up for in effort. My coach called me the "scrapper." Whenever there was a loose ball, I always seemed to come up with it.

Alyssa jumps back into the conversation: "So I met Chloe a few weeks ago. We've talked a lot at school, and we had lunch yesterday. I asked her to consider joining our group. She's a believer."

Alyssa turns to me. "So, Chloe," she says, "what we typically do here is focus on some current events and any challenges we are facing. We like to pray for each other. Meagan keeps an ongoing list of the prayer requests. One of the goals of this group is to encourage each other. About half of us are the only Christians in our families, so for us, this group has become a kind of family."

Alyssa seems completely genuine, so I relax a little and start to eat my lunch. The group begins with current events. One girl mentions the negotiations in Geneva. I am so tempted to jump in, but I hold back. I promised myself I wouldn't share my opinions for at least the first few weeks. Most of the other girls have also heard the rumors. This leads to a lively discussion and speculation about whether this could be the big one, the seven-year agreement. It's apparent from the ensuing conversation that most of them hold to a pre-Tribulation Rapture position. Some seem excited that we could be so close, believing that if this is the seven-year agreement, the Rapture could happen at any moment. Once again, I'm dying to give my opinion, but I hold back. I'm not sure from the conversation where Alyssa stands on the timing of the Rapture. She seems to have the role of a facilitator.

The group provides other updates related to new Central Zone initiatives, and there is some talk about the potential confiscation of guns. Two of the girls in the group are clearly hunters, a fact which surprises me. I never met even one girl at Addison Christian who hunted. Everyone agrees that World War III would happen if the Central Zone tries to take away our guns. I know, of course, that this is exactly what will happen. We finally get to prayer requests. The list moves me. These are not the typical Addison Christian–girl prayer requests. I'm used to hearing things like "God keep us safe on our trip to Paris this summer." These were serious requests.

One of the girls has an alcoholic dad who beats her mom several times a month. She is thinking about moving in with one of the other girls in the group for the rest of her senior year. Another girl has a sister who is into goth and is cutting herself. It begins to occur to me that I am now seeing the world as it really is. I have been protected from this my whole life. I am shocked by the raw emotions and complete honesty among these ten girls. If they are secretly working for the Zones, they are the best actresses I've ever met. I quickly decide this group is the real thing.

That evening, I provide Dad with my conclusion that these ten girls are true Christians. He seems relieved but still suggests that I keep my opinions to myself for one more meeting, and I agree.

CHAPTER ELEVEN

GENEVA

Saturday rolls around, and we head out to Mr. Harmon's house around five thirty, as planned. Jackson gets his pepperoni-and-onion pizza and seems completely disinterested in our evening plans. We get to Mr. Harmon's house around six o'clock. He welcomes us with a round of hugs.

"How have you all been?" he asks. "It's been several weeks since we last spoke. I've got a lot of new information I want to share with the three of you, but let's eat first."

My first thought is, "Let's do the updates now and the food later," but I hold my tongue. I can be impatient.

Thirty minutes later, we finally finish dinner and head to the living room. Mr. Harmon jumps right in. "I noticed you brought Chloe, but not Jackson," he says. "Should I read anything into that?"

My dad glances over to Mom before responding. "Well, to be honest," he says, "we're not sure where Jackson stands spiritually. We think he might be an atheist. We thought that it would be best to leave him out of these conversations, for now, just to be on the safe side."

Mr. Harmon looks a little concerned. I'm sure he remembers that Jackson was in on that initial conversation about Alaska.

"I think that's a prudent decision," Mr. Harmon responds. "We all need to err on the side of caution these days."

"Yes, we do," says Mom.

"Well let me start with some updates," Mr. Harmon continues. "Have you heard the rumors about the negotiations going on in Geneva between Israel and several Muslim nations?"

"Yes," we all say at the same time.

"Good," Mr. Harmon says. "Well, actually, not so good, given the context. I have a personal friend in the IDF, the Israeli Defense Forces. We went to college together many years ago. He's pretty high up there. We talk a couple of times each year. I spoke with him last night, and I asked him directly about these rumors. Keep in mind he is not a believer. Well, he tells me there is great excitement in Israel right now among people who are in the know. Very serious negotiations are happening, and they seem different than those in the past, before the nuclear war with Iran and Russia. He says that because Israel won that war, they have a very strong position in these talks. Israel is likely to get most of what they want, including the right to rebuild their temple in Jerusalem."

I feel like I could throw up. I had imagined that we might have a few more years before the clock started clicking down to the end, but it looks like I was wrong. I glance over at Mom and Dad, and they look pale. I know they are processing what this means for all of us, including Jackson.

Mr. Harmon senses our shock. "I don't know with certainty if this will be the seven-year agreement," he continues. "My friend in the IDF said that very few details are getting out. That's one of the reasons he's convinced that these negotiations are serious. In past negotiations, each side would deliberately leak details to put pressure on the other party. That's not happening this time around. It's tightly controlled. My friend doesn't even know who is facilitating the negotiations, but his guess is that it's someone from the Central Zone."

We all know what everyone else is thinking, so I just jump in and say it: "Mr. Harmon, if this is the real deal, then it's the Antichrist who is facilitating the negotiations, right?"

"Yes, that's right, Chloe," Mr. Harmon says. "But keep in mind that if and when the deal goes through, only true Christians will know this. Everyone else will call him the greatest negotiator of our time. Many world leaders, including several U.S. presidents, have tried to secure a meaningful deal and failed. In his second term, Bill Clinton tried and failed. I had heard that Clinton's draft agreement even included Israel's right to rebuild their Temple. If this deal goes through, then we will know who the Antichrist is, and we can start the seven-year countdown clock."

I jump back in: "Well, it's not really a countdown of seven years for us, more like four or five, if you believe in a Pre-Wrath Rapture, right?"

"Well said, Chloe," Mr. Harmon responds. "It will probably be closer to four years."

He continues: "I know that lots of Christians are very excited right now because they think this means that the Rapture is going to happen at any minute. They believe that Christians must be removed from the Earth before the Antichrist is revealed. I can't begin to imagine their shock and dismay if this is the real deal. They will still be here and will wonder what happened. I'm concerned that many could fall away from the Christian faith altogether. Many will say, 'Well, if my pastor was wrong about something this big, how can I trust any of his teachings?' Do you see the risk?"

We all agree that this will be a huge problem. I mention another challenge. "There are churches like the one we attend, Mr. Harmon, that never teach on end-time Bible prophecy. I think they are afraid that it's too controversial, even though the Bible itself says we are to teach the whole Bible, not just parts of it. So the challenge will be convincing Christians that the seven-year period has begun. I think many are clueless about the end-time and will think we're crazy. Do you agree?"

"I agree, Chloe," Mr. Harmon says. "That's also going to be a challenge. I'm not sure which will be more difficult, convincing a 'former' Pre-Tribulation Rapture Christian that the Rapture is Pre-Wrath or convincing completely clueless believers that the last seven years of world history has begun."

Dad finally jumps in: "I think the Pre-Tribulation Christians will be the tougher group. People like my aunt are so convinced they're right, and pride gets in the way. I think many of them will decide, at least initially, that even though a seven-year agreement is reached and the Jews get to rebuild their Temple, this is the not the final agreement. However, as events unfold, they will have to come to terms with it. It won't be pretty. I agree that some will leave the church altogether, especially when the real persecution begins. I mean, think about it. I'm sure in the past two thousand years that many true believers decided to abandon their faith rather than lose their lives or jobs or whatever. It will happen on a much greater scale this time around."

Dad continues: "So your friend in the IDF, does he have any sense of how close they are to a deal? Are we days away, weeks away?"

Mr. Harmon responds, "He told me he has no idea. The talks could collapse, or they could reach a deal tomorrow. For all we know, they have already reached a deal and are putting together an official announcement. We need to give some thought to what we'll do if a seven-year deal is announced. If it happens, or when it happens, I think we should get together immediately and talk about our fight-then-flight plans. I got the impression from our last conversation that you were leaning toward that approach."

Dad looks at Mom but responds to Mr. Harmon, "Yes, we've had several discussions about our strategy, and fight-then-flight does make the most sense. So I agree we should meet immediately if a deal is announced."

We spend another hour talking about what we should say to our Christian friends if a deal goes through. There is strong agreement between Mom, Dad, and Mr. Harmon that we should be very direct with them since most believe in a Pre-Tribulation Rapture. Given that the agreement could come at any time, I feel like asking Alyssa for an emergency meeting of our group. That will feel strange, given that I've only attended one of their meetings, but my sense is that they are in for a real shock. I feel compelled to explain the Pre-Wrath position to them before all this hits them. At least then they'll have something to fall back on when their Pre-Tribulation scenario obliterates. I don't ask for Dad's opinion. I just decide I'm going to do it.

When we get home, Jackson passes me in the hallway on my way to my room upstairs.

"How was the college planning meeting?" he asks.

"Good," I respond. "I'm shooting for UT Austin since they have a stronger business program. I think it's ranked eighth in the country or something like that."

He doesn't say anything, which is typical for him, but I'm still cautious. I need to be extra careful around him now, especially if the seven-year agreement goes through. Should we even try to tell him what it means? I know he is, at a minimum, sympathetic to the Zones. What if he is more than that? What if he is working for them? The thought of my own brother working for the Antichrist, or at least his system, is too much for me to process. I'm worried about how I can't hide anything. My face always gives me away. That could end up being a real problem very soon. It could put Mom, Dad, Hannah, and me at great risk.

As soon as I get to school on Monday, I text Alyssa and ask if we can meet briefly between second and third period. She agrees. I tell her I have some information related to the negotiations in Geneva and that I want to share them quickly with the other girls. She agrees to ask the others for a lunch meeting the next day, on Tuesday. However, she knows of at least one girl who won't be able to make a Tuesday lunch meeting. I thank her and quickly head to my third-period class. I'm completely stressed out the rest of the day, thinking about what I'm going to say and how they will respond. Most of them have only met me one time, and I said almost nothing at that first lunch meeting. I'm guessing that at least a couple of them are, at best, suspicious of me, and, at worst, they think I might be working for the Zones. I try to calm myself down and think through what I'll say.

The next day we meet at the lunch tables near the softball field. Only eight girls show up. Alyssa thinks one more might be coming late, but she's not sure. I take a deep breath and jump in: "I know you guys don't know me very well, and some of you might even be a little suspicious of me. I totally get that.

I mean, I was really concerned with Alyssa. I thought she might be setting me up. The last thing I need is to get my parents in some type of trouble at their jobs. So thank you for meeting on such short notice. At the last lunch meeting, you all talked about the negotiations in Geneva. My mom, my dad, and I have been watching them closely. It looks like the negotiations could end up as the treaty that starts the seven-year period." Several of the girls nod in agreement.

I keep going: "Well, based on what many of you said at our last meeting, I'd guess that most of you believe that the Rapture will happen before that seven-year period begins, right?"

There are lots of enthusiastic nods this time.

"My family and I used to believe the same thing, but we don't anymore," I say. "We all read a book this last spring called *The Pre-Wrath Rapture of the Church* by a guy named Rosenthal. In his book, he makes what we believe to be an airtight argument from Scripture that the church will be here for roughly the first four of the seven years."

I can see the shocked looks on their faces.

I barely take a breath and keep talking: "The Bible says that we as Christians are not appointed unto wrath, which is true. But the first part of this seven-year period is not God's wrath. It's more like Satan's wrath, or the wrath of the Antichrist. Here's an example. Most of you probably know that in the first three and a-half years, the Antichrist comes to power and ends up controlling the whole world. He starts off as a man of peace and then quickly turns to war. Something like one-quarter of the world's population is killed by the wars he starts. You see, the rise of the Antichrist is not God's doing; it is Satan's work. To call what the Antichrist does God's wrath is to make God responsible for what he does, to suggest that God is causing all of this suffering and death. Well, he isn't. God's wrath comes later, at some point early in the second three and a-half years."

Alyssa is the only one who responds initially, and, to my surprise, she doesn't disagree with me.

"I've heard something like this before from one of my uncles," Alyssa begins. "It was a few years ago. He didn't mention that book, but what he said was very similar. I was still in middle school and didn't pay much attention to it. I hadn't thought about it until now."

"Do you have a copy of that book, the Pre-Wrath book?" she asks.

"Not with me," I respond, "but I have a copy at home, and you can, of course, get it on Amazon. The reason I'm bringing this up now is that we could be close to the beginning of the seven-year period. If the deal in Geneva goes through and it includes the right of the Jews to rebuild their Temple and we're still here, then I want you all to know why. You need to know that there is a very reasonable explanation for why the church is still here. I know it's a little shocking if you've never heard this before. And again, I know that, other than Alyssa, you guys don't know me at all, so I understand if you're skeptical."

Meagan jumps into the conversation: "So if this guy, Rosenthal, is right, then what does that mean for us, for true Christians? Doesn't the Antichrist kill most Christians during the Tribulation?"

I knew this would be one of the first questions. I choose my words carefully: "Well, he kills some Christians, but definitely not most Christians. If you read Revelation, chapter six, you see that two groups show up in Heaven sequentially during this seven-year period. The first to arrive in Heaven is a group that is killed, beheaded actually, during the Great Tribulation. Then, a little while later, a second, much larger group suddenly appears in Heaven. This group is so large that no man can number them, and they are from every tribe, nation, and tongue. This second group is the Raptured church. From this passage in Revelation, we know that the Antichrist does kill many Christians, but it's probably a small percentage of the total because of the strong contrast in the size of these two groups. My dad thinks that the Antichrist will murder perhaps 10 percent of Christians between the three-and-a-half-year mark and the Rapture. I don't know if that makes you feel any better or not."

I can tell from their faces that the enormity of what I'm suggesting is sinking in. I'm sure that some of them are thinking about what this means to them personally. Others are thinking about their parents or siblings.

Meagan seems the most composed of the group and jumps back in: "How will we know if this Pre-Wrath thing is right? What if the agreement reached is not the one mentioned in Revelation?"

"Good question, Meagan," I say. "If the agreement is for seven years and gives the Jews the right to rebuild their temple, that will be a strong indication that it's the agreement described in Revelation. Also, if the man who pulls this off then achieves other major diplomatic accomplishments in quick succession, that will be another clue. If the ten Zones presidents give him authority over the entire Zone system, then we'll know with 100 percent certainty that the final seven-year period has begun."

The girls are all quiet, so I keep going: "I know this is an incredible shock and probably totally depressing. I don't know all of you yet, but I'm guessing you know Bible prophecy better than most people your age. Some of you are probably already thinking about those three kings who end up rebelling against the Antichrist. Those nations get wiped out. That's why 25 percent of the world's population dies in the early part of the seven-year period. It's not a stretch to imagine Zone One being one of the three Zones who rebels. That's part of why I'm bringing this up. We all have to think long and hard about what our personal strategies will be."

"What do you mean by that?" Meagan asks. "I mean, we will all have choices to make about how we'll respond. Let's say Rosenthal is right, and let's say this whole mess starts next week. People in every Zone are going to fall in love with this guy. They are going to buy his lies and deception. It will be the job of true Christians to expose him for who he is and for what he intends to do. There will be consequences for those who oppose him. Not initially. In the beginning, I think that people will just dismiss us or just find us annoying. However, as the Antichrist consolidates his power, he will begin to persecute those who oppose him. Once we hit the three-and-a-half-year mark and he declares himself to be God, everyone on the planet will be forced to worship him under penalty of death. So, you see, we will each have to decide how we will respond personally. There will be consequences for our decisions not just for us individually but also for our families."

Alyssa finally rejoins the conversation. "So, Chloe, you are obviously way ahead of us on this. What's your plan?" she asks.

I hesitate for obvious reasons. I need to be careful not to reveal too much about what my parents are planning. Besides, they might think the whole Alaska thing is crazy.

"I have given it a lot of thought," I answer. "I intend to fight against his lies for as long as I can. That might only be a couple of years. I believe Zone One will rebel against the

Central Zone. Since I'd like to make it to age twenty-one, I've considered some type of escape. This is sort of a fight-then-flight idea. It might not work. I don't really have a detailed plan."

"This is a lot to take in," Alyssa continues. Looking at the other girls, she says, "I can tell that you are all a little shell-shocked by this conversation. Even though I've heard this concept before, it's troubling even for me, given what's happening in Geneva right now. Let's do this. Why don't we all commit to ordering a copy of this book Chloe mentioned? Let's all dig into the topic, and then cover it in one of our regular lunch meetings. Sound like a plan?"

Everyone agrees. I thank them for meeting on short notice, and Alyssa promises to update the two who couldn't make the meeting. We all agree to keep this topic under wraps for now, but I can't imagine ten high school girls keeping any topic under wraps, especially one about the end of the world.

That evening at home, I start to wonder if I made a mistake by telling my lunch club what I think is going to happen. I don't really know them, except Alyssa. I don't even know her very well, but I feel I can trust her. It's so incredibly frustrating to me how few Christians have done any homework on the end-time. I was just as guilty. I guess I can blame it on my age. I mean, what seventeen-year-old girl wants to spend her weekends digging into the precise timing of God's wrath? It seems crazy to me even now. Every once in a while, I find myself thinking that maybe the whole concept of Armageddon isn't even true. Then logic kicks in. Everything that's happening now was predicted in the Bible two thousand or more years ago. How could all of this be just some sick coincidence? Of course, it couldn't be. I've never been that great at math, but even I know that it's mathematically impossible for these events to unfold exactly as they were prophesized to happen. I guess I'd just like all of this to go away, and imagining just for a moment that it might not be true gives me a temporary escape.

I decide that when Dad comes home, I need to tell him about my girls' club meeting. I can't imagine any of the girls being Zone watchers, but then I never imagined that I would be afraid of my own brother. I know that if Mom or Dad lose their jobs, it could complicate our plans for an escape. Or maybe it would just accelerate our plans. Part of me just wants to forget the whole "fight" part and just head for Alaska. I love the mountains. I would be perfectly content to hide out there now. But I have this feeling I'm supposed to play some role in all of this mess. Why am I the only person my age I know who understands what's about to happen? Why am I ahead of the curve on this? I need to find out why, and soon.

Dad gets home a little later than usual, and I ask him if we can talk after dinner. Of course, he agrees. I help Mom get dinner going and make small talk with her. She rarely brings up this whole mess. I feel bad about trying to draw her into a conversation about it because I know how sad she gets. And then when I see her sad, I get even more depressed. It's a vicious cycle. I can't get inside her head because I'm not a mom. How does a mom imagine the potential death of her children? And it's not a "normal" death, such as a sudden car accident or maybe cancer. It's a horrible death, where people could be fed to lions or dragged through the streets or beheaded. How does a mom imagine her children whom she carried for nine months then nurtured for another ten or twenty years having their heads chopped off in front of her? Or being burned alive in a cage? When I think of it in these terms, I can see why she doesn't want to talk about it.

Before my meeting with Dad, I make sure that Jackson is gaming and that he has his headset on. Dad and I meet in the office so we can have some privacy. I start our meeting with my little confession: "So, Dad, you know I've started meeting with a small group of Christian girls once a week during lunch. Well, I called an emergency meeting today because of these negotiations in Geneva. Eight of them were able to make it today. I didn't waste any time in the meeting. I jumped right in with a summary overview of the Pre-Wrath Rapture. I could tell that most of them were shell-shocked. They asked a lot of questions, and I think Alyssa, she's the leader, might even agree with me. They agreed to get the book. I think most of them will. I just wanted you to know, just in case."

"Just in case of what?" he asks.

"Well, you know," I reply. "What if one of them is a watcher for the Zones and she gets you or Mom in trouble at work?"

"I'm really proud of you for doing this, Chloe," Dad says. "This is exactly what we need to be doing, helping to prepare other Christians for what's about to happen. You remember our last conversation with Mr. Harmon. I think it's much better that they know up front rather than after the deal is signed. And don't worry about our jobs. We have saved enough to where if we lost our jobs tomorrow, we could still sell everything and have enough to last more than five years up in Alaska. We're covered. I don't like my job anyhow. It's breathtakingly boring and an intellectual wasteland." Dad laughs, and I feel so much better.

"Hey, Dad," I say, "not to change the subject or anything, but your comment just now made me think of one upside to all this. You've taught us how work has been under a curse ever since Adam and Eve sinned in the Garden. You've always wanted us to know that while work is a good thing and God created work, that it's a big pain in the butt!"

"So what's the upside, then?" Dad asks. I'm surprised he doesn't see the obvious answer.

"Well, the upside is that I won't live long enough to experience the curse of work!" I say. "I get a complete pass on this!"

"You have a twisted sense of humor, Chloe!" he says. "I should have seen that one coming!"

Just then Dad's cell phone rings. Normally, he wouldn't take a call while we are talking, but it's from Mr. Harmon. He motions for me to stay in the office and takes the call. I can hear Mr. Harmon's voice, but I can't make out what he's saying. Dad stops the conversation briefly, then asks me to turn on the small TV in our office. Dad's face is pale. It can't be good. Dad keeps the phone to his ear but stops the conversation with Mr. Harmon. He says there's a breaking news story coming out of Geneva. It can only mean one thing!

We have to switch channels a few times to find a network that is providing live coverage. We catch *ABC News* in the middle of an update. There has been a major agreement between Israel and several Arab nations and Iran. They have all signed a seven-year peace treaty that includes Israel's right to rebuild their Temple. The Palestinians will be granted statehood, so Israel will recognize them as a sovereign nation. The most shocking news is that Israel agrees to put their nuclear weapons under joint control with the Central Zone after the completion of the Temple and after several security requirements have been fully implemented.

My heart is racing so fast that I feel like I'm going to pass out. I don't even know if I'm breathing. Dad and I are frozen as we listen for any additional details. Of course, we are waiting for the name of the person who negotiated the deal. We're about to meet the Antichrist, and we now know beyond any doubt that the pre-Tribulation Rapture is untrue. If we are still here after the three-and-a-half-year mark, then the pre-Wrath Rapture is absolutely true. I suddenly find myself sobbing with grief. My eyes are so filled with tears that I can no longer see the TV screen. My whole body is shaking. Dad pulls me over and holds me against his chest but continues watching. To my surprise, I can feel his tears dropping onto my face. My head is spinning, and a dozen thoughts are running through my mind simultaneously. My life is over. All of our lives are over. We've had the misfortune of being born at the end of the age. I can't imagine how we'll somehow make it four plus years to the Rapture. The odds seem impossible, especially since we're in Zone One.

To our surprise, the news announcer doesn't have details on who the key negotiators were. Apparently, the Central Zone is planning an official announcement later this evening. I'm guessing we will then know who the Antichrist is. There has been speculation about this for centuries. Will Caesar Nero come back to life from hell? Will he be Jewish? Will he be a Muslim? We won't have to wait long to find out. The broadcast ends with the promise of live coverage of the official Zone announcement in a little less than one hour.

Dad switches back to his cell phone and Mr. Harmon. I hear Dad say, "I agree. This has to be it."

It sounds like Mr. Harmon will be coming over to our house tonight. My guess is that we'll all watch the official announcement together.

Dad ends his call, then switches his attention back to me. I'm sure my face looks like a puffer fish. I can still hardly see through my eyes.

"I love you, Chloe," Dad begins. "I love all of you more than you'll ever know. This marks the beginning of the end of our time together here in this life. We both know that. There's no point in avoiding the obvious. We could have a couple of years left, or we could make it all the way to the Rapture. Chloe, only God knows, and he has a perfect plan for all of us. He is always working behind the scenes for his glory and our good. Do you believe that?"

"Yes, Dad, I believe that," I say, "But I'm so afraid. I'm not just afraid, I'm terrified. Dad, we are going to be the most persecuted group of Christians in the history of Christianity. They won't just be hunting and killing us in one or two countries; they will be killing us on every continent on the planet!"

Dad is quiet for a moment and just holds me. "You're right, Chloe," he says. "But I also know that God will give us the strength to endure whatever he sends our way. Christians have been murdered for their faith for the past two thousand years. I've read so many accounts of how incredibly brave Christians have been just before they are killed. God will not put us through something that we can't endure. If we are part of the group that gets nuked or is executed, then God will give us the ability to endure either situation. And, Chloe, remember the math we talked about? I still believe that perhaps 10 percent of believers are killed by the Antichrist. Most will make it to the Rapture. We could be part of that group. In fact, given that we have an active plan to escape the Zone wars and the persecution, I think we have a better than fifty-fifty chance of making it to the Rapture."

I don't say anything and just let Dad hold me. I feel safe with him, like this evil can't reach me when he's holding me. What if he goes first? What if I end up all alone? I can't do this on my own; I can barely get myself to school on time. How could I possibly fight against the devil himself? I want to go first. I push from my mind the thought of losing my family and my Christian friends and having to face this alone. If I let myself think that way, I know I'll go insane.

Mom must have sensed something was up, as she joins us in the office, closing the door carefully behind her.

"Has it started?" she asks. I'm surprised that Mom is so direct, given how hard this whole topic has been for her.

"Today is day one," Dad responds. "There will be an official Zone announcement at eight o'clock. Everything we expected to be in the deal is there, including the seven-year time frame, of course. Mark will be over any minute now. He wants to update just the three of us on his plans. Somehow, we need to play this down around Jackson. I know that sounds impossible, but I don't want him included in our planning."

I see a profound sadness on Mom's face. Considering the possibility that Jackson could be on the other side of this nightmare is probably almost as painful for her as knowing that we're probably going to die in the Zone wars or be martyred. I still can't believe it myself. He's two years younger than I am. We grew up side by side. We attended the same churches, the same Christian schools, the same church camps. Mom and Dad treated us the same and taught us the same truths. How could he possibly end up having all of us put to death?

My mind flashes back to a news article I had read a few years back about an Islamic terrorist in Syria. His mother had tried to escape to Jordan. She was caught and returned to the city where her son was based. They brought her to the town square along with her son. He was in his early twenties. They told him that to prove his loyalty to Allah and to their cause, he had to execute his own mother. He did it. He killed his mom right there in front of several hundred people. How can this level of evil exist in the world? How does a son murder the mother who lovingly raised him?

Mom and Dad have always showered so much love on all three of us. Since becoming teenagers, Jackson and I have pretended to be annoyed by it, but the truth is it has made us feel secure. Dad used to rock Jackson to sleep almost every night when he was small. Jackson would say "soft thing," and Dad would put one of his white T-shirts on his shoulder, then rock Jackson to sleep. How could Jackson have Dad put to death? How can I even begin to fathom that kind of evil? I'm sure if I asked Dad, he would give me the obvious answer: Satan.

Mom nods her agreement with Dad's directive. By the tone of his voice, it's obvious that it's not a suggestion. Maybe Dad has already moved into survival mode. Maybe he's already thinking ahead to what he will need to do to keep us alive. I'm not there by a long shot. I'm still stuck in despair.

"We can meet here in the office when Mr. Harmon arrives," Dad continues. "He wants to update us on his plans. We can stop to watch the official Zone announcement, and then continue our meeting. We might learn something from the announcement that could impact our planning." Mom just nods her head in agreement and returns to the kitchen in silence.

CHAPTER TWELVE

THE ANTICHRIST

I decide to wait in my room until Mr. Harmon arrives. I check my phone and see several texts related to the announcement. The most recent one is from Alyssa. She's asking if I'd heard the news about the treaty. Normally, I would never respond to a text by calling someone, but this is too important and too complicated for texting. She picks up after only one ring.

"Chloe, thanks for getting back to me so quickly. Have you seen the news?" she begins.

"Yes," I respond. "My parents and I caught most of it a few minutes ago. There is going to be an official announcement this evening."

"So, Chloe," Alyssa says, "I remember what you told us, your new thinking that we'll be here for more than half of the seven-year period. This deal seems to match what the Bible says about the deal the Antichrist will put together. Do you think this is it?"

I pause for a moment. I know it's the real thing, but, for some reason, it's hard for me to say the words.

"Yes," I finally respond. "My parents and I all feel this is it. Today is Day One. In exactly 1,260 days the Antichrist will go into the rebuilt Temple in Jerusalem and declare on national television that he is God. He will require that every person on

Earth to worship him, and those that don't he will put to death. And 2,520 days from today, Jesus will return physically to the Earth. Sometime between the three-and-a-half-year mark and Jesus' return, the Rapture will happen."

Alyssa is quiet for a moment. I'm sure she knew when she texted me that this would be my answer.

"None of my family members are believers, Chloe," she says. I can sense that she is holding back tears. I hadn't thought of how this will impact those like Alyssa who are kind of on their own with no family members to turn to for encouragement. I suddenly feel so sad for her.

"I'm so sorry, Alyssa," I say. "You probably told me that before, and I just forgot. I want you to know that we can talk about this every day if needed. Maybe starting next week at school, just the two of us can start meeting for lunch on the days when our group isn't meeting."

Alyssa sounds more confident and responds that our little group will probably be meeting every day, now that the deal between Israel and her neighbors has been signed. She's probably right. I wonder if the other girls will be convinced that this is the real thing. Maybe some will be in denial, not wanting to believe that none of us will still be on the planet five or six years from now. Depending on where we are when the Zone wars start, we might have as little as two years. Some of us might not make it to our twentieth birthday. None of us will get married, or have children, or even finish college. I've never been crazy about any particular boy, but I always imagined that maybe someday I'd meet that perfect guy for me. That won't be happening.

"I'm going to text the rest of the girls and ask that we all meet before school starts on Monday," Alyssa says. "We can then continue the conversation during the lunch hour. I'll ask them to check out the news between now and Monday, so they are up to speed on the deal. I think I'll also send them the Bible references related to the treaty so they can review them prior to our meeting. I'm 99 percent sure that you and your family are right, that his is it, this is Day One, but it will be good to hear what the others think."

"Sounds like a good plan, Alyssa," I say.

Just as I start to say something else, I hear the doorbell ring. It must be Mr. Harmon.

"Hey, Alyssa, a friend of the family just got here. We are all going to talk this over tonight. What time do you want to try and meet Monday morning?"

"Let's shoot for seven," she says. "That will give us a full hour before classes start. Let's meet at the lunch tables next to the gym. If we want more privacy, we can always walk out to the football stadium."

"Sounds like a plan," I respond. "See you Monday morning."

As soon as I open my bedroom door, I can see Mr. Harmon in the front entryway of our house. Dad is talking to him very quietly. As I head down the stairs, Dad ushers him into the office. Dad motions for me to head to the office, and then heads off to find Mom. I shake hands with Mr. Harmon. He looks much more serious than in the past. I almost feel like he is sizing me up, still trying to decide if he can trust me. This whole thing was so theoretical before; now it's all very real. Before I can start a meaningful conversation with him, Mom and Dad come into the office and close the double doors. Dad pulls the office chair around to the other side of his desk, and we all sit in a tight circle, just the four of us.

Dad starts the conversation: "Thanks for coming over so quickly, Mark. This looks like the real thing. Are you convinced? Has the seven-year period started?"

Mr. Harmon doesn't answer that question. Instead, he shifts his focus to me. "Chloe, these are very serious times we're living in. The consequences for those who hold to their faith could include torture and death. As you know from Scripture, children will turn in their parents and have them put to death. Parents will turn in their children. We are heading into the evilest time in the history of humanity. I need to know that I can trust you to keep these conversations completely confidential. That means what we say here, among the four of us, stays with the four of us, no matter what. I need to know that I can trust you with what we're about to discuss."

I suddenly feel a little bit like I'm on trial, but I quickly come to terms with the fact that trust has now become the most valuable commodity in the world. Christians are going to be hunted down soon, probably within just a few years. At some point, Christians won't be able to buy or sell anything. Some will starve to death. Many will be tortured and killed. I get it. I need to convince Mr. Harmon that I can be trusted.

"I totally get it why trust is so important," I begin. "We are no longer debating the merits of the various theories on the timing of the Rapture. The pre-Tribulation Rapture was wishful thinking, it was never Biblically sound, and it didn't happen. Today is Day One of the seventieth week of Daniel, and every believer is still here. I'm ready to do whatever we agree needs to be done to fight the lies that the Antichrist will soon spread throughout the world. You have my commitment that, whatever we agree to do, those details will be kept completely confidential. I give you my word."

Mr. Harmon's face softens just a little. I can tell he believes me.

"Thanks, Chloe," Mr. Harmon says. "I needed to hear that from you, and I don't think we need to go into detail on why Jackson is not part of this conversation. Since we don't know where his loyalties lie, I agree that it's best we keep him out of the loop, at least for now."

He returns to dad's question: "So the short answer to your question is, yes, I firmly believe this is the same seven-year agreement described in the Bible. Like Chloe just said, today is Day One. We might even know the name of the Antichrist tonight. My guess is that he will not miss the opportunity to boast about this accomplishment. This will set the stage for what I believe will be several back-to-back diplomatic successes. He will probably also find a way to get the world economy growing again. After all, money is all most people really care about these days. At some point, probably within one year, the ten Zone Presidents will put him in charge of the entire system. His authority will then be absolute, and you all know what happens next. Three Zones, including Zone One, I'm sure, push back hard and get wiped out. No one can beat this guy. As you know, it is God who eventually takes him out, but we will all be in Heaven by then!"

To my surprise, Mom joins the conversation: "So, Mark, I know we've talked about this before, but how much time do you think we have until the wars start?"

Mr. Harmon responds immediately and firmly. "No more than two years," he says.

Mom continues: "So we need to have a plan that can guarantee that we'll be out in some remote area within two years, and with enough food and water to last for an additional two or three years."

"Yes, that's pretty much it," he replies.

Dad jumps back into the conversation: "So, Mark, we've talked recently about Alaska. Now that the clock is ticking, what do you think we should do now, in the next month or two?"

Mr. Harmon begins to answer Dad's question, but he looks at me, almost like he's trying to reassure himself that I can keep my teenage mouth shut.

"I have a major update on that aspect of my plans," Mr. Harmon says. "And, of course, this stays with just the four of us for now. I gave a lot of thought to Alaska. I did a ton of research. I changed my mind on the location. It's too far from Texas. We could be in a situation where we couldn't fly there. Then we'd face the challenge of trying to drive through Canada. I know the borders have been wide open since the Zones' implementation, but I think the Central Zone is going to significantly reduce our freedom of movement in Zone One. This will be especially true as we get closer to the Zone wars."

Dad looks a little disappointed. I am as well, given how much I love the state of Alaska. It's so vast that you could really hide out there for a long time without being found.

"So is there a new plan, or are you back to the drawing board?" Dad asks.

Mr. Harmon's voice sounds much more serious as he continues: "There's more than just a plan. Two months ago, I purchased a 150-acre property in Montana not far from the border with Canada. It is adjacent to the Kootenai National Forest which has 2.2 million acres. The property is completely self-contained. The house on the property is next to a river, and a hydroelectric system provides electricity. It also has a diesel generator for backup power. It is entirely off the grid. It sits at the end of a five-mile long dirt road, and there are no other homes or businesses within ten miles. This was originally a homestead property, and the original log cabin is still there. I formed a shell company and used it to buy the property, so it's not officially in my name. I know this will only slow down the Zones one day, but it will buy me a little more time. The property is almost exactly a twenty-one-hour drive from where we are sitting right now. With so much land, I can easily hide an underground shelter on the property. I have more details to share, but I can tell by the look on your faces you have questions."

"Wow, I didn't see that coming," Dad says. "Did you have to take out a loan?"

"No. I paid cash," says Mr. Harmon. "A loan would have created a paper trail for someone to follow."

I have a million questions, but I let Dad continue.

"How big is the house, not the homestead house, but the main one?" Dad asks. "How many people could live there?"

"The main house could easily take ten people," Mr. Harmon says. "The homestead house is a mess. It's not fit for living. It's very cool looking, though! Here's the deal. As you know, I've never been married, and I don't have any kids. That's why I was able to pay cash for the property, but I'm a little short in terms of money for the underground shelter and supplies. I'd like to know if you want in, at least the four of you, anyway. I'm including Hannah, of course. There's plenty of room for all of you. I'd need you to kick in maybe one hundred and fifty thousand dollars for the bunker and supplies. We would need to get started within six months, hopefully, sooner."

Dad looks over at Mom. It's amazing how they can read each other. Without her saying a word, I can tell he knows that she's in.

"Yes, absolutely, we're in," Dad says. "I mean, we don't have a plan. We only started thinking about this in a serious way last spring when the Central Zone closed the kid's school. We can definitely come up with the money. I have a 401k from my last company that I rolled into an IRA. I'll have to pay taxes and a 10 percent penalty, but I can net the one hundred and fifty thousand dollars. How soon do you want to move on this?"

Mr. Harmon is quick with his response: "I'll need a few weeks to make a final decision on a vendor for the bunker. Let's plan on maybe thirty days. I'll provide regular updates via phone. There's another thing. I need everyone to agree that we will not use e-mail or texting to discuss any of these plans. When we talk about this on the phone, let's all be careful with the words we use. I know that sounds paranoid, but I'm 99 percent sure that the Zones record every cell phone call. They might eventually scan their files for keywords. When we talk about the property, let's not provide details like the state it's in or the address. Make sense?"

"Yes, absolutely," says Dad. "That makes complete sense. It's almost eight o'clock. We should probably turn on the TV to one of the network channels, so we don't miss the announcement. It's funny. For almost thirty years, our various pastors told us not to spend time speculating who the Antichrist might be since we wouldn't be here. Well, I wonder how all of those pastors are going to respond to today's events. I'm guessing that their voice mail boxes are overflowing right about now. Can you imagine the stress? I'm sure that many of their church members won't use kind language given the situation. What a mess! They should have read Rosenthal's book!"

"I don't think very many of them would have changed their position publicly, even if they had read his book," says Mom. "Even if they were convinced they were wrong, if they had told their congregations it would have created a huge mess. Some people would agree, others would disagree, and there would be a split in their churches. I hate to say it, but it seems like most pastors in the last thirty years have been more interested in growing church attendance than in the truth. In fact, most don't even teach on end-time prophesy. I wouldn't want to be in their shoes right now!"

Dad finds a network news channel, but there are just commercials. It's so surreal to think that I could be looking at the face of the Antichrist in a matter of minutes! I've read in the Bible that he will be intelligent, charismatic, prideful, and downright evil. He will probably speak multiple languages. My hands are shaking. I feel like my face is flushed. Mom, Dad, and Mr. Harmon are talking about the property in Montana, but I can't concentrate on what they're saying. I'm so engrossed in the moment. I always come back to that thought about why I have to be alive right now. Why do I have to live through this nightmare? I probably won't make it to my twenty-first birthday. None of my friends will, either. We're all marked for death or the Rapture. I wish I knew which one applies to me! I don't want to be tortured to death. I don't want to fear my brother. I just want to be ten years old again. I want all of this to go away, but I know it won't.

Suddenly the news anchor comes on and says there will be a Central Zone update in just a couple of minutes on the peace deal. My stomach really hurts, and I feel like I could pass out.

I want to sit in Dad's lap, but that would be awkward with Mr. Harmon here. We all start to calm down. I look at Mom and I see a look of profound sadness on her face, but she seems to have abandoned her avoidance, her denial of this mess. I feel like she is coming to terms with it, like she's finally ready to face it head-on. I guess that's always been Mom's personality. Dad always loves to speculate about everything. Mom never goes there with any of us. Her attitude is always "We'll cross that bridge when we come to it." Well, we're definitely at that bridge now.

I look over at Dad and Mr. Harmon, and they look so serious. I know they are both curious to see the man who will wreck the entire planet. In one sense, the Antichrist will be the greatest leader in world history. I guess it only makes sense that we are all intensely curious. It all seems so twisted. The news guy is talking again. The Central Zone will be making the announcement from Jerusalem. My heart is pounding. My hands are shaking. This is it. I see his face!

Jet-black hair and penetrating blue eyes are what I notice before anything else. His name and title appear at the bottom of the screen: Hussein Salam, Central Zone Negotiator. He looks young, too young to have just solved the most intractable issue in the world. He can't be more than thirty years old. He's speaking a language I don't recognize. Is it Arabic? I look toward Mr. Harman and mouth the words, "What language?" He whispers, "Hebrew." We are all reading the English subtitles. He is talking about the great history of the Jewish people. He starts with Abraham and begins to summarize the key events in their three-thousand-year history. He then talks about Abraham's first son, Ishmael, and describes his descendants in equal detail. Although I recognize the details on Israel's history, almost all of what he is saying about the descendants of Ishmael is foreign to me.

I don't notice the change, but Mr. Harmon briefly mentions that when he began describing the history of Ishmael's descendants, he switched to Arabic. Both languages sound so similar to me that I have no idea he had changed languages. He suddenly changes to English just as he begins describing the historic agreement. Israel has agreed to implement a two-state solution within thirty days. Palestine will be recognized as its own nation. The Central Zone will run the government of Palestine for the first twelve months, and then gradually hand over control if certain security measures have been achieved. The Palestinians have agreed to turn in all weapons to the Central Zone. East Jerusalem will be given to the Palestinians and will become their capital. Israel will be allowed to rebuild their Temple after the Central Zone constructs a separation wall between the Dome of the Rock and what will become the new Jewish Temple. The Central Zone has agreed to complete the wall within thirty days. Israel has acknowledged the possession of roughly two hundred nuclear warheads and will allow joint control of these with the Central Zone on two conditions: the completion of the Temple and complete adherence by the Palestinians to all security agreements.

Hussein Salam's English is perfect. He has no accent. I don't know for sure, but my guess is that his Hebrew and Arabic are perfect also. He speaks with great confidence, but there is almost a subtle humility about him. He gives most of the credit for this historic agreement to the Jews and Arabs who participated in the negotiations. He flatters them for what seems like an eternity. He closes by saying that the full text of the agreement, including the lengthy security requirements, will be available in about an hour on the Central Zone's website. He closes by once again thanking those he calls his "partners in peace."

Dad lowers the volume but keeps the television on. We are all very quiet for a moment. A feeling of despair hangs in the air. We have now seen the man who will have millions of believers in Jesus put to death in the most horrible ways imaginable.

I break the silence. "He's physically attractive. Of course, you would expect that. And he's not from Italy. At least his name is not Italian. He doesn't look European, either. I thought the Antichrist was supposed to be from Europe?" I ask.

Mr. Harmon is the first to respond. "His name is not European, but we don't yet know where he's from. I suppose he could have grown up in Europe. However, I've read a lot of commentaries in the past few years that suggest the Antichrist could be a Muslim. The Bible has some vague references in Isaiah and Micah about an Assyrian in passages that many believe are about the Antichrist. The ancient Assyrians lived in Iran and Iraq. Many Muslims believe that, in the last days, their messiah, they call him the Mahdi, will rule for seven years just before a final day of judgment. They believe that Jesus will return to the Earth as his prophet and that the two of them will require the whole Earth to convert to Islam."

My head is about to explode! I have never heard this before.

"That is so completely twisted!" I blurt out. "So Muslims will accept the Antichrist as their Messiah and the False Prophet as Jesus? That is so messed up!"

Dad finally joins in. "Chloe, it makes total sense if you think about it. What does Satan do twenty-four/seven? He deceives people. Satan has always known about the Antichrist and the False Prophet. Doesn't it make sense that he would create an end-of-days scenario within the false religions of the world that seems to match what he knows will happen? That's just what he's done here in order to convince almost two billion Muslims to worship the Antichrist as some kind of holy Messiah."

"That's exactly what Satan has done," adds Mr. Harmon. "Satan has also convinced the Jews to believe that any man who allows them to rebuild their Temple must be their long-awaited Messiah. Most Muslims and Jews, and the rest of the world for that matter, will believe this lie. Because they have rejected the one true God of the Bible, God will send them what the Bible calls a 'strong delusion' to believe this lie. It's a type of punishment. When people have the knowledge of the truth and then knowingly reject it, they will believe almost anything."

"So, Mr. Harmon," I continue, "what do you think of the Antichrist? Is he what you expected? I mean he wasn't spouting out a bunch of blasphemies or boasting about his negotiating prowess. I thought the Antichrist was supposed to have a foul mouth and be full of pride. This guy seems gracious, almost humble."

Mr. Harmon is quiet for a moment. Then, he says, "Chloe, I'm not sure what I expected. I did expect that he would speak multiple languages. Regarding his seeming humility, remember that the Antichrist begins as a charismatic man of peace. After the ten Zone Presidents hand him the keys to the world, he will quickly change to a man of war. If I had to guess, I would say he will control the whole Zone system in less than one year."

Mr. Harmon continues: "He is younger than I expected. He can't be more than thirty years old. I can't wait to do some research on his background. I'm surprised the Central Zone didn't provide a brief bio for him. Maybe they'll release that information tomorrow. I must admit that something about him was captivating. He projects an intense amount of self-confidence but without appearing arrogant. I found myself wanting to believe him, to trust him. If I weren't a believer, I'd be very complimentary of what he just accomplished, given his age. I can see how the whole world, minus true Christians, of course, will fall in love with this guy."

My hands have stopped shaking, but I'm sure my face is still flushed. So this is it. This is Day One. The only thing keeping me from a complete meltdown is the knowledge that we have a very specific plan. We know what we're going to do on Day Two. What about the millions of other believers all over the planet who know this guy is the Antichrist but never imagined they would be here to see him? I can't even begin to imagine their horror, their feelings of hopelessness. I'm sure many are in denial, trying to convince themselves that this deal will collapse just like all the previous ones. Someone needs to explain all of this to them and fast!

Mr. Harmon changes the subject just a little. "I know that you're 100 percent committed to our plans for Montana. Now that this thing has begun, I feel we need to move fast. Ray, how quickly can you liquidate that IRA?"

Dad doesn't hesitate. "I can submit the request electronically this evening, and it will process tomorrow. I should have access to the funds by Thursday."

"Great," says Mr. Harmon. "I'll call the company that I've contracted with for the bunker and see how much money they'll need to get started. The total cost is one hundred thousand, and I'm pretty sure they will want 50 percent up front. I'll call you later tomorrow and let you know for sure. I'm going to head home. There are several other things I need to get going on, now that this thing is in motion. And just for the record, even though I might not show it, I'm just as shell-shocked as the three of you. I knew this day would come, but it's still hard to believe." We all nod our heads in agreement. The enormity of this moment is just beginning to sink in.

We walk Mr. Harmon to the door and say goodnight. To our surprise and relief, Jackson never leaves his room during the broadcast or our impromptu meeting. I'm so afraid that he'll know we're hiding something from him. I'm a terrible liar. I'm sure he will eventually hear all of the speculation about Salam being the Antichrist. In fact, he loves to keep up with what he calls the Wacko-Right-Wing-Christian websites so that he can make fun of them. It seems to be his favorite pastime. Will his new pastime eventually be killing Christians? The thought is so abhorrent to me that I push it out of my mind.

Dad reminds me to keep all of this between the three of us and Mr. Harmon. If Jackson starts asking questions about Salam being the Antichrist, we will all just say that it's an interesting idea and that we'll need to look into it when we have the time. As soon as I get to my room, I Google "Israeli Agreement Hussein Salam." I see several articles with links to the news conference, but I can't find anything on Salam's background. It's like he's a ghost. Maybe he's Caesar Nero back from the dead. Maybe he's a demon. This last thought is incredibly disturbing, and I can't get it out of my mind.

My phone rings, and I see that it's Alyssa. I had a couple of texts from her earlier but didn't have time to respond because of the Zone press conference.

"Hey, Alyssa," I say. "I'm sure you saw the broadcast, right?"

Her voice is shaky, less confident when she responds: "I did, Chloe. I watched the news for a while before and after. It's seven years. They get to rebuild their temple. Jerusalem gets divided in two, one part for Israel and one for the Palestinians. I ended up in an English language Israeli chat room after the conference call. Don't ask me how. Anyway, I read posts from a bunch of Jews speculating that this Salam guy is the Jewish Messiah! What's that all about?"

I remember what Mr. Harmon told me and began to explain it to her: "So here's the deal. Apparently for the last thirty years or so, if you had asked religious Jews how they will know their Messiah when he arrives, they would have told you that it's the person who helps them to rebuild their Temple. They are expecting their Messiah to be a man, not the son of God. It gets worse. I also learned, and this totally blew me away, that the Muslims will accept Salam as 'their' Messiah. And when the False Prophet shows up at some point, they will think he is Jesus!"

"That's just crazy, Chloe," Alyssa says. "I thought the Muslims are all into Mohammad. Do they think Salam is Mohammad come back from the grave?"

"No, they don't," I continue. "Their Messiah is an entirely different person. And get this, they are taught that their Messiah will cut a seven-year deal with Israel and then break it. Don't you see? Satan has created a false end-time scenario in order to deceive almost two billion people. It's brilliant if you think about it. They are going to believe that Salam is their Mahdi. That's the name they have for their coming Messiah."

Alyssa is quiet for a moment. I'm sure this is a lot for her to process.

"So, Chloe, I've received calls or texts from all of the girls in our group," Alyssa says. "Most have read the Pre-Wrath Rapture book. So have I. They all agree with our idea to meet early tomorrow morning before school starts instead of waiting until our Thursday meeting. Are you good with that?"

"Sure, Alyssa."

"Great," she continues. "Prepare yourself for a very emotional meeting. This has hit most of us like a ton of bricks! Most of us were Pre-Trib, or indifferent. Our bubble has popped, and we're all in shock. As you know, most of us don't come from Christian families, so we only have each other for support. I have a feeling we are going to be meeting every day. I know the other girls will want you to walk us through the sequence, you know, what happens next. Are you good with that?"

"Of course, Alyssa, I'd love to," I say. "I'm no expert, but I'll cover the stuff I'm most familiar with. It might be a little high-level."

"Thanks so much, Chloe. I'm going to send a group text for the meeting. I'll tell them we'll meet at seven. Sound good?" she asks.

"It does," I say. "Thanks, Alyssa. I'll see you first thing tomorrow morning."

CHAPTER THIRTEEN

DAY TWO

There is much more hugging than usual as we gather for our meeting at seven. All of the girls actually hug me, which is a little awkward since I hardly know them. I can tell that some of them have been crying, probably on the way to school. It feels like we're a group of girls getting together after a classmate has died. It's so somber. Alyssa thanks everyone for being on time. We have almost a full hour, so we can cover a lot of ground. She asks if everyone either saw the broadcast from last night or read about it. Everyone has. She tells them that she's convinced this is the real thing and that we are on Day Two of the Tribulation. One girl whose name I can't remember starts to tear up. Of course, it's contagious. It takes almost five minutes for us to compose ourselves. Alyssa asks me to explain as much as I can about what's next.

My voice is shaky as I start: "So I guess I'm in a little bit of a different place than all of you, because I saw this coming. I can tell you that although it's a different place, it's not a better place. To be honest, this all really stinks. I know I shouldn't say that. I know God has me here at this time in history for a reason. But you know what? There are a lot of cute guys out there, and I sort of planned on landing one of them someday!"

Everyone laughs, and the mood lightens just a little.

Someone says, "Boys are overrated." More laughs.

"Well, I guess some things are off the table now, like college or having our own families," I say. "We'll all have to process through that in the coming weeks and months. I want to talk about the sequence of events, sort of on a high-level time frame. Let me start with what Salam will probably do next."

For more than thirty minutes, I walk through the major events. I talk about how Salam will probably solve several long-standing conflicts in rapid succession, winning the admiration of the Zone presidents. At some point, probably in less than one year, they will put him in charge of everything. He will then solve even more challenges and implement a short period of worldwide peace and prosperity, but that will be followed quickly by war. I tell them my suspicions that Zones One, Three, and Four are probably the three kings, or Zones, mentioned in the Book of Daniel that push back and get wiped out. I explain the different options like fight, or fight then flight. I'm careful not to reveal our family's plans. I just start getting into the timing of the Rapture when we run out of time. They are literally hanging on my every word. This is such a strange new role for me. I'm not sure I'm up for it. They decide they can't wait until the next school day for more, so we agree to meet during the lunch hour.

When we meet again at lunchtime, I can tell they have spent all morning digesting what I told them before school, because they hit me with a bunch of questions right away:

Are you 100 percent sure that this seven-year deal is THE deal? Yes, absolutely.
Revelation says 25 percent of the world's population gets wiped out in the wars and famine that follow,

so why is that more than the populations of Zones One, Three, and Four? I don't have a great answer. My best guess is that the Zones who rebel manage to inflict damage on the Central Zone before they are wiped out. Another possibility is that the plagues that follow the war end up impacting other Zones.

How much time do we have until the wars start? My guess is at least one year but not more than two.

When will Salam require everyone to take his mark? At exactly the three-and-a-half-year mark. I explain that these will be years of 360 days, not 365 days.

When does the heavy persecution of Christians begin? I'm not really sure on this one. I tell them my guess is that persecution will heat up once Salam implements his One World Religious system. I would guess that starts in just over one year. But I'm pretty confident that the executions don't start until after the three-and-a-half-year mark, but I could be wrong.

How long until the Rapture? About four or five years.

I can tell they have many more questions, but, in the interest of time, Alyssa asks me to continue with the time line of key events. Since the timing of the Rapture is where I left off in the morning, that's where I pick up. I explain the sequence of events leading up to it. Since none of us will be around after that, I don't walk through post-Rapture stuff. The truth is, I'm not completely sure what happens after the Rapture. I don't really care. I guess I care a little, since Jackson might still be around. From the little I do know, he won't last long once we're gone. It will be hell on Earth.

We run out of time before we run out of conversation. I'm sure this will be true for many weeks to come. During the rest of the week, our focus begins to shift from an understanding of what's going to happen to what each girl plans on doing. Alyssa accurately senses my hesitation with providing details on what my family has decided to do. The other girls are less perceptive, and I get hit with these questions several times. I tell them that my family is still undecided about what actions to take. I feel really bad for the seven girls in our group who don't have other family members who are Christians. They don't have anyone at home to help them process all of this. I get the feeling that they want our group to come up with a collective plan. I can't go there. My plan is Mom and Dad's plan. I can't have two strategies.

CHAPTER FOURTEEN

CHURCH

On Saturday, Dad mentions that we should plan on getting to church really early on Sunday morning. At first, it doesn't occur to me why; then it hits me. Tomorrow is the first Sunday service after the announcement. It's going to be chaos. Dad mentions that all members received an e-mail on Friday from the church, saying the first service will start thirty minutes earlier and run thirty minutes longer than normal. The second service will start at its normal time but run longer. At both services, the entire time will be used for questions about the Middle East deal signed last weekend and what it could mean.

I decide to ask Dad what he thinks will happen at church tomorrow.

"So, Dad, I think the services tomorrow will be absolute chaos. Our church never taught us about the end-time, so I think things could get really ugly. What do you think?" I ask.

Dad has a really sad look on his face as he begins to respond: "Chloe, I hate to admit it, but you're probably right. I don't think the services will be as rough as they will be for churches who have been teaching a pre-Tribulation Rapture. They will have it much worse tomorrow. My guess is that during our services, one of the first questions will be, 'Why didn't you tell us this was coming?' I think some members will be really angry. This will be the most difficult question for Pastor Jon to answer. Someone might point out that pastors are instructed by the Bible to teach the entire Bible, including books like Revelation. Clearly, our church hasn't done that. I think our church will both lose and gain members in the coming weeks."

"Dad, I can't imagine our church, or any Christians for that matter, talking about anything other than the Tribulation from this point forward," I say. "What would be the point? The clock is ticking now for all of us. Even those who make it all the way to the Rapture have maybe four years. I think a lot of pastors are going to either quit or get fired in the next few weeks. I know our church is so incredibly gracious and friendly, but this is a big miss. I don't see this ending well. And you know how emotional Pastor Jon gets. He might cry the entire time!"

"Chloe," Dad says, "Mom and I talked about church and decided that we are no longer going to force Jackson to attend with us. You know he hates going. He always complains. If he goes now and hears details on what's about to happen, it might cause him to pay closer attention to our meetings and conversations with Mr. Harmon. That could spell trouble for all of us later on. I just wanted you to know ahead of time. I'll let Hannah know as well and ask her not to bring it up."

I try not to imagine the trouble Jackson could create for us, and I just respond that he will be thrilled he gets to sleep in every Sunday. I can't help but think how smart Jackson is, however. Mom and Dad have been fighting with him about attending church for years. He will suspect that something is up. I won't be surprised if he goes online and watches one of the services. I think we're kidding ourselves. He's not fooled so easily. As soon as he gets conflicting answers from any of us, it will be really hard to hide our planning from him.

In the morning, we leave for church much earlier than normal, and we arrive about fifteen minutes before the second service starts. The first sign that something unusual is happening is the traffic. It's backed up for a quarter mile from the entrance to the church. This is a first. As we inch closer to the parking lot, it's clear that it's full. The local police, who manage traffic at both services each Sunday, direct us to the parking lot of an industrial building next to our church. Dad points out that there should be people leaving the first service by now, but we don't see any open spaces. We all guess the obvious. The first service hasn't ended.

As we enter the church, we don't get more than twenty feet inside before we run out of room. The place is absolutely packed. Everyone is looking up at the screens that display the service going on in the sanctuary. Pastor Jon is asking the first service attendees to exit through the side doors rather than the main entrances. It's obvious why. There's no way they could make it past the thousands of us crammed into the lobby area. I'm sure we're violating multiple fire codes.

I watch the monitors as more than three thousand people slowly exit the main sanctuary. Almost ten minutes later, ushers finally open the main doors, and we begin moving inside. By the time we get inside, there are only a few seats left on the far left side. Just as we take our seats, the ushers begin asking what must be a thousand people to move back out to the lobby area. They will have to watch the service on the video screens. I'm relieved we got four seats. I want to be inside for something this important. I can't imagine a more impactful service in the history of any church.

Pastor Jon comes onto the stage, and the sanctuary goes quiet. I've never been in the middle of a group this large that didn't make a sound. It's actually really creepy. I can tell by the look on Pastor Jon's face that the first service was rough. He looks completely beaten down. He opens the service with a prayer asking the Holy Spirit for wisdom. After the prayer, he jumps right into the obvious.

"I want to welcome all of our family members and the many, many guests who have joined us this morning. Thank you for coming. It's not a coincidence that you're here today, and I believe God has something for each of us. I've received more than a thousand e-mails this week with questions concerning the agreement signed last weekend between Israel and several Muslim nations. Our pastors and staff have all received hundreds of e-mails and calls as well. Because of the overwhelming volume, I apologize that we have not been able to respond to each one individually. As most of you know, on Tuesday, I decided to send a generic e-mail response to the many inquiries we continue to receive related to last weekend's developments. For the benefit of those who did not receive my response, I'd like to start by reading it. I'll provide some additional details; then, we can move to questions and answers. But let me start by reading the e-mail I sent out last Tuesday:

"Thank you for contacting Carrollton Bible Fellowship with your questions and concerns related to the Central Zone announcement from last Sunday. As you know, a seven-year agreement between Israel and several Muslim countries was signed that includes the right of the Jews to rebuild their Temple. Many Christians feel that this is the agreement mentioned in the Old Testament Book of Daniel that marks the beginning of a period of time the Bible calls the Seventieth Week of

Daniel. It is also referred to as the Tribulation. Many, perhaps most, evangelical Christians believe that the Rapture will occur **before** this final seven-year period begins. In my twenty years as the senior pastor at Carrollton Bible Fellowship, I have never directly addressed the issue of the timing of the Rapture. This was a mistake on my part. Knowing that there were differing opinions, I avoided the subject altogether. I didn't want our church to experience divisions over this issue, but my avoidance was clearly a mistake. This was both a failure and a sin on my part, and I humbly ask for your forgiveness.

"Most of the e-mails and calls we have received this week asked if this seven-year agreement is indeed the event that signals the beginning of the Tribulation or Seventieth Week of Daniel. My senior leadership team and I are meeting daily this week to pray and, with the help of the Holy Spirit, determine the correct answer to this important question. Please pray for us as we seek to find the truth. I hope you can join me in person or online this Sunday as I will provide an update on our thinking. God bless you, and I'll see you all on Sunday."

Pastor Jon looks up from his letter and addresses the congregation.

"In my e-mail, I mentioned we have been meeting daily this week, reviewing the details in the agreement and comparing them to the relevant biblical passages in the Old and New Testaments. As you can imagine, these meetings have been complex, emotional, and exhausting. We prayed multiple times during each meeting. I can report that, in the end, there was no deadlock. We ended our final meeting at ten o'clock last night with unanimous agreement. We believe that the Seventieth Week of Daniel began one week ago today. Today is Day Eight of the seven-year Tribulation."

There is an audible gasp from the audience. I can hear people beginning to cry. Several people leave the sanctuary, holding their hands over their mouths like they're about to throw up. I feel strangely calm, maybe because none of this is new to Mom, Dad, and me. We knew this was coming. We had done our homework, albeit belatedly. I know it's wrong, but I have something like a condescending feeling for the vast majority of the people in this room, those who never bothered to look into this on their own. They must be absolutely crushed right now. I wonder how many of them have any idea at all what's coming next: the wars, the famines, the executions. I can't imagine Pastor Jon mentioning any of that now. It would be too much for them to bear.

Pastor Jon's voice begins to crack as he continues: "In the coming weeks, we will dedicate every Sunday service to this topic. Also, as some of you know, it has been fifteen years since we had a Wednesday evening service. Those services will begin again, starting this Wednesday. We'll meet at seven. We are changing the times for our two Sunday morning services, adding thirty minutes to each service. We'll have the website updated with these changes by Tuesday. I want to assure you that we will make a 100 percent effort to get you the answers you need in the coming weeks. For now, I'd like to start with questions from all of you. We have several pastors with mobile microphones, so let's get started."

Hands go up everywhere, more than I can count. How will Pastor Jon ever get through them all? I know he won't. The first question comes from a woman near the front, just to the left of Pastor Jon: "I don't know a whole lot about the Rapture or the Tribulation, but I always believed we would be gone before this seven-year period started. Since that didn't happen, is there going to be a Rapture, and when will it happen?"

I want to jump to my feet, grab a microphone, and tell them! I feel like I'm going to explode! I look over at Dad, and I can tell he's feeling the same way. Does Pastor Jon even know about the Pre-Wrath Rapture? Dad said he sent Rosenthal's book to Pastor Jon several months ago, but he has no idea if he read it.

"Thank you for your honest question," Pastor Jon begins. "It's a question we grappled with this past week. We didn't spend a ton of time on it, but I believe we have identified the various possibilities. Our pastoral staff will be meeting every day again this week, and we will try to figure this out quickly. I promise that if we reach a strong consensus during the week, I will provide an e-mail update to everyone and post it on our website."

The woman continues. "So you **do** believe that there will still be a Rapture, is that right?" she asks.

"Yes, absolutely" responds Pastor Jon.

Pastor Jon points to someone to his right for the next question. There is some confusion as to whom he selected and then some nervous laughter. A middle-aged man takes the microphone. "Pastor Jon, I have been a member here for nine years. I have to be honest with you that I'm still really— 'angry' is probably not the right word. I'm just so upset that you didn't teach us about end-time Bible prophecy. I read your e-mail, and I get it that you wanted to avoid creating any kind of division in the church, but I think that the truth is more important than unity. It seems to me that churches today are more interested in head count than telling the truth. I know it's too late now, but look at the mess we are all in! I'm sorry.

I know we are supposed to ask questions, but I just had to say how incredibly disappointed I am." Even from this distance, I can see that his hands are shaking violently. The man hands the microphone back to a staff member.

I can see Pastor Jon starting to tear up. He is very emotional on a typical Sunday morning, so I can't even begin to imagine how he'll get through this service. My guess is that he got a similar comment during the first service. People are outraged. I'm sure they feel like he has committed some kind of pastoral malpractice, a term I heard my dad use this past week. I wonder how many will leave the church altogether. Mr. Harmon talked about this scenario. His thinking is that many will say "If my church was wrong about something this important, then I don't trust anything they have to say." I guess this situation is a little different since Pastor Jon simply avoided the topic altogether.

"Thank you for your honesty," says Pastor Jon. "I take full responsibility for this. It was my decision to avoid this topic. Some of our pastors and a couple of our Elders brought this up occasionally over the years. They encouraged me to consider teaching on it. I always pushed back. I said I wasn't ready, wasn't mature enough. Those were just excuses. I was wrong. I intend to work very hard in the coming months to earn back your trust." Amazingly, he makes it through his response without crying.

Pastor Jon points to someone in our section. From this distance, it's impossible to know which hand he is pointing to, so a staff member just picks someone in the general area, a young woman.

"I know you'll be trying to figure out the timing of the Rapture soon, but do you have any idea how bad things are going to get for Christians before we're taken out of here?" she asks. "Doesn't Revelation say that a bunch of Christians are beheaded during the Tribulation?"

"Yes, that's right," Pastor Jon begins. "The New Testament Book of Revelation does talk about Christians who are beheaded for their faith. Those who believed in a pre-Tribulation Rapture called these people Tribulation Saints or Tribulation Martyrs. Well, we now know, of course, that these are Church Martyrs. I think it's absolutely true that some of us, I have no idea how many, will be put to death for our faith."

A sound goes up from the audience that I've never heard before and can't describe. It's kind of like a muffled gasp, sort of like the sound you hear in movies from a character when that character dies. It's horrible. It's as if the shadow of death just entered the room. I can tell that Pastor Jon senses the gravity of his comment.

"There are no coincidences for Christians. Everything happens for a reason," he continues. "God promises in his Word to never test us beyond what we are able to endure. If he knows that we cannot endure being put to death for our faith, then he won't allow it. Please remember that God is still on his throne. He is still calling the shots in this world. He will give each of us the grace to endure whatever comes next."

Just as Pastor Jon finishes his sentence, I thrust my hand into the air. It's completely involuntary, like someone is pushing it up for me! Because Pastor Jon was already looking in our direction as he answered the last question, he sees me and points directly at me. I can feel my heart pounding in my ears. I don't even know what I'm going to ask until he hands the microphone to me. My voice breaks a little as I begin to speak: "Pastor Jon, my family and I all knew that the church would be here during the first part of the Tribulation. We read a book many months ago called *The Pre-Wrath Rapture of the Church*. The book makes an airtight argument from Scripture that the Rapture happens roughly four years into the Tribulation, just before God pours out his wrath described at the end of Revelation, chapter six. My dad sent you a copy of the book. It is super important that you read it. I'm sorry to ramble on about this. My question is: do you still have this book my dad sent to you?"

I can feel my body shaking. I am terrible at public speaking. I have never spoken in front of more than thirty people, and I just spoke in front of three thousand here in the room and another one thousand in the lobby! I keep standing as I wait for his response, but my legs feel weak, like they will give out on me at any moment.

"I want to thank your dad for sending me this book," Pastor Jon begins. "Yes, I received it, and, yes, I still have it. And this might surprise you, but I've already read it twice."

Someone in the audience says somewhat forcefully, "What's the title?"

"The title is *The Pre-Wrath Rapture of the Church*, and the author is Marvin Rosenthal," Pastor Jon continues. "As I mentioned just a moment ago, our leadership team did spend a few hours on the topic of the timing of the Rapture. The scenario in Rosenthal's book is one we discussed. I don't want to get too far ahead on this, since we'll be meeting throughout the next week to discuss the Rapture. We will absolutely be looking at the Pre-Wrath scenario carefully, along with the other major ideas. Just so everyone knows, the other two ideas for the timing of the Rapture are mid-Tribulation, right at the three-and-a-half-year mark, and post-Tribulation, right at the end of the seven-year period. We will be closely analyzing all three."

I realize that I had not handed the microphone back yet, so I simply say, "Thank you," pass it back down the aisle, and sit down. My dad takes hold of my left hand and squeezes it firmly. There are a dozen words in his small gesture. He knows how terrified I am of public speaking, so I'm sure he is incredibly proud of me. I don't hear the next question because I'm still processing what just happened. I'm not the one who pushed up my arm! I felt someone, or something, push it up. Even though that should have totally creeped me out, I wasn't afraid at all when it happened. Did the Holy Spirit do this? I can't wait to tell Dad after the service! I am so relieved that Pastor Jon read Rosenthal's book. Pastor Jon is super smart, and I'm convinced he will believe it's true. My guess is that he already believes it but wants to wait until he can do a full analysis with the other pastors. If only he had read this book ten years ago! If he had, this would have been a very different Sunday morning church service!

The questions keep coming for more than an hour. Some are really interesting and thoughtful, like one asking if Salam is a man or a demon, and some are just bizarre, like one asking if Salam is Elijah. Pastor Jon's voice is so raspy toward the end that we can hardly understand his answers. One frustrating thing is that, given how detailed his answers are, it's clear that he already knows a lot about what's going to happen in the next seven years. From one of his answers, it's also clear he concluded a long time ago that the ten Zones are the ten kingdoms mentioned in the Old Testament Book of Daniel. If he knew so much, why didn't he teach on this? I'm sure there are three thousand other people in this auditorium thinking the same thing. I wonder how many of them will actually forgive him? I wonder if our church will shrink in the next few months or double in size?

Even though they added thirty minutes to the service, we run fifteen minutes beyond that. Pastor Jon looks like he could pass out at any moment. A tall man I don't recognize finally walks up next to him from behind the stage and suggests into the microphone that he close us in prayer. Pastor Jon nods his head in agreement and moves slightly to his left. The tall man prays for unity and grace, two things that might be in short supply in the coming months.

It's so crowded that it takes us forever to get out of the building. I notice as we are leaving that a large number of people remain in their seats. Some are crying, and some look like they are praying. For the first time since all this mess started, I find myself feeling sorry for someone other than myself. My mind flashes back to that meeting with Mr. Bradley, when I asked him if he believed the Pre-Wrath Rapture was true. I remember the dread that overwhelmed me in the seconds after he answered my question. That's what's happening all around me at this moment. They now know what I've known for months, and they're devastated. The worst part is that I have no idea how to help them.

As soon as we're in the car, Dad begins telling me how surprised he was to see me raise my hand.

"I didn't raise my hand, Dad," I say.

He looks at me in the rearview mirror with a confused look on his face.

"I didn't raise my hand, Dad," I repeat. "I am terrified of public speaking, and I wasn't even thinking of a question when my hand went up."

My mom turns her head all the way around and looks directly at me.

"We don't get it," she says. "You *did* raise your hand. What are you talking about?"

"Mom, I felt someone, or something, raise my hand for me. For a split second, I didn't even know it was my hand that was in the air! This should have totally freaked me out, but it didn't. I felt really calm. I didn't have a question in my mind until the microphone was in my hands."

Mom looks over at Dad, and the expressions on their faces change at the same moment. They know exactly what happened. The Holy Spirit was not going to let those three thousand people out of that service until they all knew six words: "The Pre-Wrath Rapture of the Church." We are all quiet the rest of the drive home. I'm thinking to myself that if God has already used me to influence three thousand people, what else does he have planned for me? I'm excited and terrified at the same time. I'm no leader. I'm just someone who's done my homework on all of this.

As we walk into the house from the garage, we run into Jackson in the kitchen. I avoid eye contact. He looks toward all of us and asks, "How was church today?" My head is about to explode! Jackson never asks about church. He hates going. Of all days for him to ask, why today?

"It was packed today Jackson," says Dad. "You should have been there. It was a really interesting service."

"What did they talk about?" asks Jackson.

Even though I'm not part of the conversation, I can feel the blood rushing to my face. I turn away from him, hoping he doesn't notice.

Before Dad can respond, Jackson says, "I watched it online. Hey, Chloe, I can't believe you asked a question! You almost passed out your sophomore year giving your Shakespeare presentation in front of like twenty-five people! YOLO!"

For a second, I consider telling him that I wasn't the one who raised my hand. I know he'll just make fun of me, so I leave out that detail when I respond: "I wanted everyone to know about that book we all read last spring. Remember? You read it, right?"

"Yeah, I did," he responds. "Shocking that I read a book I didn't have to. A first for me. So it looks like Christians are all worked up about Salam being the Antichrist."

He's clearly baiting us. If we tell him what we think, then the conversation could go in a direction that could be dangerous.

Dad responds before I can think of something to say: "Jackson, many Christians think Salam is the Antichrist. Many others are still trying to make up their mind. What do you think?" Dad is so smart to turn this around and put the question back on him. I would never have thought to do this.

"I think that every hundred years or so, some great leader comes to power and shakes things up," says Jackson. "Regarding the end-of-the world stuff, I'll believe all of that junk when I see the flying scorpions that crazy Bible teacher at Addison Christian always talked about!"

None of us respond to him. We just act like nothing happened and we each make ourselves something for lunch. We rarely sit together at a table when we eat, and today is no different. If all five of us are in the kitchen, most of the time we all make something different to eat, and we usually just stand around the kitchen island when we eat. I always had the feeling this made Mom sad, but she never mustered the energy to change it. Jackson grabs a leftover sandwich from the fridge and heads back upstairs. Mom, Dad, and I all look at each other but don't say anything. I'm sure we're all thinking similar thoughts. Jackson is watching us, keeping track of what's happening with Christians. What's he doing with that information? Is he passing it along to the Central Zone? By telling us he watched the service, is he making some type of veiled threat? Is he interested in what we believe but too prideful to talk about it? How can we possibly know?

With Jackson back in his room, we are free to have a real conversation.

"Chloe, it's so amazing what happened today in church," Dad says. "I have a feeling that Amazon is going to run out of copies of the Pre-Wrath book this week!"

"Dad, do you think our church will come to the same conclusion we did?" I ask.

"I believe that they will, Chloe. Last spring, when we all started looking into this, I did some research on the Mid-Tribulation and Post-Tribulation Rapture ideas. Neither of them makes any sense. If the Rapture were Mid-Tribulation or Post-Tribulation, then we would all know the exact day, but the Bible says no one knows the day or the hour. I can't imagine anyone believing either of these two options. In retrospect, there have only been two possibilities, Pre-Tribulation and Pre-Wrath, so all that's left now is Pre-Wrath. My guess is that since God knows that Pastor Jon is going to announce this week that the Pre-Wrath is correct, he wanted everyone to have access to Rosenthal's book so they could see his arguments for themselves."

Dad ended up being right. The following Thursday, all church members receive an e-mail from Pastor Jon, confirming what we knew they would conclude—that the Rapture will occur at some point after the three-and-a-half-year mark and just before God pours out "his" wrath on the Earth. It's the longest e-mail Pastor Jon has ever sent, and it includes a detailed Question and Answer section at the end. On the same day, Dad receives a personal e-mail from Pastor Jon, asking if he would be willing to meet in person on Saturday. This is quite a surprise. Since Pastor Jon lives just one mile from our house, they agree to meet at his house. Dad asks if I can join the meeting, and Pastor Jon quickly agrees.

On Saturday, we drive the brief mile to Pastor Jon's house.

"Dad, I'm nervous about this meeting," I say. "I don't know what to say. I'm afraid I'll say something dumb and embarrass myself."

"Don't stress out, Chloe," Dad says. "He's a super nice guy. My guess is that he will want to thank us for sending him the book."

Before we can have much of a conversation, we're already there. His house is right next to a park I used to play in when I was in elementary school, that's how we figured out where Pastor Jon lived. We mentioned that park to some friends, and they told us he lived right next door to it. Ever since I was born, Dad has had this funny habit of naming all of the parks in our neighborhoods. This one was appropriately named "Pastor Jon Park."

I'm still really nervous as Dad rings the doorbell. Pastor Jon opens the door with one hand while holding back a very large dog with the other. I absolutely love dogs, so I instantly feel more relaxed. He welcomes us into the living room and introduces us to his wife and his youngest son. His son is my age, but we've never met. Even though we both attend Hebron

High School, I have never known what he looked like. Also, our high school is so huge that the odds of us running into each other are negligible. All three of them stay in the living room, so it looks like the conversation will include the five of us.

"Thank you so much for coming over," Pastor Jon begins. "It's great that you live here in the neighborhood."

"We love the community," Dad says. "We've lived here almost eight years."

There is some small talk about kids, college, where everyone grew up; then Pastor Jon moves the conversation to the book: "Thank you for sending me the Pre-Wrath book. As you might guess, I receive dozens of books in any given year. I only have time to read a small number of them. In the weeks leading up to when you sent me the book, I had been thinking a lot about end-time Bible prophecy. To be honest, I always leaned toward the pre-Tribulation Rapture idea, but I began struggling with several inconsistencies."

Pastor Jon continues: "Something that had always bothered me was the Magog invasion from Ezekiel, chapter thirty-eight. One of the tenets of the Pre-Tribulation Rapture was that no prophesied event had to take place before the Rapture could occur. My struggle was that we knew from Ezekiel that, after the war, the Jews would use the weapons from the war as fuel for seven years. In order to avoid saying that the war would happen before the Tribulation, the Pre-Tribulation Rapture group would say that the war will start just after the Rapture, maybe even the same day. Well, that didn't make any sense to me.

"At the three-and-a-half-year mark, we know that the Jews will all flee to Petra in southern Jordan for the remaining three and-a-half years, where God will protect them. Because of that, they would only be able to use the weapons for three and a-half years, not seven. If you put the war at some point during the seven years, that didn't work either. It seemed obvious to me that the Magog war had to happen at least three and a-half years *before* the start of the Tribulation. That conclusion then destroyed the idea that the rapture could happen at any time. There indeed *was* a prophesied event that had to occur before the Rapture, the Magog war. We all know now, of course, that the war did occur several years before the start of the Tribulation.

"Another huge one was Matthew chapter 24, the famous passage where Jesus' disciples ask him what will be the sign of his coming and the end of the age. Jesus lists numerous signs, including false Christs, wars, famines, and earthquakes. He says that many Christians will be persecuted and killed. But what is fascinating is that he makes an obvious reference to the Rapture, and it is listed *after* all of these other signs. He says, 'Two men will be working in a field. One will be taken and the other left.' If the Rapture were supposed to happen before the Seventieth week of Daniel, then Jesus would have started his extensive list of signs by saying, 'Two men will be working in a field. One will be taken and the other left,' but he didn't.

"It was these inconsistencies and many, many others that caused me to question the Pre-Tribulation Rapture. Your book arrived just as I was having this struggle! When I opened the packaging and read the title, I had this feeling come over me that this was it, that this was the answer I had been looking for. I immediately cleared my calendar, which is not an easy thing to do, and read the entire book in one sitting. My mistake after reading the book was sitting on this for several months, and now that we're into the final seven years, it's a little late.

However, as I mentioned a moment ago, I am so grateful that you took the time to send it to me."

"You're welcome," Dad responds. "I understand your hesitation to bring this to the church. After I had concluded that it had to be true, I tried talking to Christian friends and relatives about this. It definitely was not well received. Only a handful of them were willing to read the book. I didn't find many Bereans out there, if you know what I mean. You have an incredibly tough road ahead of you, given what we know comes next: the wars, the famines, and the persecution. Please know that we will be praying for you."

We all talk for more than an hour about what we believe will be the sequence of events from this point forward. I even get a chance to talk about the group of girls I meet with at school. I'm surprised that, in a few areas, Dad actually knows a little more than Pastor Jon. I never imagined that I would get the chance to have a meeting of such consequence at my age. As I have so many times lately, I keep wondering what the next surprise will be.

In the coming weeks, church attendance grows substantially—so much so that they add a third morning service in addition to the new Wednesday night one. Every service is packed, with folding chairs in the entry area. Getting there earlier doesn't help much because the service right before always seems to go long, and it takes forever to find a parking spot. My dad tells me that after 9/11, the church Mom and Dad attended in California saw a huge increase in attendance, but it lasted only for a couple of months. Dad says this looks completely different. He thinks attendance will continue to grow in the coming months and years.

CHAPTER FIFTEEN

FINAL PLANNING

As we expected, in the next few months Salam solves several worldwide conflicts through skillful diplomacy. The one that puts him over the top is the peaceful reunification of North and South Korea, something that seemed as impossible as the Middle East nightmare. The world has fallen in love with him. Within a few weeks of this win, the ten Zone presidents vote to make him chancellor over the entire Zone system. The ten Zone presidents have the power to recommend new regulations, but Salam has the final word. The more frightening change is that Salam is given the authority to implement new policies on his own. One of the first things he does is move the entire world to a single currency, the Euro. Canada, the United States, and Mexico had already moved to one currency years earlier. It was called the North American Dollar. This change to one currency, coupled with the elimination of all major conflicts around the world, leads to incredible economic growth. Dad had been expecting this and had decided to wait a while to put our house up for sale, knowing that prices would increase.

As the world gets better economically, it gets uglier spiritually. Salam announces the creation of a Zone-wide religious convention. He claims that since the major world conflicts have now been resolved, we must prevent future ones by eliminating religious intolerance and hate. He argues that many of the problems in our world have, as their root cause, the belief by some that their beliefs are superior or more accurate than those from other groups. Only by combining the religions of the world into one system can conflicts be avoided, he argues. Even the atheists are on board since their nonbelief system is also embraced as long as they tolerate the religious among them. Salam's catchphrase is "peace today, peace forever." With the exception of born-again Christians, the world embraces his thinking wholeheartedly.

Gradually, born-again Christians begin to stand out as the only group that seems opposed to peace. People in every Zone start using the word "haters" to describe Christians. My group at school decides it's no longer safe to meet on campus. We begin meeting during the lunch hour at Alyssa's house since she only lives a few minutes from school. Both her parents work, so their place is empty during the day. Mom and Dad begin describing a significant change at work. Employees are now required to attend mandatory Central Zone tolerance training classes. They both think that, at some point, employees will have to sign tolerance commitments with wording that violates their personal Christian beliefs. They are fairly certain that those who won't sign will be fired.

The Central Zone inches closer and closer to confiscating all guns in every Zone. We begin to hear of people being prosecuted for not registering their guns. At first, people are only fined, but then we start to hear of arrests and jail time. It's becoming almost impossible to legally purchase a firearm, even a rifle. Ammunition is only available on the black market. The Central Zone makes it a crime to make your own guns or ammunition, but I hear that people are doing it anyway. The anger in Texas is growing by the week. Dad senses that we're getting close to the Zone wars, so he arranges for a meeting at Mr. Harmon's house. Although we have been communicating regularly for months, this meeting is different.

We arrive at Mr. Harmon's house on a Saturday around noon. We drop Hannah off at a friend's house, so it's just Mom, Dad, and I. It has been several weeks since our last face-to-face meeting.

"It's great to see you all again," Mr. Harmon says as he opens his front door. "Let's meet in the living room."

We all take turns shaking his hand. I'm sure he can sense the apprehension in my eyes. I sense this meeting could be the one where we pick a date.

"Well, just to bring you up to speed," says Mr. Harmon, "everything is in place up in Montana. The bunker is in and fully stocked. The main house is also fully stocked. We have enough food in both to make it three years. What I mean by that is we could live on just what I have in the house for three years, then move to the bunker and last another three years. At some point, we have to assume that we'll have to move into the bunker. I have several rifles, two handguns, and lots of ammunition. so we could make it even longer by hunting. I just had a complete inspection done on the both the hydroelectric system and the backup generator. Both are in good shape and should last for several more years without an overhaul. I have a few spare parts for both. I'm no expert on either system, but I'm pretty sure I can accomplish minor repairs on my own.

"I've installed two security gates on the private road to the property. If either is forced open, it will set off an alarm in the cabin. From the time the first gate is breached, we would have about ten minutes before someone arrived at the house. That should give us plenty of time to be out of the house and well on our way to the bunker. It's about a twenty-minute hike to the bunker. I made sure that the bunker isn't close to any hiking or game trails. We'll have to bushwhack our way there, but that will help cover our tracks. Once we are all settled in the cabin, we'll need to practice the whole routine, both during the day and at night. Our process will need to include making sure the house doesn't look lived in when we leave. That won't be easy. It will take some thinking.

"I'm sure you've noticed that things are heating up not just here in Texas but all over Zone One. I'm hearing about a lot or arrests, mostly for illegal guns. My guess is that a new law allowing confiscation could come any week now. I think it's time to start planning our escape. Here's one other new update. I sold my house. The escrow closes in three days. I'll be staying in an extended-stay hotel until we leave. I think you should consider listing your house this week. With the economy still really strong, it should sell quickly."

I am hanging on his every word. I'm really excited to be heading to the mountains. It's so incredibly stressful everywhere now. School is awful. I can't wait to leave.

"I agree with you completely," Dad says. "I'll put the house on the market next week. I already have an agent lined up. I'm going to list slightly below market to ensure a quick sale. With a thirty-day escrow, we should be able to leave in about six weeks. Even if that's much earlier than we need to leave, I don't care. Things are getting ugly. I hear people talking about taking up arms, about trying to leave the Zone system through force. If they announce confiscation, that will be the trigger that starts it all.

"What is also concerning me is that we don't see the large increase in Zone forces you would expect with all the unrest lately. That only confirms my fears that the war, when it comes, will be nuclear. I'm sure Salam will pull his people out quickly just before he hits Zone One. He doesn't even need to use dozens of nukes; he could just set off a few high-altitude nukes and create an Electro Magnetic Pulse or EMP. We've talked about this before. That would wipe out all electrical systems. That would push Zone One back to the 1800s. Millions would starve to death. We have got to be out of here well before this happens, or we will never make it all the way to Montana."

Dad redirects the conversation: "There's one big challenge we need to discuss. It's what to do about Jackson. If we list the house for sale, he will go on high alert. He will ask a lot of questions. We obviously can't take him with us. He's almost an adult. It breaks our hearts to know that we have to leave our son behind, but I can't think of another option. The challenge is how do we pull off our escape without him knowing what we're doing? To be honest, I've considered not even selling the house and just leaving one day while he's at school. We have enough money without selling it, and besides, once Salam requires his mark on the right hand or the forehead, no one will be able to buy or sell without it. Our money will eventually be worthless anyhow. What do you think?"

Mr. Harmon is quiet for a minute. It's a lot to process. Then he says, "You're right that we can make it without the extra money. From what we already have between our two families, we can more than cover any needs in the coming four years. As you know, I paid cash for the property. We can pay the taxes up until the point where Salam's mark is implemented; then, we can head to the bunker. I can't think of a way for you to sell the house out from under Jackson and get away without him knowing."

I look over at Mom, and she has this incredibly sad look on her face. While the guys are working through the logistical junk, I know what Mom is doing. She's trying to process the fact that she will have to abandon the son she loves in a few short weeks. Once we leave, it's unlikely any of us will ever see him again, in this life or the next one. She won't be able to say good-bye. She won't be able to hug him or tell him how much she loves him, and I have no doubt that this realization is breaking her heart. Even though he's a jerk, I love him, too. Mom and I look directly at each other, and both of us begin to cry.

Dad figures it out right away. It takes Mr. Harmon a little longer.

"We all love Jackson," Dad begins. "Chloe, I know that you love him, too. It breaks my heart to have to abandon him like this. If we stay, we could all die in the war that we know is coming. Even if by some miracle we survived the war, Jackson could end up turning us in, and we would all be executed for our faith. If we leave, there is a chance we could make it all the way to the Rapture. It's not a guarantee, but it's a chance. We will never stop praying for him. As long as he has not taken the mark, there is hope for him. God is in the business of doing miracles. God can still save him."

Dad turns toward Mr. Harmon and says, "I agree with you, Mark, that it's probably too risky to sell the house. I'll call my real estate broker on Monday and let him know we've decided to hold off on selling for now. Since your house will close in about three days and we're not selling, can we go ahead and set a tentative date for our escape? It needs to be on a school day, and I think we should plan on leaving as early as possible—after Jackson leaves for school. Chloe, we'll have you stay home sick that day so Jackson will drive in by himself. Mom and I will pretend to leave for work, and then come back within thirty minutes. Let's look at a calendar."

Mom pulls up one on her iPad.

"I think we should shoot for two weeks from Monday," says Mr. Harmon. "That will give us a small buffer in case my closing gets delayed."

"That's May 15," says Mom.

"We can't go much later than that because the school year ends at the end of May," Dad says. "It will get more complicated with Jackson once he's out of school."

Everyone agrees that May 15 is the date. Mr. Harmon reminds us never to use this date in any of our texting, e-mails, or phone calls. For months now, we have been referring to our escape as our summer vacation plans. I guess it was a fitting cover story, given that we'll be escaping right at the beginning of summer. At least the weather should be good for the long drive. No snow.

"Now that we have a date, there are a couple of other logistical things to discuss," says Mr. Harmon. "You can only take what will fit in your SUV. With the four of you in there, that won't leave much room. You'll need to avoid packing up stuff in any obvious way, because that could tip off Jackson. I'd suggest filling some suitcases ahead of time but keeping them out of sight. Sometime in the next couple of days, you'll want to withdraw all the cash available in your accounts. This might not sound very biblical, but you might consider taking out the maximum cash advance on your credit cards. For the next few years until the Rapture, we are all going to be off the grid.

You'll have to leave all of your credit cards behind or cut them up after you take out the cash advances."

Mr. Harmon looks at me and says, "Chloe, I know this will be painful for you, but all of the cell phones have to stay behind. They can track us if we take them along."

My heart sinks as the reality sets in. In just over two weeks, I will never see or talk to any of my friends again, not in this life.

"That's a good point," Dad says. "I hadn't thought of that."

Mr. Harmon continues: "Also, be sure and remove your toll tag transponders the morning we leave. Those can be used to track us as well. Lastly, I know this sounds a little crazy, but I have a coating I'm going to put over the license plates on both cars. It looks like mud. You might not know this, but between here and Montana, we will be videotaped dozens of times. By covering the license plates, we can cover our tracks. And of course, we'll use cash from here on out so there won't be a record at any of the gas stations along the way. Effective the day we leave, we are all 100 percent off the grid for good."

It will seem like a strange question to Dad, but I ask what will happen to our house. I really love our house, especially my room.

"I have the mortgage and utilities set up for auto-pay," Dad says. "We'll leave enough money in our checking account to cover these charges for about one year. After that, the bank will foreclose on the house, meaning they will take possession of it. My guess is that the wars will start long before then. I'm going to leave some cash behind for Jackson, as well. I haven't decided how much. I'll put it somewhere that will take him a few days to find it. I feel we owe that to him. The bottom line is Zone One will be gone before Jackson no longer has a place to live."

"Can we all leave him individual goodbye notes, Dad?" I ask.

Mr. Harmon answers before Dad can get out a word, "I don't think that's a good idea, Chloe. We want to leave as few clues behind as possible. We need to be safely in the cabin before the authorities get involved. There will be some confusion at first. I figure that we'll have been gone for at least seven hours before he gets home from school. It's a twenty-one-hour drive to the cabin. We need him to be guessing at what might have happened for the next fourteen hours. By the time he gets the Zone or local police involved, we should be safely in Montana."

He can tell I'm disappointed by his answer. I know he's right. I don't tell anyone, but I decide to write him a note anyhow but hide it somewhere he will eventually look, like maybe under a computer keyboard. I'll pick a place I'm sure he won't look in for the first twenty-four hours.

"I know you're disappointed, Chloe," Mr. Harmon says, "but we all need to switch to survival mode now that we have a date. That means avoiding any conversations or actions in the next two weeks that could compromise our escape. It's business as usual until we leave. Don't do anything at work, at school, at home, or with your friends, even Christian friends, that could create suspicion. Don't say a word to Hannah. At her age, she won't be able to keep any of this to herself. Remember we're not the only Christians in Texas planning an escape. I hear things all the time. Some people have already left without saying a word to family members and friends. I've had people try to draw me into conversations about hiding out or moving to another Zone. I never go there with any of them. I know that sounds harsh, but you don't know who you can trust."

We all nod is agreement. As always, I'm worried that I am a terrible liar. I'm sure Mom and Dad are a little concerned, as well. What about my small group at school? With the school year winding down, we have started making plans for weekly meetings throughout the summer. Alyssa and I have become really close. She has no one at home for support, and I have become her closest friend. We tell each other things that we would never tell anyone else. Not just Zone stuff, but personal things. She has become like a sister to me. The thought of just leaving without saying a word to her breaks my heart. It will break hers as well. I don't bring this up with Dad or Mr. Harmon because I know what they'll say.

Since our escape is two weeks away, we agree to meet again at Mr. Harmon's house in exactly one week. Mr. Harmon suggests we have all of our packing done, secretly of course, before our next meeting. Mom and Dad will pull out all of the cash they can just before we meet again. As we head out the front door, Mr. Harmon gives me a hug. I'm a little surprised. As I turn to leave, I say, "Since we'll all be one happy family in about two weeks, can I start calling you Uncle Mark when we get to Montana?"

He chuckles, gives me a second hug, and says, "Of course, and you can start now! And I might even call you by your nickname, Lolo, once in a while."

"It's a deal," I say as I walk toward our car.

CHAPTER SIXTEEN

SAVING ALYSSA

By early the next week Alyssa senses a change in me. I am trying my best to hide the fact that our time together is short, but she can read me like a book. I'm convinced everyone can. That's quite a liability in the times we are living. At the end of our lunch session on Thursday, she asks if I can stay at her house for a few minutes after the others leave. We'll both be late to fourth period, but who really cares? Within a year, there won't be any schools in our Zone anyway. There might not even be anyone alive. I agree to stay.

As soon as we're alone, she goes right to where I knew she would: "Chloe, we've grown really close this school year. I think you know this, but I consider you my closest friend. The other girls in our group are terrific, but our relationship is special. Maybe it's because of how we met. I don't know. But I can tell that something is up with you. I'm not sure if the other girls can tell, but I can. You have been avoiding eye contact with me, and you seem really distracted. Given the world we now live in. I'm sure there are things you can't tell me, but is there anything you can tell me?"

My heart sinks. I rack my brain. What can I say to her?

"You're right, Alyssa, I have been distracted lately," I say. "And you're also right that there are things I can't tell you. It's not because I don't trust you. I totally trust you—more than any of my friends, and I also consider you to be my closest friend. You have become like a sister to me. During the school year, all eleven of us have talked about our plans. Some of the girls have no plans to leave. Not necessarily because they don't want to, but they just can't. They don't have the money or anyone to help them leave. It's different for me. My family, well most of us, will eventually leave. That's why I'm so distracted. That reality is starting to set in. I'm going to miss you terribly, Alyssa!"

We both start crying. I knew we would. I never used to cry. Before Addison Christian closed, I might have cried ten times in my entire life. In the past year, I must have cried a hundred times. It's pathetic.

"You have become like a sister to me as well, Chloe," Alyssa says. "I consider you to be more my family than I do my own parents. I've known for a while that you would eventually leave. Just the thought of it breaks my heart. I've never been closer to anyone before. Maybe it's the times we're living in. Relationships are so much deeper when you know your time together is short."

We sit for a long time crying and holding each other's hands. I want so desperately to tell her everything, but I can't betray my family. But Alyssa is my family. She is more family to me than my own brother. How can I leave her behind? How can I abandon her? She will be completely alone. It seems so incredibly wrong. At that moment, I hear a voice in my mind whisper, "Take her with you, Chloe." It startles me. I stop crying. Of course. Why not? We have room in our car. We should have plenty of food. If we are a little short, we can buy more after we get to Montana. I don't say a word to Alyssa about taking her with us, but I do tell her that I'm going to talk to my family and ask for permission to give her more details on what we're planning. That seems to brighten her spirits just a little. We decide to blow off school for the rest of the day and head out for ice cream. Just what we both need after a good cry.

That night I corner my dad as soon as he walks in the door from work.

"Hey, Dad, can we talk privately for a few minutes?"

"Sure," he says.

The weather's nice, so I suggest we walk across the street to a small park next to our house. It's empty. We sit on a bench facing the playground. I grew up in this playground. It seems like a lifetime ago. I try not to think about it.

"Dad, do you remember all those movies we used to watch about World War II—the ones about people hiding Jews from the Nazi's?"

"I remember some of them," he says. "Why?"

"God used many Christians, and even some non-Christians to save thousands of Jews. Well, I want to save someone. Before you ask any questions, let me explain. You know I've become close friends with Alyssa, the girl in my high school group. We have become like sisters."

"Chloe, I think I know where you're heading with this. The cabin's not Noah's Ark. We can't stuff it full of every Christian friend we know."

I interrupt him midsentence: "Dad, please let me finish. We were talking today during lunch after all of the girls went back to school. She has sensed that something is up with me. I told her that our family would eventually leave. And don't worry; I have never given her any of the details. We both started crying as we realized that our time together was ending soon. As we sat there quietly, I heard a voice speak to me, and it said, 'Take her with you, Chloe.' Dad, that had to be the Holy Spirit! No demon would tell me to rescue another Christian! And it wasn't my voice that I heard! Don't you see? It's just like when my hand was pushed up at church. It's not me, Dad. It's God. God wants us to rescue Alyssa!"

Dad is quite for a long time. I can't imagine what's going through his mind. Maybe he has thought of Christian family members he would like to take along. He has an aunt who lives just forty-five miles north of us. Of course, we can't take everyone. But we have to take the ones God tells us to take. I'm convinced of that!

"I am going to pray about this," says Dad. "Please don't say anything to Mom or Mr.— I mean, Uncle Mark. I'm not saying no, Chloe, but this is really big. We're talking about adding her to our family for three or more years. There are other considerations. You know, food and all that. I promise to pray hard about this. Okay?"

"Thanks, Dad. I will continue to pray as well, and I won't say anything more to her until you give me the green light."

Just for fun, I ask him if he wants to go on the teeter-totter with me, for old times' sake. He agrees, and for a moment I'm ten years old again.

It doesn't take long for Dad to make up his mind. The next day he tells me she can come but asks me to say nothing to her until after our follow-up meeting with Uncle Harmon. I ask Dad what convinced him that we should rescue her. He says that, in the last twenty-four hours, the name Alyssa has shown up a dozen times, at work, while reading news articles, and on television. The clincher happened just that morning. He has an open position at work. When he logged into his Intranet site to pull up the candidates who had applied, three of the seven candidates had the same first name: Alyssa.

While waiting for our final meeting with Uncle Mark, I sort of break my promise to Dad and give Alyssa a few more details on our plans, privately of course. I'm careful not to mention the date or the location. I can tell she wants more information, but I hold back, and she doesn't pry. I find myself thinking a lot about Jackson. Because we are just under two years apart in age, we truly grew up together. We had so many 'firsts' together, like parasailing, skiing, surfing, and scuba diving. He is part of every major memory I have. How did he become what he is? How could we have so many shared experiences but now be on opposite sides in this big mess? I remember Dad saying that atheists are born, not made. Maybe he's right. Maybe nothing could have prevented Jackson from falling in love with evil, but I already miss him so much! In just two weeks, I know that I'll probably never be able to see or talk to him again. I find myself mourning for him like you would for someone who has died.

I know he will search for us. I'm not sure if his search will be motivated by revenge for us leaving him or loneliness. After we're gone, I'm sure he will realize that there was no way we could take him with us. If he does manage to find us at the cabin, I can't imagine that ending well. The thought of how that could play out is so disturbing. Will he kill us all? Would he be like Judas and bring others who will then kill us? I try to put it out of my mind.

The week passes quickly, and we are back at Uncle Mark's house. Dad asks me to let him bring up Alyssa. Uncle Mark gets right down to business.

"So let's go through the checklist" he begins. "Were you able to pull out all of your cash?"

"Yes," says Dad, "and I took your advice and made the cash advances on all four of our credit cards. All in all, it's roughly one hundred thousand dollars."

"Great," says Uncle Mark. "That's more than I was expecting. I have about the same amount. With the cabin and food already paid for, we should be good for four years—maybe even five years."

"I agree," says Dad, "but I don't think we'll be around five years from now."

Uncle Mark works his way through the other items, and it looks like we're in good shape.

"So does everyone feel we can stick to our May 15 date?" asks Uncle Mark.

"We all feel good about that date," Dad says. "So it's one week from Monday."

"I'll come to your house," says Uncle Mark. "Is eight o'clock a good time? Will Jackson be gone by then?"

"Yes," says Dad. "He leaves for school no later than seven-thirty most days."

Dad glances over at Mom and me, and his expression changes. Immediately, Uncle Mark knows that something is up.

"What is it, Ray?" he asks. "Has something happened? You aren't having second thoughts about leaving Jackson behind, are you?"

"No, it's not that," says Dad. "It's something else. There will be five of us going to the cabin, five, not including you, but the fifth one won't be Jackson; it will be a girl named Alyssa. She and Chloe are best friends. Alyssa is solid. She's a strong Christian. We've prayed about this all week. Chloe and I are convinced that God wants her to go with us. I won't go into the details, but some stuff has happened to confirm it for us, some supernatural stuff."

Uncle Mark has a concerned look on his face. I get the impression he's a big planning kind of guy and this last-minute change is throwing him off.

"So we'll need to buy extra food for her once we get there," he says. "There's room in the cabin for her, but the bunker is a question mark. I think we can make it work. Good thing you made those cash advances on your credit cards; that should cover the food. As long as you're convinced that this is what we should do, I support you, but let's all try not to take in any more strays in the next seven days, agreed?" Of course, we all agree. After all, what could happen in one week?

"There's one more thing," says Uncle Mark. "I know we're only one week away from our escape, but you never know what could happen. We need a protocol for what to do if we have to leave earlier. My thought is that if any of us, you included, Chloe, see or hear anything that would cause us to accelerate our plans, we send each other a group text. We just need to agree on what it will say. We'll have to be careful about the wording."

"How about something like, 'There is no time like the present,'" I suggest.

"Well, that sounds cryptic enough for me," says Uncle Mark. "So if anyone in our group of five, or I should say six now with Alyssa, sends this, then I suggest we meet at your house, assuming Jackson isn't there. If it turns out to be a false alarm, we can all stand down. Agreed?"

"Agreed," we all say.

Dad and Uncle Mark agree that I can bring Alyssa up to speed on the details, including the group text, but they ask me to be sure and communicate all of this in person, not over the phone. As soon as we're back home, I call her and ask if we can meet for a couple of hours. She quickly agrees. I pick her up, and we drive to the donut shop in my neighborhood, and luckily, it's still open. We grab a seat in the corner away from the six other customers in the store.

"So here's the deal, Alyssa, you're in!" I say.

Her eyes start to get watery, so I jump into the details before she can start crying: "Alyssa, it's super important that you don't write any of this down. You need to memorize everything I'm about to tell you."

She nods her head in agreement.

"First, the date. We're leaving next Monday, May 15. We're all meeting at my house at 8:00 a.m."

Alyssa looks puzzled. "Who's we? Who all is going?" she asks.

"So it's my mom and dad, my sister Hannah, and a friend of our family, plus you," I tell her. "So six all together."

I keep going: "We'll be taking two cars. You'll be driving with us. You need to leave your cell phone behind but turn if off before you leave, and hide it! Everyone knows that no teenage girl would ever go anywhere without her phone. In fact, you might just chuck it in a creek on the way to my house. Just don't bring it."

"Is it so we can't be tracked?" she asks.

"Yes. We are going to spend the next three or four years completely off the grid. No phones, no Internet, not even any gas or city electricity."

Alyssa hangs on my every word.

"So can I ask where we're going?" she asks.

"Yes, of course," I say. "We're going to the extreme backcountry in Montana."

I spend the next thirty minutes going through the other details, including the emergency text. I give her everyone's cell phone number. I remind her to pack really light, just one large suitcase. And, most importantly, I ask her to leave no notes, not for anyone, including her mom and dad. I explain that we need to leave as few clues behind as possible so we can get to the cabin before the police start looking for us. It's a twenty-one-hour drive without traffic, and we will only have a seven-hour head start. It's going to be tough playing it cool with the other nine girls in our group at school.

CHAPTER SEVENTEEN

ESCAPE

I find it impossible to concentrate in school on Monday. I stopped turning in my homework assignments two weeks ago. Dad would be upset at me if he knew, not because he cares about my grades but because it could tip off my teachers that something is up. Several kids I know have left the school in the past two months without giving any notice. I'm sure there are many more I don't know about. It's such a huge school that anyone hardly notices. I keep my phone with me in class just in case. If any of my teachers catch me, they'll take it until the end of the class.

Just before the end of my fourth-period class, I hear a kid in the back of the room say, "No way! They're going to take everyone's guns!" Our teacher tries to shut him up, but everyone starts hitting him with questions. He claims to have just received a link to an article saying that the Central Zone has voted for a complete confiscation of all personal firearms in all Zones. There will be a voluntary thirty-day period where gun owners can turn in their weapons. Those who don't comply within the thirty-day period will face arrest. I slowly back away from the group and move out into the hallway. I have no way of knowing if this is true or just more speculation. I try to call Dad, but he doesn't pick up, so I try Uncle Mark. He answers.

"Uncle Mark, have you heard any news today about confiscation?" I'm careful not to use the word gun in my call.

"No, but give me a second, and let me take a look," he says. I ask him to call me right back.

My hands are starting to shake. This could be it. What about Jackson? If we go now, we'll only have a two-hour head start, not a seven-hour one. The seconds seem like hours as I wait in the hallway for Uncle Mark to call me back. The fourth-period bell rings, and the hallway is so loud I won't be able to hear my phone ring. I move outside. I text Alyssa and ask her to meet me right away at the softball field. Within minutes, we're together, and I tell her what just happened. Her face turns pale. We both begin searching the Web with our phones for any news articles. We can't find anything official. Just then, my phone rings. It's Jackson!

I hesitate for a second but then pick up.

"Hey, Jackson, what's up?"

My voice is really shaky. I'm sure he can tell.

"Hey, Chloe, tell Mom I'm going home with David after school," he says. "I'm going to help him finish up his short-film project, okay?"

"Sure, no problem. What time will you be home?" I ask. This is something I wouldn't normally ask, but I need to know how much extra time we'll have in case we leave today.

"Maybe around ten," he says. "It depends. I have a key."

Just then my phone rings again, and its Uncle Mark.

"Hey, Jackson, I have to pick up another call. I gotta go."

I hang up and take the call from Uncle Mark.

"Uncle Mark, what did you find?" There is panic in my voice. Alyssa leans in to try to hear what he is saying.

"This doesn't look official, Chloe," Uncle Mark says, "but people are acting like it is. This isn't good. Just the rumor could set things off. I'm going to send the text now. You know what to do, right?"

"Yes, absolutely. I'm good. We're good. See you soon."

I look at Alyssa. She heard. We're going.

"This is it, Alyssa!" I say.

Just as I say this, the group text hits both of our phones.

"Do you have your luggage in your car like we planned?" I ask.

"Yes," she says.

"Good. Let's get to my car quickly, and I'll drive over to yours. We'll pick up your luggage and head to my house." She nods in agreement but doesn't say a word.

We walk quickly to my car. I'm tempted to run, but I restrain myself. Two minutes later, we are at her car, and we grab her luggage. I see several students leaving the campus, which is unusual for this time of day. Maybe it's the gun confiscation rumors. Maybe their parents told them to head home. If this thing gets crazy, it might be really tough to get out of the city quickly. We arrive at my house right at two o'clock. Mom is working from home today, so she's already there. We all hug the second I walk in. Mom looks nervous and sad. Everyone is supposed to reply to the group text with two words: "Too true." Everyone has responded except Dad.

"Mom, I'm concerned. Dad hasn't responded!" I almost scream the words.

"I know," Mom says. "I tried calling him, but he didn't pick up. That's unusual. Why don't you try calling him?"

I try, but he doesn't pick up. My heart is pounding.

"I have to run pick up Hannah," says Mom. "I'll be back in about twenty minutes."

As she pulls out, a car pulls into the driveway. It's Uncle Mark. I give him a hug, and we walk quickly into the house. He sees Alyssa and says with a broad smile, "So you must be our new family member?" Alyssa relaxes just a little and introduces herself. They shake hands. I guess it's too soon for hugs. Uncle Mark looks concerned.

"Have you tried calling your dad?" he asks.

"Yes," I reply. "Mom and I both tried. He isn't picking up! It's been twenty minutes now since your text."

"How far is the drive to his office from here?" he asks.

"About thirty minutes," I say.

"I saw your mom pulling out just as I pulled in. She's getting Hannah from school, right?"

"Yes," I respond.

We all pace around the room. It's almost two thirty. We're losing precious time!

"Why don't we head over to—"

Before Uncle Mark can finish his sentence, my phone rings. It's Dad! His phone froze up, and he just got the text. He couldn't reply to our text or call out from his phone until just now. He left work twenty minutes ago, and will be home in less than ten minutes. What a relief. Mom should be back with Hannah in about the same amount of time.

"The second your mom and dad get here, all the phones go off," Uncle Mark says. "We'll find a place to toss them as we leave the neighborhood. I should have turned mine off before I headed over here. Not that it matters, but if they dig into our phone records, they'll know that your neighborhood was the last place my phone and Alyssa's phone pinged a cell tower."

I have an idea and voice it: "Uncle Mark, what if we have you and Alyssa leave your phones on; then we can head south for a few miles. You can then kill your phones, and we'll do a quick U-turn?"

"Not a bad idea, Chloe," he says. "It will cost us an extra twenty minutes, but I think it's worth it."

Just then Uncle Mark looks at his watch, and his face turns pale.

"What about Jackson?" he asks. "It's almost 2:45. Won't he be home soon?"

"We're covered," I quickly respond. "He's going to a friend's house straight from school to work on a project, so he won't be back here until around ten o'clock. Assuming we leave in the next fifteen minutes, we'll still have the seven-hour head start we were hoping for."

Uncle Mark relaxes just a little.

I see Dad pulling into the driveway, so I run to the front door. By the time I get to the driveway, Mom pulls in with Hannah. As soon as they are both in the house, Dad says, "It looks like we have everyone. We need to move fast. Jackson could be home at any minute!"

I bring him up to speed on Jackson and our plans to head south, then turn off the last two phones, then head north for Montana. We all start to head for the front door, but Mom stops us. She asks Dad to go with her to Jackson's room for just a minute. I don't need to question why. It's her way of saying good-bye to her only son. Despite who he has become, I know she loves him with all her heart. Uncle Mark and I don't say a word. Hannah looks confused. Alyssa, Uncle Mark, Hannah, and I wait by the front door.

When Mom and Dad come out of Jackson's room, their eyes are filled with tears. I can't hold back my emotions, and, within seconds, I'm crying. Alyssa quickly joins in. I'm sure she's thinking about her family. She'll never see them again. I feel so bad for Uncle Mark. I wonder if he wishes he had gone solo on this whole thing. It's too late now. We're a family.

Hannah interrupts the collective meltdown by asking why we're not taking Jackson with us on vacation.

"I'll explain it to you in the car," Mom says.

I have no doubt that conversation will lead to another emotional meltdown. We'd better save that one until we've crossed the state line.

Uncle Mark takes charge again. He reaches into a small duffle bag and hands Dad a walkie-talkie. I didn't know they still made these. They look really expensive.

"These are top-of- the-line Motorola walkie-talkies," Uncle Mark explains. "They have a maximum range of twenty-three miles. The batteries will last us all the way to Montana, with plenty of power to spare. Once we're in our two cars, let's only communicate using these. No cell phones. If we get separated, we'll use these to find each other."

Uncle Mark pulls out a map from his bag.

"Since we won't be navigating by our phones," Uncle Mark says. "I've purchased two identical maps and included written directions to the cabin. If we get separated for some reason and can't communicate via the walkie-talkies, then I want you all to go directly to the cabin. On the back of the directions is a hand-written map showing you where I've hidden a key to the cabin."

I've actually never seen a fold-out map like this before. I guess this must have been the way people traveled before cell phones.

"Let's head south on Highway 121 for three exits," Uncle Mark says. "Once we pull off to do our U-Turn, we all need to turn off our phones. We'll also need to peel off the toll tags from both cars. Everything needs to be tossed at that point. There is a grocery store where we'll be doing the U-Turn. We'll toss the phones and the toll tag transponders in a trash bin behind the store. Just follow me and stay close. Any final questions?"

Hannah speaks up again. "Why are we throwing away our phones?" she asks.

She gets the same answer from Mom: "Honey, I'll explain everything to you in the car."

Hannah doesn't look satisfied with Mom's answer and just nods her head. We all move out the front door, and Dad hesitates just for a moment. It's hitting all of us, I'm sure. We can never come home again. Dad locks the front door, and we load our suitcases into both cars. Since Uncle Mark has more room, we put most of them into his Jeep. I've never seen him driving this car before. I'm guessing that he just bought it. The four-wheel drive could come in handy.

Just before we pull out, Dad and Uncle Mark test the walkie-talkies. The reception is excellent. We follow Uncle Mark out of our neighborhood. As we pull away, I look over my shoulder for one last look at our house. Within five minutes, we are heading south on the freeway. We're all completely quiet. The silence shatters when Alyssa's phone rings! It's her mom calling! Alyssa looks around the car as if to ask what she should do.

Dad doesn't hesitate. "Don't answer it, Alyssa! Let it go to voice mail!"

She complies, but I can tell this unsettles her.

"Can I listen to the voice mail?" she asks

"Sure," says Dad. Alyssa listens to the message.

"Mom was just letting me know she'll be home a little late tonight from work," Alyssa says.

We all relax a little, but I can tell that Alyssa is really sad. I'm sure she wasn't expecting to hear her mom's voice again. I'm sure Hannah is really confused by our cryptic behavior.

Within just a few minutes, we exit the freeway and follow Uncle Mark into the parking lot behind a grocery store. He walks to our car and collects Alyssa's phone.

"It's turned off, right?" he asks.

"Yes," she responds.

Uncle Mark puts her phone and the toll tags into a bag with the other phones and tosses them into a large trash bin. He walks back to our car quickly like he forgot something.

"Shoot! I forgot to cover our front and back license plates!" he says, almost in a panic.

He then says, "This will only take a minute. I have a spray that looks like mud. I'll cover the left side of your front and back plates. I'll spray the fenders, too, just to make it look less conspicuous. I'll do your car first, and then mine."

I find myself scanning the back of the grocery store for cameras. I see two. We've barely started our trip, and we've already been filmed at least once. Uncle Mark was right to cover part of our license plates.

We pull out of the parking lot and pull back onto the freeway, this time heading north. That's it. We're off the grid for the rest of our lives. It feels so strange not to have my phone, not to have any phones. I've never been without a phone since sixth grade. It's really strange. In this moment, so much has changed about life. My self-reflection is cut short by the sound of Uncle Mark testing the walkie-talkies again. The reception is still great, but I'm guessing it should be, given we are only forty feet behind his car.

I want to check the time but realize I don't have a phone. I look at the dashboard on our car. It's 3:15. My high school just let out. Jackson will be on his way to David's house. We have our seven-hour head start. Alyssa's mom said she'd be home around seven, but her dad usually comes home by six. We'll have a three-hour head start on her family. I look at the map. Uncle Mark has highlighted the path in yellow. We'll head northwest up through Amarillo, then into the northeast corner of New Mexico. Dad says we'll be in Colorado within nine hours. Factoring in stops for food and gas, Dad thinks we'll be at the cabin in roughly twenty-four hours. Mom and Dad are going to take turns driving.

This time, Hannah breaks the silence: "Mom, why aren't we taking Jackson, and why did we throw away our phones? Those cost a lot of money! I thought I was going to get Chloe's phone when she's done with it. Does this mean I don't get a phone?"

Since Hannah is in the very back of the Sequoia and Mom is in the front passenger seat, Mom climbs all the way to the back of the car. This is a conversation that needs to happen face-to-face.

"Hannah, I'm not sure where to begin," Mom says. "This vacation we are taking, it's not really a vacation. We're going to live in another state. We're going to live in a cabin in Montana."

Hannah has a very confused look on her face and asks several questions. "Why do we need to move, Mommy? And if we're moving, why didn't we sell our house? And what about your work and Dad's work? Won't you get in trouble at work?"

Mom stops her before she can ask another question.

"Let me explain, Hannah. It's no longer safe for us to live in Texas. It's no longer safe for us to live in a big city. There is a war coming soon, and we are going to live in the country where we'll be safe."

Hannah gets quiet, so Mom keeps going: "We know that the war is coming because it's in the Bible. We also know that Texas and the other states won't win this war. Hannah, many people are going to be killed in this war. We are going to a place far away from the major cities where we'll be safe."

"But won't Jackson die in the war?" Hannah asks. "Why did you leave him behind if he is going to die when the war comes?"

This is going to be a really complicated conversation. I have no idea how Mom's going to put this into words that a nine-year-old will understand.

"Hannah," Mom explains, "in the next few years, life is going to be tough for Christians. Some Christians are going to be killed just because they believe in Jesus. In just over two years, there is a man who will make everyone in the world worship him. He will tell everyone that he is a god. Anyone who doesn't worship him he'll put to death. You know the Bible says we are only supposed to worship God, and not people, right?"

Hannah nods her head.

"Well, if we stay in a city," Mom continues, "then one day they will tell us to worship this man, and if we don't, they will try to kill us. The Bible says that some children will tell on their parents during that time. They will have their parents arrested and turned into the police for refusing to worship this man."

"Are you afraid that Jackson will turn us in to the police?" Hannah asks. "Why would he turn us in? We are his family. He loves us."

"Well, Hannah, you know how Dad and Chloe and I all believe in God? Well, Jackson doesn't believe in God. Even though we have always told him the truth about God, he doesn't think God is real. If we took him with us to where we're moving, he might decide to turn us into the police for not worshiping that man I mentioned a second ago. Do you understand, Hannah?"

"So people who don't believe in God are going to turn in people who do believe in God, right?" she says.

"That's right, Hannah," Mom says. "It won't happen right away, but since we're getting close to when this will happen, we needed to leave now."

"Does that man who will say he is God start the war, Mommy?" Hannah asks.

"Yes, he will," says Mom.

"Does he win the war?" asks Hannah.

"Yes, Hannah, he does."

Hannah is quiet for a minute.

"Will I ever see Jackson again?" she asks.

"I don't think so," Mom says as her eyes fill with tears. They hold each other, and both cry for a long time.

CHAPTER EIGHTEEN

THE CABIN

I n the first couple of hours of our drive north, I tell Alyssa what I know about the cabin. She has never heard of a hydroelectric system that can generate electricity from a stream. I don't know much about the inside of the cabin, so I can't provide details on where the two of us will be sleeping. I tell her what I know about the hidden bunker. She seems concerned about how her joining our group will impact our food supply. She opens her purse and shows me a stack of twenty dollar bills.

"I've brought my life savings," she says sheepishly. "It's almost two thousand dollars. I thought we could use this to buy extra food when we get there."

I feel almost embarrassed for myself. Our family has always been well off financially, but I know that Alyssa's family has always struggled. She must have worked really hard to have saved this much money.

"That's a very good idea Alyssa," I say. "From what Uncle Mark told us, between the food in the cabin and the food in the bunker there is enough for five adults to last six years. Since we are about two and a half years away from the midpoint of the Tribulation, we should have plenty of food. Your money will definitely put us over the top."

Alyssa seems relieved to know that we already have more food than we need to last three or four years. I can't help but wonder, though, what could happen in the next two years. Once the war breaks out and Zone One loses, people will begin to starve to death. Some of them will be Christians. What if some of them find their way to the cabin and ask for help? How could we turn away Christians who are starving to death? I'm sure Dad and Uncle Mark have thought about this, as well. Maybe that's why they bought way more food than we need.

My thought is interrupted by Uncle Mark's voice on the walkie-talkie.

"We'll need to stop for gas soon," he says. "I'll pull off at the next exit."

"Sounds good. We're low, as well," Dad says.

We have been on the road for almost five hours, and it's just starting to get dark. As I look out the window to my left, I catch a glimpse of a beautiful sunset. It occurs to me this will be my last Texas sunset. In just about four hours. we'll be in New Mexico and then in Colorado an hour later. As we pull into the gas station, Dad asks all of us to use the restrooms. Since we're on a 'cash' system now, both Uncle Mark and Dad go inside to pay for gas.

Alyssa and I buy a couple of snacks for Hannah and us. As I'm in line, I see Jackson's favorite gas station snack, beef jerky and cheese sticks. I feel a profound sadness envelop me. In two hours, he will come home and find the house empty. What will he think? What will he feel? Will he be able to sleep tonight? Will he start calling and texting all of our numbers? He's really tech savvy, so he'll see that his texts are not delivered. He'll know that my phone is turned off, which will provide him with a clue. I just saw him this morning, and yet I miss him terribly.

Alyssa must have sensed something is up because as soon as we're back in the car, she asks, "What was going on back there in the store, Chloe? You totally zoned out when we were in line."

"I know it will sound bizarre," I respond, "but when we were in line, I looked down and saw Jackson's favorite gas station snack. I started thinking about how much I'm going to miss him. I was also wondering what he'll feel in the next couple of days as he figures out that his family has abandoned him. I started imagining myself in his shoes. There are no words to describe how devastated I'd be if I came home and my family was gone for good. So that's why I zoned out."

Alyssa is really quiet for a while. I wonder if she is having the same thoughts about her parents. It has to be worse for Jackson than for Alyssa's parents. Her parents still have each other. Jackson is completely alone. I try not to think about it for now. I'll think about it when we're at the cabin.

"Our next stop will be somewhere in Colorado," Dad says as we pull back onto the highway. Mom decides to stay in the back with Hannah rather than ride up front with Dad. I wonder what Hannah is thinking. I try to imagine how I would be dealing with this as a nine-year-old. Mom talks to Hannah about the cabin and the state of Montana. She tells her about the time she and Dad vacationed there before any of us kids were born. I haven't heard this story before, so I listen in. Mom describes how beautiful Montana is in the summer. She tells a funny story about how Dad wanted to take Mom hiking on a remote trail in Glacier National Park. Mom whined the whole time about how there were probably grizzly bears everywhere on the trail. They only made it five minutes into the hike before Mom convinced them to turn around. Mom loves looking at the outdoors but not living in them. I wonder if she'll ever leave the cabin.

About an hour later I hear Uncle Mark's voice again. He's asking Dad to turn to a news radio station. Uncle Mark says things are heating up in Texas. Dad finds the station, and we listen for details. The rumors are flying about the possible forced confiscation of guns in Zone One. The guy on the radio says there are estimated to be more than three hundred million guns just in the United States. I had no idea there were so many out there! That's almost one gun for every person in our country. A few Texas politicians are asking all working Texans to skip work tomorrow and to join protest rallies in each of the major cities. Politicians in at least twenty other states are calling for the same actions.

Uncle Mark comes back on the walkie-talkie and says, "They are calling for protests tomorrow in every state we will be passing through in the next fifteen hours. I'm concerned about Denver. We'll be driving through there around four o'clock tomorrow morning. I can't imagine any trouble that early in the morning."

"I think we'll be through Denver before any trouble breaks out, but what about Wyoming?" Dad asks. "I don't know that state very well. Are we going through any major cities?"

"I don't think there are any major cities in Wyoming," Uncle Mark responds. "That doesn't mean there won't be challenges. Wyoming is a huge gun state. I would guess that the protests there will be as big as here in Texas. It could slow us down. I hope not. Let's continue to monitor the news and see what develops. We have good maps. If needed, we can always take a longer route that avoids any of the larger cities along the way."

I find myself instinctively reaching for my phone. Since the sixth grade, I've only been without it twice, both during school camps. I feel naked without it. How did people ever manage without them?

"I keep wanting to look up the news on my phone," I say to Alyssa.

"I feel the same way," she says. "I think we're both going through some kind of withdrawal. I wonder how many weeks it will be before we stop missing our phones."

"Months," I say, and we both laugh.

"Alyssa, did you ever talk to your parents about your Christian faith," I ask her.

"A couple of times," she replies. "I wish I had done more. My mom and dad have always seemed indifferent. They never argued with me about it. They just didn't seem to care one way or the other. I did ask Mom one time if she wanted to go with me to church, but she said it wasn't her thing. Now that I'm gone, I wish I had pushed harder."

Alyssa lowers her voice as she continues: "Chloe, please don't say anything to your parents. but I left my parents a note. Don't worry; I didn't say anything about our plans, and I hid it in a place where it will take them a few days to find it." I find myself instinctively whispering my response.

"What did you tell them?" I ask.

"It was a really long letter," she replies. "I wrote it over a week ago. Since I wasn't sure exactly when we might be leaving, I hid it in my closet a few days ago. I'm glad I did since I ended up going straight to your house from school. I told them both how much I love them. I thanked them for both working so hard to provide for me. I don't think I ever told you, but my mom works two jobs. I said that I have to go away because the

Bible says a war is coming soon. I actually went into a lot of detail on what's coming next. I provided them with a copy of Rosenthal's book. I attached my letter to his book. I know it's a little odd since neither of them are Christians. My guess is that the book will sound crazy to them, but I wanted them to know what's coming. Maybe they'll believe me and store up food and water. Maybe they'll survive the war. I know I wasn't supposed to do this. I'm sorry."

"Well, since we're doing the whole confessional thing, I'll tell you a little secret," I say. "I left a note for Jackson. I know how smart he is, so I put it in a spot where I know it will take him a few days to find it. He got in trouble once, and my mom hid his phone from him for several days in a row as punishment. I think it took him on average about four minutes to find it each day! It became this hilarious game that Mom always lost! Jackson and I laughed about it for weeks. Even Dad thought it was incredibly entertaining. I know how good he is at anticipating where we might hide stuff like a note, so I was careful. I didn't talk about what's coming, like what you did in your letter. He's heard all of that a thousand times before. I just talked about how much I enjoyed growing up with him. I told him that I always felt more brave, more willing to try new adventures because he was with me. I didn't say that I was leaving explicitly, but I did say that I will miss him more than he can imagine. And I told him that I love him, which is something I don't think I've ever done before, at least not in writing."

I can tell that Alyssa feels better knowing that I also broke the rules, but I'm sure it's different for her. My parents aren't going to stop loving me or stop being my parents when I mess up, but Alyssa has only been part of our family for a week. I'm sure she's afraid of messing things up and being rejected or perhaps not trusted.

Before Alyssa can respond, I hear my dad say loudly, "Oh no! We're getting pulled over!"

Dad grabs the walkie-talkie. "Mark, I've got a cop behind me. He has the red light on us. I'm pulling over."

"We aren't speeding so it's probably the license plate," says Uncle Mark. "You know, because I covered most of it. I'm going to get off at the next exit and wait for you."

My heart is pounding. As we pull to the shoulder, Alyssa asks, almost in a panic, "What if they ask about me? I'm only seventeen."

"Don't panic" Dad says. "I'll just tell them we are on a family vacation and that you are Chloe's best friend. No big deal. Try to relax."

The police officer seems to take forever to walk up to our car. Maybe it's because he can't read our license plate. Maybe he is calling for backup. Finally, he walks slowly toward our car with a flashlight in his left hand. Dad rolls down his window.

"Hello, Officer," Dad says. "Was I speeding?"

"No," the officer says. "I pulled you over because I couldn't read most of your license plate. It looks like you hit some mud or something along the highway. I'll need to see your registration, license, and proof of insurance. Where are you all headed tonight?"

"We're taking a family vacation up to Montana," Dad says.

My heart is really pounding now. The police officer must know that schools aren't out for another two weeks. What if he looks in the back and sees us?

Dad provides the documents, and the officer asks us to wait while he runs our information. This isn't good. Now there will be a computer record indicating what direction we are headed. I look over my shoulder and can see him at the back of our car. It looks like he's checking our license plate number against the registration. After just a couple of minutes, he comes back to the window and gives Dad back the documents and his license.

"Are you planning on driving through Denver tomorrow?" the office asks.

"Yes, that's our plan," Dad says. "It's the most direct route."

"You might want to take an alternate route around the city," the officer says. "I'm hearing that the highway might be closed down early tomorrow morning to prevent protesters from getting into the city."

"Thanks for the tip, Officer," Dad says. "And I'll get the license plate thoroughly cleaned up at our next gas stop." Of course he won't.

As we pull back on the highway, I say, "Dad, won't there now be a computer record of us heading north? And you told him we are going to Montana! What if he puts that into his computer?"

"Relax, Chloe," Dad says. "He didn't run our information. After he took my registration, he walked to the back of the car and wiped off the license plate just to be sure they matched. We're not in his computer. We're fine, and besides, remember how everything happens for a reason? Well, now we know to avoid Denver." Dad's right, and I relax just a little.

"Mark, we're back on the highway," Dad says into the walkie-talkie. "How far is the next exit?"

"Eight miles," I hear Uncle Mark say.

"Okay," Dad says. "We'll be there soon. You were right. It was the license plate. I told the officer I'd clean it up at the next gas stop. You'll need to pull out your map, Mark. We can't go through Denver. The officer told me they are going to be closing the downtown section of the highway to keep out the gun protestors tomorrow. We'll talk more in a few minutes. Where are you parked?"

"I'm in the back of the McDonald's parking lot. You can't miss it," I hear Uncle Mark say.

In just a few minutes, we're pulling off the highway. We're barely six hours into our escape, and we already had our first close call. I'm worried there will be more.

Dad and Uncle Mark agree on a route to the east of Denver. It will add an hour to our drive, but we can't chance getting stuck in the city. Uncle Mark applies more of his special mud to our rear license plate, again covering up most of the left side. We decide that since we've already stopped to take a quick bathroom break at the McDonald's, this will be our last stop in Texas. After this little incident, I can't wait to cross the state line.

Finally, just over seven hours into our drive, we cross into New Mexico. I check the map and see that we'll only be in this state for about an hour and a half. A couple of hours after that, we'll take our detour to avoid the downtown Denver area. I realize it's now ten o'clock. I turn back to Mom. Hannah is almost asleep.

"Mom, it's ten o'clock," I say. "That means Jackson will be getting home now."

She doesn't say anything. I wonder if she has been having the same thoughts as I—about how Jackson will feel when he discovers we have all abandoned him.

"Mom, I feel really sad for him. Even though he's not very nice to any of us, I still feel sorry for him. Even though he would never admit it, I think he likes having all of us around."

"You're right, Chloe," Mom says. "This will hit him really hard. Either it will wake him up and cause him to think long and hard about what we've been trying to tell him, or he'll just get really angry at all of us. We need to keep praying for him. Your dad and I deliberately left extra food and water around the house and in the garage. When things get bad, when the fighting starts, maybe this will be enough to keep him going for a while. He's very resourceful. I want to believe he'll find a way to survive."

"What if he starts looking for us, Mom?" I ask. "I know we've covered our tracks pretty well, but you never know. For all we know, he might have hacked our phones months ago. He's really good with the tech stuff, and ever since that church service, he seems to have been watching us more closely."

"I have no doubt that he'll look for us, Chloe," Mom says. "Wouldn't you? We've been careful. Mr. Harmon, I mean Uncle Mark, used a shell company to purchase the property. Jackson would have to hire a lawyer to unravel all of that, and with rumors of war growing by the hour, I don't think that will even cross his mind. He'll do an Internet search, for sure, but I don't think he'll find anything. Uncle Mark has been doing Web searches on his name for weeks now just to be sure that nothing related to Montana shows up. He last checked just a couple of days ago, so we should be okay. Given that we had talked openly with him about Alaska, my guess is that's where he'll start his online search, but there's nothing to find since we didn't pursue it. I suppose he might try to contact dad's aunt and uncle up there, the ones we stay with when we go to Alaska."

I find myself getting exhausted, even though it's not quite eleven o'clock. I rarely get tired until close to midnight, but all of the emotions from today's escape have worn me out. I know we'll stop again for gas at around two in the morning, so I let myself drift off to sleep. The words "bathroom break" wake me from my sleep. I look at the clock. It's 2:15 in the morning.

"Are we in Colorado?" I ask.

"Yes," says Mom. "We have been for the past couple of hours. I'm going to drive now for a while so your dad can take a break. Be sure and use the restroom. It will be another five hours before we stop again."

It's too dark, and I'm too tired to enjoy what looks like a gorgeous detour around Denver. I've always loved our Colorado vacations. I suddenly remember that Dad has a brother in Denver.

"Hey, Dad," I ask, "what's the deal with Uncle Don in Denver? I remember we've stayed with him a couple of times in the past. Is he a Christian?"

"I'm not sure, Chloe. I wish I knew. He never calls, so the only time we talk is when I call him, which isn't very often. He claims to be a Christian, but whenever I bring up something from the Bible, he doesn't seem to follow any of it. I know he has attended church most of his life, but he doesn't seem to get it. It's like he's clueless about the Bible. I considered talking to him about the peace treaty, just to see if he understood the significance but decided against it. It's too late now, of course, since I have no way to contact him."

I suddenly have another epiphany. Now that we're at the end of the age, there is this clear dividing line in the world. There are only two types of people on the planet, those who are true Christians and those who are not. Biology no longer matters. Friendships no longer matter. Family no longer matters. For Christians like us who have decided to survive until the Rapture, the only people we can trust are other believers. Parents will soon turn in their children to the Central Zone authorities. Children will turn in their parents and have them put to death. Everyone has to decide which side they will be on. There's no middle ground. Even some agnostics and atheists will eventually be executed. What will Jackson do? He's an avowed atheist. Will he take the mark rather than starve to death, assuming he survives the war?

A few hours later, I feel myself waking up as the sun hits my face.

"Where are we now?" I ask.

"Wyoming," Mom says.

She's still driving. Dad is up front, but it looks like he's asleep.

Alyssa and Hannah are both asleep, so I talk quietly: "Can we stop soon, Mom? I need to use the bathroom."

"Sure, Chloe. We're getting low on gas." She hands me the walkie-talkie.

"Ask Uncle Mark if he can take the next exit that has a gas station," Mom says.

It takes me a minute to figure out how to use the thing.

"Hey, Uncle Mark, it's Chloe. Can we stop at the next gas exit? I need to go to the bathroom."

"Good timing, Chloe. I was going to stop soon anyway," he says.

"Great," I say.

The view out the window is amazing. It's so incredibly beautiful. If I still had my phone, I'd take a picture of the sunrise and put it in my Snap Chat story. Despite the sadness of leaving everything behind, I feel this sense of wonder over all of this beautiful landscape that God has made. I wonder if Montana will be even more beautiful. I can't wait to be living in the woods. I've never liked cities, and I've always wished we could have lived in the country. It took the end of the world for me to get my wish! How will we all spend our time? All I know how to do is study, surf YouTube, and Netflix binge. Maybe Uncle Mark can teach me survival skills. I'd love to learn how to hunt. I already know how to fish. Dad made sure of that. I remember one time when we went to a really upscale resort in San Antonio. We walked down to a little dock at the river. Dad challenged me to make a homemade fishing pole from whatever I could find in the dirt next to the river. Within ten minutes, I found some fishing line, a hook, and a bobber and assembled my Tom Sawyer fishing pole! He was impressed! Only Dad would assign me something like this at a five-star resort!

I hear Uncle Mark say he's getting off at the next exit. Mom asks me to wake everyone up. We all look terrible. In our family, we call it "car face." It usually kicks in after ten hours in the car. We grab some snacks at the gas station and within a few minutes, we're back on the highway. In less than ten hours, we'll be at the cabin! I'm starting to get really excited. Based on our progress and the little detour, Dad says we should get there before it gets dark.

Finally, almost twenty-four hours after leaving Dallas, we pull off the highway onto a small road in Montana. After about thirty minutes on a paved road, Uncle Mark pulls off onto a gravel road. This must be it. This must be the final road to the cabin! After another twenty minutes, we pull onto a dirt road. One minute later, we stop at a gate. Uncle Mark walks back to our car and asks us to all walk up to the gate. It feels good to stretch our legs.

"Pay close attention to this," says Uncle Mark. "Look closely at this latch on the right side of the gate. Do you see how it's pushed up? If I leave it up while I open the gate, it will set off an alarm at the cabin. Do you see this small box near the ground? It has a transmitter and a battery. I'll have to change the batteries once every couple of months. This is how we'll know if someone opens this first gate."

Dad says, "So I'm guessing we need to flip the switch to the down position each time we come through the gate, then back up again after we close the gate."

"You got it," says Uncle Mark. "I have the same setup on a second gate about four miles ahead. Also, I have double locks on both gates. I'll give you all keys, of course. This will slow down whoever tries to come in without our permission, and I estimate that from the first gate alarm, we'll have just under ten minutes to get out of the cabin. I think I mentioned that the bunker is about a twenty-minute hike from the cabin and, of course, we'll practice this, but not today. I know you're all sleep deprived, and so am I."

"So are we just ten minutes from the cabin," I ask?

"Yes, we're almost there!" says Uncle Mark.

"I'm excited to see it!" I say.

"Well, let's get going then!" he says.

I ask if I can ride with Uncle Mark in his car the rest of the way, and he agrees.

As we drive the last few minutes to the cabin, I ask him how he found this place.

"It was kind of a miracle, Chloe. I was actually looking online at a property in Eastern Washington. I accidently moved my mouse to the right, and I saw one dot, one property, all by itself. It looked like a remote area. When I clicked on it and saw the hydroelectric system and the backup generator, I knew this was the perfect property for us. I had already formed a shell company, so I made an offer through the business I created. Because I made a full cash offer, they accepted it quickly, and it was mine within three weeks. I didn't even ask for an inspection before making an offer. I knew this was the place for us!"

We make a sharp turn to the right, and I see the cabin. We're not even inside yet, and I can tell it is even better than I imagined! There are so many trees that it kind of blends in with the landscape. As we pull up to the back of the cabin, I see what must be the original settler cabin off in the distance. As soon as I step out of the car I hear the river! I'm so excited that I grab Alyssa and the two of us take off toward the water. I hear Uncle Mark say not to go far because there are a lot of bears in the area. Even better, I think to myself. The more wildlife, the better. Maybe missing college won't be so bad after all!

The main cabin has four bedrooms, but Hannah, Alyssa, and I will have to share a room because the fourth bedroom is stacked almost to the ceiling with food and other supplies. The kitchen is large and has a fantastic view of the river. Uncle Mark warns us about the river. Since it's late spring, the water level is high. He thinks we could probably get out safely if we fell in but asks us to be extra careful. He shows us several battery-operated radios. "This is how we'll keep up with the outside world," he says. "We won't have TV or an Internet connection, so this is it. I've written down the numbers for all of the local news stations I could find."

Given that each of us only brought one large suitcase, it doesn't take us long to unpack. Everyone is so exhausted from the drive that we decide to wait until tomorrow to head into town.

"It's about a thirty-minute drive into town," says Uncle Mark. "You just head back toward the main highway, then head north for about twenty minutes or so. The town is really small, maybe a thousand residents. They have a good-sized grocery store and a sporting goods store. With Alyssa on board, we'll need to stock up on food and a few other items" he says.

"I brought all the money I have," says Alyssa. "It's around two thousand dollars. I'd like to pay for my own stuff."

"That would be terrific, Alyssa," says Uncle Mark.

Just doing some math in my head, I'm sure this won't cover her food for the entire time we're here, but I know that Mom and Dad will cover the rest.

Uncle Mark says, "I mentioned to Alyssa and Chloe to be careful about wandering around in the woods. There are probably a dozen grizzly bears in this area and mountain lions, as well. You're fine as long as you are here, close to the cabin, but don't go any further into the woods alone. Always go with at least one other person and always bring bear spray. It's under the kitchen sink. In the future, when things start to get ugly, we'll have to be even more careful. As people get desperate for food they might wander onto the property."

His comment gets me thinking. What will we do if people try to forcibly take our food or other supplies or try to hurt us? Will we shoot them? Is that what God would want us to do? I don't know if I could actually kill someone. What if it was the Central Zone police coming to arrest us? Would I be willing to shoot them? Probably. Uncle Mark must have read my mind because he mentions the weapons in the cabin.

"In the next few days," he says, "I'll show you all of the firearms I have here in the cabin. They are all locked up so don't worry about running into a loaded gun. I have plenty of ammunition, and everyone except Hannah will need to practice with live bullets. I also have a rifle, two handguns, and lots of ammo in the bunker. I'll show you the bunker in the next few days."

All six of us are so exhausted that we're in bed by nine. Even though I'm incredibly tired, I have a hard time falling asleep. My thoughts drift back to our house in Dallas and to Jackson. We've been gone more than twenty-four hours, and tonight is the second night since we left. Did he sleep at all last night? He must know by now that we've left him for good. Has he started searching for us? Is he searching our house right now for clues? He has probably stopped calling and texting our numbers by now, realizing that our phones are turned off. I find myself feeling really sad for him—sad that he's alone now. Tears fill my eyes, but I don't make a sound. Will I ever stop feeling guilty for leaving him? Will I ever stop missing him? If only he had believed what we believe, he could be safe with us in this cabin right now.

CHAPTER NINETEEN

THE END OF AMERICA

Early the next morning, voices in the kitchen wake me up. As I walk into the kitchen, Mom, Dad, and Uncle Mark are listening to the radio. From the looks on their faces, I can tell something has happened.

"What is it," I ask. "Has something happened?" There is an audible fear in my voice.

Dad looks over at me and says, "We got out just in time. We don't yet know what has happened exactly, but it looks like the east and west coasts were hit with nukes a couple of hours ago."

My whole body starts shaking.

"What about Texas? What about Jackson?" I ask.

"From what we are hearing," Dad says, "the middle of the country didn't take a direct hit, but electricity is out everywhere. The entire grid is down. We are only able to pick up news from two stations on the radio, and they don't seem completely sure of what's happened."

"If the middle of the country was hit with an EMP device, then our cars won't work, right?" says Dad.

Dad and Uncle Mark grab the keys to both cars and head outside. Mom and I follow close behind. Uncle Mark tries his car first. Nothing. Then Dad tries our car. Same thing. Both are completely dead. We all look at each other but don't say a word. I break the silence by asking why we still have electricity in the house.

"On my last trip up here about a month ago," Uncle Mark says, "I installed EMP protection on the hydroelectric system and the backup generator. It must have worked because the hydro system is still running. We need to see if the generator is still working."

We all head out to a small shed behind the cabin. Uncle Mark unlocks the shed and flips the 'on' switch to the generator. Nothing.

"I don't know why it's not working" says Uncle Mark. "I protected it in the same way I did the hydro system. Let's not worry about that now. Let's get back inside and see what we can learn from the news."

It turns out that the information we're getting on the radio isn't from a news station but from individuals who are communicating with personal radio transmitters. News is being passed along from other parts of the country by individuals, not from the formal media outlets. Those appear to all be offline. From what we hear, the east and west coasts are gone. Very few people in the major cities are still alive. On both coasts, some people are starting to move inland on foot to escape the radiation. There doesn't appear to be any working electricity anywhere in the country. It's clear that the people we hear from on the radio are people like us, who moved to more remote places.

Alyssa comes into the kitchen.

"What's happened?" she asks. "Has the war already started?"

"I wouldn't call it a war," says Uncle Mark. "I'd call it an extermination."

"What has Salam done?" Alyssa asks. She has a look of panic on her face.

"We don't know for sure," Uncle Mark says, "but it looks like he nuked both coasts and hit the middle of the country with an EMP device. An EMP is a nuclear weapon that is detonated at a very high altitude. It wipes out all electronic devices. Salam has killed almost everyone on the coasts and pushed the rest of the United States back to the 1800s. We don't know yet about the rest of Zone One. If he didn't hit Canada and Mexico, my guess is that people from the United States will be pouring into those two countries soon."

"So people in Texas are still alive but without electricity, is that it?" Alyssa asks.

"Yes," says Uncle Mark.

"Will they be able to survive without any electricity?" she asks.

"Not for very long, Alyssa. Our whole society runs on electricity. Without it, you can't put fuel into trucks to get food from farms to grocery stores. You can't get clean water into people's homes. Within about one week, people will begin running out of food and drinking water, and stores will be empty. My guess is that every grocery store is being looted right now, including the one in the town near us. People who live near large farms will be able to last a while, but not forever. As I mentioned, if Mexico wasn't hit, then I think people in Texas will start heading south on foot. Millions of Americans are dead, and millions more are going to starve to death" says uncle Mark.

Alyssa starts to cry uncontrollably. Mom and I walk over to her and wrap ourselves around her. I'm sure she's thinking about her family, and I'm sure Mom is thinking about Jackson. Despite the strained relationships we all had, I know that we wish he could be here. Dad said that he left extra food and water in the house for him, but my guess is that will only last him for a month or two. What will he do then? It must be chaos in Dallas right now. I doubt there is widespread violence yet. It's too early. People are probably in shock and trying to figure out what's happened. However, my guess is that within a couple of weeks, things will get really ugly.

"I need to check our gate alarms," says Uncle Mark. "My guess is that they no longer work. I have backup alarms here in the house that I'll take with me. Let's check the walkie-talkies and see if they still work." They no longer work, but Uncle Mark says he has another set in the generator room that might still work, since the shed had some EMP protection. Fortunately, the ones from the shed still work.

"I'm going to grab a handgun from the safe," says Uncle Mark, "and Ray and I will walk back up the road and test the gate alarms. We'll call you on the walkie-talkie once we get to the second gate."

About thirty minutes later, we hear Uncle Mark on the walkie-talkie.

"I'm opening the second gate now. Do you hear the alarm there in the kitchen?" he asks.

"Nothing," says Mom. "I don't hear anything."

"Okay, give me a few minutes to replace the transmitter, and we'll try again," says Uncle Mark. This time it works. The sound of the alarm startles me. It's almost as loud as a fire alarm. About twenty minutes later Uncle Mark replaces the transmitter on the other gate and successfully triggers that alarm. About an hour after that, Dad and Uncle Mark are safely back at the cabin. The first alarm woke up Hannah, but none of us seem ready to tell her what's happened. I'm sure Mom will talk to her later today. Her world has already been so broken.

All the excitement from the night before about being in this beautiful place is gone. Probably half the people in our country are already dead or will be soon, and we have moved into survival mode. Within days, people could begin wandering the countryside, looking for food and survival supplies.

"I wasn't planning on us practicing an escape to the bunker for a few days, but with what's happened I'd like us to do this now," says Uncle Mark. "I need everyone to put on your best hiking shoes and lots of bug spray. Let's all meet in the backyard in five minutes."

"So you all know what the alarm sounds like except Ray?" asks Uncle Mark. "Ray, I'll play it for you after we get back from the bunker. Here's the challenge: Now that cars are no longer working, no one will bother opening the gate. Anyone who comes here will come on foot. I'll need to rig up a new system, some type of trip line on the main road that will trigger the alarm. I'll probably need to put in more than one. The challenge with this is that larger animals like deer and elk tend to use the roads around here because it's easier than walking through the forest. We could end up with a bunch of false alarms. I'm not sure what I'll do. But we need to practice getting to the bunker both in daylight and at night, so let's get started."

We head to a small bridge that crosses the stream. The water is really high and almost touches the bottom of the bridge. Once across, we head north. Uncle Mark shows us notches on trees near the ground level. These mark each side of the path. At first, they are hard to see, but after a few minutes, we can spot them more easily. We are not on any kind of path, so it's tough going. It's uphill the entire way. After twenty-five minutes, he stops us.

"So let's have a contest," he says. "The bunker is within eyesight of where we're standing right now. Let's see who can find the entrance first, and remember it's close, so don't wonder off and get lost!"

We all separate and begin looking for the entrance. This is the first fun thing I've done in a very long time. I scan the ground for anything that doesn't look natural. It would have to be in some type of clearing. I see a tree stump that looks like it's been cut by a chainsaw. This must be the area. I walk slowly, kicking the ground with my feet. My fight foot hits something hard. I reach down and clear away the leaves and soil. It's metal! It's a latch.

"I found it!" I call out in excitement.

As the rest of the group approaches me, Uncle Mark gives me a side hug and says, "Well done, Chloe."

"Uncle Mark, if I was able to find it so quickly won't others be able to as well?" I ask.

"I don't think so, Chloe. First off, no one knows there's a bunker on the property. Second, the property is over one hundred and fifty acres. Lastly, the land we're standing on right now isn't our property! We're in the Kootenai National Forest, which has over two million acres! Finding this bunker would be like finding a needle in a haystack!"

Uncle Mark continues, "Let me show you how to open the door. It's a foot higher than the ground around it to avoid flooding."

We all take turns opening it, except Hannah. The door is way too heavy for her. As we descend the stairs, Uncle Mark flips on the lights. It's much bigger than I imagined but crammed full of food, water, and survival gear. There are three small bedrooms, a small kitchen, and a common area with a couch. When he closes the hatch, it's completely silent in the bunker. I feel a little claustrophobic, but it's not overwhelming.

"How do we get fresh air," I ask.

"The bunker has two ventilation pumps, one on each end of the bunker," Uncle Mark says. "They run on batteries but can also be manually pumped if necessary." He shows Alyssa, Hannah, and me our room. He shows all of us where the various food supplies are stored.

"Given that the war has already started, I think we should move some additional food and water from the cabin to the bunker, just to be safe," Uncle Mark continues.

After our tour, we all take turns closing the bunker and covering the entrance with sticks and leaves; then, we head back to the cabin. Once we're back in the cabin, Dad immediately turns on the radio, and we huddle quietly, listening for more news. The news is sketchy, but it appears that people on the coasts are moving into the middle of the country to escape the radiation. So far, people aren't walking into Mexico and Canada, but Uncle Mark thinks they will as food becomes scarce. The areas not hit directly by the nukes all appear to be still without electricity. Given that we are so close to Canada and have lost electricity, my guess is that the whole country is blacked out. The areas on the fringes of the nuclear strikes sound like they are in chaos, with no official control.

"Ray, I think the two of us should walk to town and see what we can learn," says Uncle Mark. "We can get there on foot in just over two hours. We'll both need to carry concealed handguns to be on the safe side."

I look over Mom, and I can tell she doesn't like the idea.

"You might be outside of the walkie-talkie's range," Mom says with concern in her voice. "How will we know if you're safe, and what do you hope to gain by going into town? I mean, we have everything we need already in terms of food and water."

"I think we need to get a sense for how desperate things are out there," replies Uncle Mark. "We're only one day into the war, so I'm guessing things are still fairly stable. People in town will still have food and water. If I'm wrong and things are already turning ugly, we'll need to know that. We'll need to take more precautions here at the cabin."

"Let's do this," Dad says. "Mark and I will walk to town, but we won't actually go in unless things look stable. We'll stay on the edge of town and just observe things from a distance. We have binoculars here somewhere. We'll have walkie-talkie coverage most of the way."

I can tell Mom's still not sold on the idea.

"Look, honey," Dad says. "Mark's right. We need to know if things are already getting crazy out there. If there is widespread looting in town, it could spill out into remote places like here. We need to be prepared. I promise we won't go into town unless it looks completely safe, but it wouldn't hurt if you could pray for us the entire time we're gone."

"Of course we will," I chime in.

Since it's already late in the day, Dad and Uncle Mark decide to wait until tomorrow to set out for town. Uncle Mark has Dad do some practice shooting with one of the handguns. Since the four of us will be alone at the cabin for a few hours, Uncle Mark shows us how to load and fire one of the rifles before they leave. They will both have the guns concealed under their shirts when they go. The next morning, about thirty minutes after the first light of the day, we walk with them to the main road.

"Remember your promise," Mom says. "No going into town unless it looks safe."

"You have my word," says Dad. "We'll check in on the walkie-talkie every thirty minutes."

We watch them walk down the dirt road until a bend in the road takes them out of sight.

"Let's all stay close to the cabin while they're gone," says Mom. "No wandering off. I'm going to keep one of the rifles loaded and near the back door. Hannah, I don't want you going near any of the guns. They're dangerous! If something happens, we won't be able to get help for you since none of the cars work. Okay?"

"Yes, Mom. I promise," says Hannah.

Mom keeps the walkie-talkie clipped to her jeans, and about thirty minutes later, Dad checks in. They haven't seen anyone yet but did spot a deer. Both are good signs. Dad says he'll check in again in thirty minutes. Alyssa and I decide to relax on the back porch and talk.

"How are you holding up, Alyssa?" I ask.

"Well, I can't believe this is all happening," she says. "It seems impossible to believe that millions of people in our country are dead. And millions more are about to starve to death. There is no more United States. It doesn't seem possible. Do you think Salam hit Zones three and four?"

"I'm not sure," I say. "We probably won't know for a while. If Canada didn't get hit, then they will know. Maybe we can try and pick up a Canadian radio station later and find out. The Bible doesn't say if all three Zones will get taken out at the same time, so maybe only Zone One got hit so far. It makes sense that we would get hit first. Dad said there are almost as many guns as people in our country. Salam had to take us out first. What a stupid move to give up control of our nukes. I don't know why Salam only hit the coasts. That doesn't make any sense to me. Why not hit us in every state? I guess it really doesn't matter now, since the whole country is back to 1850."

"I'm so thankful that Dallas was spared a direct hit, Chloe," Alyssa says. "That means your brother and my family still have a fighting chance, and so does our small group from school. I wish I could talk to the girls right now. I wish I could encourage them. Some of them suspected that I was planning to leave. They started asking me questions in the last few days before we left. I felt terrible being evasive with them. It felt wrong, but I didn't want to mess up our escape plans."

"I know what you mean," I respond. "I have, or I should say had, this awesome history and English teacher at my Christian school. We became really close in the past year. I had planned on calling him to say good-bye, but then we left so suddenly. I miss him. I miss Jackson, too. I'm sure he's found my note by now."

"What was that?" asks Alyssa. We both hear a sound coming from the forest to our left.

"Quick, get the rifle," she says.

I almost trip over the entrance to the back door, trying to get into the cabin.

"Mom, something's out there!" I say.

I pick up the rifle, and Alyssa and I walk back onto the back porch slowly.

"Where's the safety on this thing," I say out loud to myself.

I find it, but my hands are shaking so much it takes me a second or two to flip the safety off. We both stand completely frozen on the back porch, staring intently into the woods. We hear something or someone moving through the trees. I place the end of the rifle on the railing and point it in the direction of the sound. I'm shaking so hard that I couldn't hit an elephant.

"It's an elk!" I hear Alyssa say. Her voice startles the elk, and it runs off into the forest.

"Thank goodness," I say. "My heart was pounding so hard that there's no way I could have hit anything!" We both laugh, and I turn the safety back on.

"Chloe, what are we going to do when it's desperate people coming through the woods?" asks Alyssa. "We aren't going to shot them, are we? I mean, that's not what God would want us to do is it?"

"No," I say. "I don't think we'll shoot any starving people, but if they start shooting at us first, I'm sure we'll shoot back."

"But what if starving Christians show up, Chloe?" Alyssa asks.

This is really complicated. I'm not sure what we should do.

"I think God would expect us to help them, even if it meant that we might not have enough food for the six of us," I say.

"I think God would want us to help them, just like your family helped me," says Alyssa. "And I think if we do, he'll provide us with more food, like that elk that just freaked us out!"

"I'm sure you're right," I say.

To our surprise, Dad and Uncle Mark are still able to reach us on the walkie-talkie right up to the edge of town.

"Things seem mostly normal," says Dad. "No one is driving around, and it looks like all of the electricity is out. People are milling around, talking. It looks safe. We're going to turn off the walkie-talkie and head into town and see what we can learn."

"Be safe!" Mom says.

It seems like an eternity before Dad comes back online. In reality, it's only forty-five minutes.

"We have some news," Dad says. "This is a really small, tight-knit town, so people are working together. A couple of people have radios similar to ours and know what's happened. They know that no help is coming, so they're developing survival plans. They have three groups in charge of hunting and two in charge of fishing. A few people have set out on foot for Canada, but most people are staying in town."

"You didn't tell them about where we're from did you?" asks Mom. There is a nervousness in her voice.

"Uncle Mark told them we were from a town to the south," Dad says, "and that we were heading north into Canada. They seemed to buy our story."

"Good thinking," says Mom. "Please hurry back. An elk came near the cabin and almost gave us all a heart attack!"

"Did you shoot it?" I hear Uncle Mark ask.

"No. We were just relieved that it wasn't a person," says Mom.

"He'll be back," says Uncle Mark. "We'll get him next time, or her, whichever it was."

Two hours later, Dad and Uncle Mark get back and provide some additional details. They met a couple of people who are probably Christians. Interestingly enough, they appear to have also seen this coming and have done some preparation, but they were careful not to provide too many details. People are bringing water up from the river and boiling it for drinking. Others are planting large gardens since it's early in the growing season. They saw lots of people carrying rifles, but no one seemed threatening. I wonder if that will still be true six months from now. Dad and Uncle Mark agree that they should walk back to the edge of town in two months but not actually go into town. Mom agrees, reluctantly.

CHAPTER TWENTY

THE STARVING FAMILY

As the summer wears on, the news from our radio gets more concerning. All major cities around the country have mostly run out of food. Many people in the northern and southern states have left for Mexico or Canada. The people who have stayed behind are becoming more desperate. Major cities are in chaos, with roving gangs killing people and taking what little food they have left. The rural areas seem to be in slightly better shape. There is word that the Central Zone has established several major military bases in a few Midwestern states. No one is sure what they are plotting. There are rumors that they are trading food for weapons. There is very little information about the other Zones. It's been two months since Dad and Uncle Mark last went into town, and they have been talking about going back. One evening at dinner, Dad brings it up again: "It's been almost two months since we last went into town. We need to know how things are going here locally. The news on the radio is sketchy, and they usually only have updates on major cities around the country. Mark and I have been talking it over, and we think it's a bad idea for us both to be away from the cabin at the same time, in case something happened here."

"I'll go," I say, without even thinking about it. I can tell from Dad's response that he was going to ask me to go with him.

"I've been practicing with the handgun," I say, "and I'm a pretty good shot now and, besides, people will feel less threatened by a father and daughter than by two men," I say.

"What do you hope to learn from going into town?" Mom asks.

"We need a firsthand look at how desperate people have become," Dad replies. "If it's really bad, then I think we should move more of our food from the cabin to the bunker. Also, we might need to consider having someone on guard all the time, even at night. We could work in shifts." None of us will admit it, but part of wanting to go into town is curiosity and boredom. Our only contact with the outside world for the past two months has been our radio.

"I want you to promise me you won't go into the town unless it looks completely safe," Mom says with concern in her voice.

"I promise," says Dad. "We'll leave early in the morning, before sunrise. We'll check in on the walkie-talkie every thirty minutes. When we get to the edge of town, we'll check it out, using our binoculars. We'll watch the town for an hour and then only go in if it looks completely safe. We'll each carry a concealed handgun. If we go into town, we'll limit our stay to no more than an hour. The whole round trip should be no more than five hours."

Mom nods her head in agreement but doesn't say anything.

In the morning, voices from the kitchen wake me before dawn. I wander into the kitchen and find Mom, Dad, and Uncle Mark talking over coffee.

"Hey, Chloe, I was just about to wake you," says Dad. I give him a side hug and pour myself some coffee. I started drinking coffee in middle school. I grew only to a height of five feet five inches, and Jackson always messed with me by saying that my early coffee drinking stunted my growth. As he grew taller over the years, he would always remind me of our height difference, almost seven inches now.

"How long until we leave dad?" I ask.

"We should plan on leaving in about twenty minutes," he says. "Be sure and eat a good breakfast. It's a long hike."

Before we head out, Dad reviews our plans, including what we'll do if we run into people along the way. His plan is for us to quickly move into the forest if we see anyone along the way, that is, if they haven't spotted us. If we run into anything that could be a major threat, like a larger group of people with guns, our plan is to warn everyone at the cabin using the walkie-talkie, then get back to the cabin as quickly as we can.

"What do you think we'll find in town, Dad," I ask.

"I'm not sure, Chloe. It's been a couple of months. Given how close we are to Canada, I think a lot of people will have headed north already. We'll know soon enough."

We both give Mom an unusually long hug good-bye. Alyssa is up by the time we leave, so I give her a hug as well.

"Be safe," Alyssa says.

"I will," I respond.

As we head out, there is just enough light to see the contours of the dirt road that leads to our cabin.

"Chloe, keep an eye out for any movement on the road," Dad says. "Not the human kind. I'm talking about animals. Predators like bears and mountain lions hunt in the evenings and early mornings. If we run into a grizzly bear, we would have to both empty our handguns to stop it." As soon as Dad says this, I go from mostly awake to completely awake and a little freaked out.

"And I'm relying on your amazing skills as our family spotter," Dad says.

He's right. I've always had this uncanny ability to spot things, mainly wildlife. On every family vacation we've taken to remote wilderness areas, I am always the first one to spot a bear or a deer. My first success as a spotter came when I was only three years old. I followed Dad into our garage from the house. I pointed to something small near Dad's foot and asked him what it was. He looked down, and a couple of inches from his foot was a scorpion. Since then, my skills as a spotter have become something of a family legend.

After an hour on the dirt road, there is plenty of light, and we walk cautiously and keep an eye further down the road for any signs of people. We pass by both gates, and the locks are still firmly in place, which is a good sign. We slow down as we approach the main road that leads to town.

"Let's move into the trees, Chloe, so we can't be seen as we approach the main road," says Dad. We leave the dirt road and move into the forest about one hundred yards from the main highway. It's much slower going, once we leave the road. Dad slows down our pace considerably as we approach the road. We stop about fifteen feet into the tree line.

"Stay here, Chloe. I'm going to move slowly toward the main road and see if there are any signs of people."

I nod my head in agreement.

"Dad, remember to turn down the volume on your walkie-talkie," I say.

"Great reminder, Chloe. I totally forgot about that," he says.

Dad lowers the volume and walks cautiously toward the highway. I can see that there hasn't been any maintenance along the highway. The grass is almost three feet high. Dad uses it to his advantage and conceals himself by crouching down. Before I can have another thought, I see Dad quickly scrambling back into the tree line.

"Dad, what is it?" I whisper.

"There are people a few hundred yards to the right, heading up the road toward us," he says.

"How many," I ask.

"I'm not sure. Maybe five or six. I couldn't tell. They will be here in just a few minutes. They won't be able to see us from where we are. Just to be sure, let's back up another few feet." We crouch down behind a large fallen tree and wait. We are wearing camo, so I'm sure they won't have any idea we're here.

After a few minutes, we hear footsteps. We have to stand up a little to get a good look at the group. There are five of them. They look like a family. They look completely worn out. They appear to be carrying what look like homemade backpacks. There are three children, and the youngest looks about seven years old.

"Dad, it's a family," I whisper. "It looks like they're in bad shape. Maybe we should talk to them. Maybe they can tell us what's going on."

"I don't think that's a good idea," Dad whispers back. "Let's just let them pass, then we'll see if it's safe to head toward town."

A moment later, they are right next to us on the road. We stay completely still.

"Ouch!" I yell. The little girl in the road looks right at me, then screams.

"Who's there?" the man asks. "We're not armed! We're just a family."

Dad looks at me with a bewildered look on his face.

"What happened?" he asks.

"Something bit me on the leg, Dad!" I say. I feel terrible. We both look back at the family. They are frozen in fear in the road, staring in our direction.

"Dad, they don't look dangerous to me. Let's go talk to them. Maybe we can find out what's going on."

Dad doesn't say anything to me but slowly stands up. I do the same a moment later.

"We are a family, as well," Dad says to them. "This is my daughter. We don't mean you any harm. Can we come down to the road?"

"Yes," the man says.

We shuffle down the embankment and through the tall grass next to the highway. I can see that Dad is keeping his right hand near his shirt, where his gun is holstered. We stop in the road about twenty feet from them. They look exhausted and scared.

"My name is Ray, and this is my daughter," Dad says.

"I'm John, and this is my wife, and these are our three children." They all nod slightly, and we do the same.

"Where are you headed?" Dad asks.

"North, to Canada," the man says.

"Where are you from?" Dad asks.

"We're from Denver."

Dad and I both look at each other in disbelief. Denver is almost nine hundred miles to the south of us.

"Have you walked here all the way from Denver?" I ask.

They all shake their heads in the affirmative.

"How long have you been walking?" I continue.

"Today is the thirty-first day, so basically a month," the man says.

Dad and I look at each other again. I know we're both thinking the same thing. How could they have made it this far on foot?

"After the electricity went out two months ago," the man says, "we initially thought it was some type of regional blackout, but then when we discovered that nothing electrical would work; we figured something worse had happened. A few people in our neighborhood had battery-operated radios. Within hours, we learned that it was an EMP attack. I had no idea what that was, but some of our neighbors did. They told everyone that it could be years before the power came back online. There was no way to confirm any of that, of course. At first, most people didn't believe it, but as the days turned into weeks, we knew it was probably true. Most people had enough food to last about one month. A couple of weeks after we lost power, some of our friends decided to walk to Canada. It sounded crazy to me, but as our food supplies got lower, I realized it was our only chance. We had to go in the summer, when the weather was good. I figured it would take us just over a month to get there. I don't know what we'll find in Canada, but it has to be better than what we left behind."

I have a million questions I want to ask them, and I'm sure Dad does, too.

"We have a ton of questions we'd like to ask you, but I can see that you're completely exhausted," Dad says.

"I have an idea," Dad continues. "Would you be willing to rest for one day at our place before you continue north? We have a cabin just over one hour from here. We would be willing to give you some food to take with you, enough to last you for a week. You're only a few days from the border with Canada. I guess what I'm suggesting is a trade: food and rest for information. We'd really like to know what you've seen in the last two months."

The man turns to his wife, and the two have a private conversation. I can see from the kids' faces that they're starving. I feel so terrible for them, especially given how well we've been eating for the past two months. My heart breaks for them. How many more children are there just like these three? There must be millions. How many will starve to death? My thoughts are interrupted by the man's response.

"That's a fair trade," the man says.

The faces of his three children light up just a little.

"Did you say it's about one hour?" he asks.

"Yes," Dad says. "The dirt road just up ahead to the left goes right to our property. Why don't we get started before anyone else comes down the main road?" They all nod their heads wearily in agreement.

As we get started, Dad says that our questions can wait until they have had a chance to eat and get a little rest. He also tells them that he will need to call ahead on his walkie-talkie to let everyone at the cabin know what's happening, so there are no surprises. I can tell from Uncle Mark's voice over the walkie-talkie that he's concerned with this unexpected turn of events. The smallest girl looks to be about seven years old. She looks like she could collapse at any moment, so about halfway home, I offer her a piggyback ride the rest of the way. She looks over at her mom, who nods in agreement, so I scoop her onto my back. Even though she looks close to Hannah's age, she weighs almost nothing. I find myself getting angry again. Salam did this. He killed our country.

"We're almost there," Dad says as we get close. "It's just around this bend in the road." As we approach the cabin, I can see Uncle Mark watching us cautiously from the south side of the cabin. He relaxes a little when he sees what bad shape this family is in. He makes a gesture toward the front window of the cabin, and Mom, Alyssa, and Hannah come outside to greet us. The family relaxes when they see them. Dad makes introductions, and Mom invites them into the cabin. As they walk through the back door, they all notice the same thing simultaneously.

"You have power?" the man asks in disbelief.

"We do," says Uncle Mark. "We have a hydroelectric system down in the river. It gives us enough electricity to run the lights and the electric stove and oven. It also runs a pump that brings up water from the river." They seem completely amazed. I had forgotten for a moment that they hadn't had electricity or running water for two months.

Mom encourages them to wash up and directs them to our kitchen table. They put all of their homemade backpacks in a corner of the living room before washing. They wash not just their hands but their faces. It seems to bring them back to life just a little. I can tell by the look on Mom's face that she is holding back tears. The sight of these poor emaciated people is almost too much for her. Mom asks Alyssa and me to help set the table for them. Mom puts enough food in front of them to feed ten adults. At the sight of so much food, the mom buries her face in her hands and begins sobbing. Her two girls join in, and, of course, so do Mom, Alyssa, and I. Once we all regain our composure, the dad asks if we would be okay with him thanking God for the food. His prayer is so moving that we almost start crying all over again.

Given how small the children are, I am absolutely amazed at how much food they are able to put down. As they are eating, Dad asks us to get together enough food for them for one week. Even though it would only take two of us to do this, I'm sure I know why Dad assigned it to everyone. He wants to give them some privacy while they eat. After they finish eating, they look like different people. Their eyes brighten, and they seem more coherent. Dad gathers all eleven of us in our small living room. Having kept our end of the bargain, Dad's ready with questions. So am I.

"Can you tell us what you saw during your walk from Denver?" Dad asks.

"I can tell you that we prayed for a long time before we left," the husband says. "We only had enough food to last for two weeks, and we knew it would take us more than a month to walk to Canada. Even though many others were walking along the highway, it still wasn't safe. There were thousands of abandoned cars on both sides of the road. At first, we thought about sleeping in them at night, but then we heard that gangs would attack the cars at night and kill people for their food. We saw bodies along the side of the road. It was terrible. We decided not to use the cars and instead slept in the forests each night about fifty yards from the highway. We could hear things at night. People being attacked. Screams."

"Hannah, let's take a walk down to the river," Mom says. Hannah looks disappointed, but she knows better than to argue with Mom in front of our guests. Once they are out the back door, the man continues. "We learned from others along the way that the Central Zone is establishing large military bases in several Midwestern cities. No one seems to know why. After all, the United States is defeated. What's the point? Attacks along the main highway got so bad that I decided we should move to smaller roads. That's how we ended up on the road near your cabin. It added time to our trip, but moving to the smaller roads has been much safer. Also, we've been able to find some food along the way. About a week ago, one family gave us some meat from a deer they had shot. Unfortunately, I don't own a gun, so I haven't been able to hunt along the way. I've never handled a gun before, so it probably wouldn't have done us any good."

"What did you do for work in Denver," asks Uncle Mark.

"I managed a team of database administers for a Web hosting company," the husband responds.

"Now that we're back in the 1800s, I'm guessing there won't be much demand for my skills," he adds with a chuckle.

"Have you heard what it's like up in Canada?" Dad asks.

"It's sketchy, but from what I've heard, they have power. I don't know if it's true, but it can't be any worse than staying in Denver and starving to death."

"Good point," says Dad.

"Are all of you from Montana?" the man asks.

"No, we're from Texas. We saw this coming and decided to get out of town before the war started."

They all have a shocked look on their faces.

"How did you know?" the man's wife asks in disbelief.

"It's all spelled out in great detail in the Bible," Uncle Mark says. "Between the Old Testament Book of Daniel and the

New Testament Book of Revelation, you can get a pretty good picture of how things are going to play out."

The conversation shifts from us asking about the outside world to how the world will end. Dad walks them through the sequence of events, letting them know what's coming. It's clear from the conversation that they are believers but their church, like ours, never discussed end-time Bible prophecy. Everything we tell them is new information. The man asks if we have an extra Bible he can take with them. We have several, and he picks one of the lighter ones. Given the amount of walking ahead of them, it makes sense not to pack up the ten-pound family version.

Dad invites them to spend the night, and they readily agree. They all sleep together in the living room. It must seem like the Ritz Carlton to them after sleeping in the woods for a month. Mom makes them a huge breakfast the next morning before they head out. We pray with them before they leave. Mom starts crying as they turn the corner and disappear out of sight.

CHAPTER TWENTY-ONE

OUR NEW CHURCH

Given what they told us about the killings along the main highway, Dad decides it's too risky to head back into town. Dad and Uncle Mark set up some trip lines around the cabin to give us some warning if anyone approaches unexpectedly. Also, Dad and Uncle Mark agree that the two of them should start a rotation, with one staying on guard all night while the other one sleeps. Uncle Mark volunteers to take the night shift. That works out great because Mom, Hannah and I can then have time with Dad during the day.

As the summer turns into fall and then winter, news from our radio gets much worse. Countless numbers of people have now starved to death or died of diseases. Cities that were not hit directly by nukes appear to have only a fraction of their former populations. There is word that the Central Zone has now set up bases in every major city in the states that were not nuked. Salam has made participation in the one-world religious system mandatory. There are rumors that Christians are facing heavy persecution.

As winter turns into spring, I begin to regret that we never really initiated the 'fight' aspect of our plan. We simply ran away to the woods. I spend some time reading sections of the Old Testament Book of Daniel. In chapter twelve, I read about how, during the Tribulation, Christians will turn many people to righteousness. We aren't doing any of that. We're just hiding out, waiting for the Rapture. I decide to bring it up during our weekly family Bible study. We each take turns picking a section of the Bible to study. Since it's my week to choose, I ask that we read Daniel chapter twelve. As soon as we read it, I jump into my thoughts with everyone.

"I've been thinking a lot lately about this chapter. It talks about how we will eventually be delivered which is, of course, a reference to the Rapture, but it also talks about how we Christians will turn many people to righteousness during the time we are in right now. We aren't really doing that. Remember our fight-then-flight plan? Well, it feels like all we did was run away. Salam is deceiving people. I think we should be out there telling them the truth about who he really is. We're getting close to the three-and-a-half-year point. People need to know what's coming, that he's going to declare himself to be God and require everyone to worship him or be killed."

There's a long silence as the implications of what I'm suggesting begin to sink in. We're relatively safe here in the cabin, but in the cities, Christians are probably being rounded up by the Central Zone authorities. Many people are desperate and starving. I'm sure things are about as bad as they can get right now. Of course, they will get much worse, especially once Salam declares himself to be God. Uncle Mark is the first to respond.

"It's interesting that you bring this up because I've been having similar thoughts," he says. "As a single person, I feel I have less to lose than the rest of you. I know that you all depend on me to keep things running here, like the hydroelectric system and the security stuff, but you could get by without me."

I nod my head in a kind of resigned agreement. I turn to Dad, knowing that his opinion will carry a lot of weight.

"Dad, do you agree? Should we be doing more?"

He's quiet for a moment, then responds, "I think that we should all pray about something this big. If some of us go out into the various communities around here, there's no guarantee we'd ever come back. It could be a one-way ticket."

"A one-way ticket to Heaven," says Alyssa.

"Exactly," says Dad. "I'm all for getting to Heaven, given the condition of our world right now, but we need to make sure this is what God would have us to do right now."

I look over at Mom. As usual, she seems so sad. This is not the future she imagined for our family. In a "normal" world she'd be planning our travel for our summer vacation right now. Maybe a trip to Maui or Colorado. Instead, she's having to consider losing more members of her family, after already losing Jackson.

"I agree that we need to pray about this," says Mom. "We also need to think through the practical aspects. Most of the towns around here are small and miles apart. Whoever goes out can only carry enough food and water for about one week. The Zone authorities could secretly follow any of you back here to the cabin; then we would all be compromised. We just need to give this a lot of careful thought and prayer; that's all."

Since I started this conversation, I feel obligated to keep it going.

"So, Dad, how many days would we need to cover that town that is closest to the cabin?" I ask.

"Probably four or five," he says. "We would need to plan on one day of travel each way, then maybe two days talking to people in town. We could carry enough food and water for that many days. I'm guessing there is drinkable water in the river that runs next to the town. That could extend our trip by several days or more."

We spend the next thirty minutes talking about how we would spend our time and the logistics, including an escape plan if things got ugly. We agree that if we had to return to the cabin quickly and under threat we would travel at least two miles south of the cabin on the dirt road, then arc back home through the woods. The thought of actually doing something is so much more appealing to me than just hiding out here in the woods. I'm glad I'm not the only one feeling this way.

We have a follow-up discussion a few days later and decide that Dad, Alyssa, and I will do a test run to the nearest town. We decide only to observe the town, and only for two days. We'll use the walkie-talkies to relay details as we collect them. Based on what we see, we'll decide whether to go into the town on a future trip. I'm so excited the night before we leave that I only sleep a few hours. We're all up about one hour before dawn. We each will carry one backpack with food, water, and other supplies. Dad's pack is larger since he has to carry the tent. We all pray together; then, the three of us head down the dirt road near our cabin.

We check the trip wires that Uncle Mark installed near the cabin. All of them are still in place, which is surprising. I would have thought a deer, an elk or a bear would have tripped at least one of them by now. When we get to the main road that leads into town, we decide to walk along the tree line rather than on the highway. It will slow us down a lot but will allow us to disappear into the woods if we see anything suspicious. Dad is carrying a loaded handgun in a holster under his shirt.

When we are about one mile from town, we use the walkie-talkie to check in with everyone back at the cabin. We tell everyone that we haven't seen anyone on our dirt road or the highway yet. We did see a couple of deer when we first left the cabin. Last fall, Dad and Uncle Harman began shooting some of them to supplement our food supply. It was the first time I had ever seen a deer cleaned. It was gross and fascinating at the same time. I told them I'd like to clean the next one they shoot.

As we get closer to town, we move into the woods to avoid being seen. We find a good spot on a ridgeline where we can set up the tent and also see most of the town. We take turns using Dad's binoculars. The town looks mostly empty. We see a handful of people sitting outside what used to be a gas station. There are no signs of Zone authorities. Given how deserted the place looks, I'm not sure we'll have many people to talk to, if and when we actually go into the town. I remember that the last time we tried to go into town, there were people heading north on foot on the main highway. We don't see any the entire first day. I guess anyone who had planned on walking to Canada is already there or has died trying.

The entire first day is pretty uneventful. Even through the walkie-talkie, I can tell that Mom is relieved that we haven't seen much activity in the town. Dad and I put up the tent. It's small for three adults. It's still getting down into the forties at night, so we had to bring our sleeping bags. We can't make a fire for obvious reasons. We eat homemade jerky from the last deer Dad shot and some mixed nuts. We take one last look at the town just as the sun is setting. We see light from a couple of fires, mostly from outside the main part of town, but not much else. I had so little sleep the night before, so I fall asleep quickly.

At first light, we are awakened by a sound we haven't heard in almost two years, the sound of motorized vehicles. We scramble out of the tent, almost tripping over each other. Three large vehicles are pulling into the town. It's still too dark to see what they are, but they have to be Zone vehicles. Who else would have three identical military vehicles that still work? Six men exit each of the vehicles, all armed with military rifles. It's the Zone police. I see several people running into the woods on the far north end of town. My heart is pounding in my chest. Even though there is no chance of us being spotted, it's still terrifying.

They use powerful lights from their trucks to illuminate the buildings as they drive slowly through town. The men on foot are entering each building. After a few minutes, the sun comes up, and there is more light. I can see that they have pulled a few people out of one building and are questioning them. They seem to be looking for something or someone. Maybe guns or something like that. For almost an hour, they work their way through the town, searching every structure. I can't help but think what would have happened to us if we were in town when they arrived. They would have found the gun Dad is carrying. I'm sure they would have arrested him. Maybe they would have shot him right there on the spot.

Suddenly two of the Zone police officers fall to the ground. A second later, I hear the gun shots. Someone has just shot them! The Zone police take cover and begin firing into a two-story building near the edge of town. The three military vehicles open fire with large machine guns mounted on top of each one. In less than one minute, the building is filled with holes. They finally stop firing and go inside. I see them pull two bodies out the front door and lay them in the street. One of the Zone police officers shoots both of them in the head. I'm sure they were already dead. I've never seen anyone killed before. I feel sick, and the shock is almost too much to bear.

We hear a lot of yelling; then, about twenty minutes later, we hear a helicopter approaching. The two Zone police officers are loaded onto the chopper. It's clear that one of them is dead. I think the other one might be alive. A second helicopter lands and additional Zone police jump out. Together with the ones already there, they search the remaining buildings. They all appear to be empty. Through our binoculars, we can see that they are using their own binoculars to scan the woods in every direction. Dad quickly puts down his binoculars and has all of us get as low as possible.

"They might catch a reflection from the glass in our binoculars," he says. His words are the first ones spoken since the Zone police arrived.

Dad motions for us to stay down, then slowly lifts his head to get another look. After a minute or two, he gestures with his hand, letting us know that it's safe to look again. The soldiers begin entering the trucks, and they turn south, heading back the way they came. Within minutes they are out of sight.

"Dad, I can't believe what we just saw!" I say. "What if we had been there in town when they arrived? I think they would have arrested us, or maybe shot us!"

"You're probably right, Chloe," Dad says. "They certainly would have arrested me once they found I had a gun, and they might have shot me right there on the spot."

I look over at Alyssa, and her face is pale. She looks like she could pass out.

"Are you okay, Alyssa?" I ask.

"I think I'm going to throw up," she says. I'm worried that she might go into shock. I give her a reassuring hug for several minutes.

"We'll get through this, Alyssa," I tell her. "God protected us today. We could have been down there when the Zone police came in, but we're safe." She doesn't look convinced.

"Dad," I ask, "what do you think the Central Zone is up to? Do you think they have a large base near here? Do you think they are looking for Christians or just people who still have guns?"

"I'm not sure Chloe," Dad says. "From the looks of it, they were looking for weapons. I'm concerned that they might be doing a sweep of this area. I need to warn everyone back at the cabin." Dad gets on the walkie-talkie and tells everyone to go immediately to our underground bunker and spend the night there, just to be safe. He reminds them to test the air circulation system before closing the hatch.

"We need to learn more about what's happening," Dad says to Alyssa and me. "I think I should go down into town and find someone willing to talk." My heart starts racing again.

"Dad, it's too dangerous!" I blurt out much more loudly than I should. I calm myself down before continuing. "What if the Zone police come back when you're in town? What if they search you and find your handgun?"

Dad is quiet for a minute. I'm sure he's weighing the risks and formulating a strategy.

"I think it's worth the risk," he says. "I'll leave the handgun with the two of you. You both know how to use it. We have two walkie-talkies with us. I'll take one with me, and you can be my eyes from up here on the ridgeline. If you see anyone approaching, you can let me know. I'll turn the volume down on mine so that only I can hear you. I'll stay within the tree line until I get close to the town. If I see anything suspicious, I'll turn back."

"Dad," I say, "I think anyone who might still be near the town would feel less threatened if Alyssa or I were with you. I should go along. Alyssa can be our eyes."

I turn to Alyssa, and she has a concerned look on her face. I can't blame her. Dad also turns to her.

"Are you up to this Alyssa?" he asks.

"I think so," she says. "I've only used the handgun twice. Can you go over that with me again, and can you show me how to use the walkie-talkie? I've never handled it before." Dad spends a few minutes showing her how to use both. Surprisingly, she seems more comfortable with the gun than with the walkie-talkie. She practices talking into it a couple of times and then Dad lowers the volume on both.

I give Alyssa a long hug; then, Dad and I slowly move down the ridgeline toward town. We both keep an eye out for any movement. After ten minutes, we're within one hundred yards of a building on the south end of town, away from where the shooting took place.

"I don't think we should run from here," Dad says. "Let's just walk quickly to the side of that two-story building, the one with brown stucco." I take a deep breath, and we cover the space in about thirty seconds. We move to the front of the building and look both ways for signs of life.

"What are you doing here?" a voice asks from behind us. I almost come out of my skin! We turn around slowly, deliberately, with our hands out to our sides.

"Why are you here?" a gruff-looking man asks us again. He doesn't appear to have a weapon, so we relax just a little.

"My daughter and I heard some shots earlier, and we came into town to see what was happening," Dad says. "We don't want any trouble. We were hoping to get some information, to find out what's been happening lately.

"Show me the backs of your hands," he says. We both look at each other and then comply. The man finally relaxes a little.

"Why did you want to see our hands," I ask?

"The Central Zone has been rounding up people for a year now, doing interrogations," the man says. "If they decide you're not a threat, they put a mark on the back of your hand. It's done with lasers." I look at dad. We're both thinking the same thing. It's too early for the mark. We're not yet at the three-and-a-half-year point.

"What happens if they don't clear you," I ask.

"Then they use you for target practice," he says.

The man makes a brief bird-like sound, sort of a whistle, and within seconds, several other people appear from nearby buildings. He must have given them some type of all-clear signal because they look somewhat relaxed as they approach us. They pepper us with questions, but Dad is evasive about where we are from and where we are living. Dad asks about what happened in town. A much younger man steps up and begins talking. He can't be much older than I. "The Central Zone has been building up bases throughout the Midwest. About eight months ago, they started doing sweeps through smaller cities and towns. That's why most of us live in the woods. We've heard that they already run the larger cities. They are feeding people who will declare loyalty to Salam and who are willing to turn in those who are against him.

People will turn on their own mother when they're starving to death."

"How have you managed to survive," Dad asks.

The same young man answers, "We have survived by hunting, but it's getting harder every month to find game. We have to go further into the backcountry each time. I'm guessing this is how most of the people who are still alive in our country are surviving, at least the ones who refuse to pledge allegiance to Salam."

"Is it safe for us to be here in town right now?" Dad asks. "Do they ever come back soon after a raid?"

"The pattern so far is that they stay away for a few weeks after a raid," the young man says. "We should be safe for now, but let's head into a small clearing in the woods, just in case."

I'm tempted to ask his name, but since no one in this group has offered any personal information, I decide it's best not to ask. The young man must have read my mind, because as we are walking toward the woods, he says, "You can call me Jason."

I smile and say, "You can call me Lolo. It's a nickname my dad gave me when I was three years old."

"Nice to meet you, Lolo," he says as he shakes my hand. Once we're in the clearing, we sit on several logs and continue our information exchange.

There is one question I have to ask, so I do. "That mark that they put on people who are cleared, do you know if people have to worship Salam as a God in order to get it?" I ask.

They all have a confused look on their faces.

"No," says Jason. "It just means they did a background check of some kind on you and have decided that, for the moment, you're not a threat. At least that's what people have told me who have been cleared. Why do you ask? Why would someone think Salam is some type of god?"

Daniel chapter twelve flashes in my mind. Now's my chance. Without even looking at Dad, I jump right in. "This is going to sound a little strange if you've never heard it before, but everything that is happening right now was predicted in the Bible. When I say everything, I mean all of it. The one-world government, Salam, the Zone Wars. Most of the details are in the Old Testament Book of Daniel and the New Testament Book of Revelation. I'm sure you've all heard the term Antichrist. Salam is the Antichrist. The reason I asked about that mark is that he is going to declare to the world that he is God and then require everyone on the planet to worship him in just over six months. Those who refuse will be killed. It sounds like the mark they are giving out to people they clear is not the final one."

I'm not sure what they're thinking. They all look a little dazed. Dad jumps in. "I know things are bad now, but you need to know they are going to get much worse. According to the Book of Revelation, roughly 25 percent of the people on our planet have died in the past two years. Within four years more than three-quarters of the people who were alive two years ago will be dead. Many of these will be Christians and any others who refuse to take his mark and worship him. God is going to take all of the Christians to Heaven soon in something called the Rapture.

"Have you ever heard of it?" Dad asks. Several people say they have.

"Well," Dad continues, "God is going to remove Christians, and then he is going to pour out his wrath on everyone who has taken Salam's mark. Not the current mark, but the one you take when you agree to worship him as a god."

"I saw that movie with Nicholas Cage," says the older man we first met, "the movie called *Left Behind*. It's been a few years now, but in that movie, all the Christians disappear before the wars and Antichrist stuff. At least I think that's what happened in the film. I had been drinking pretty heavily when I watched it, so I don't remember all of the details, but that's not what's happening now. I assume you two are Christians, and you're still here. What gives?" he asks.

I decide to jump back in. "For more than fifty years, most Christian churches have been teaching that the Rapture happens *before* the start of this final seven-year period we are in right now. In the last ten years, many people, like us, began to have doubts. Well, to state the obvious, the majority of Christians were dead wrong on the timing of the Rapture."

"We would love to spend an entire day with all of you, and anyone else in your group that isn't here right now," Dad says. "We can read you the specific passages from the Bible and show you how they relate to what's happening now. We don't have the time today, and we don't have a Bible with us."

"Could we meet back here or somewhere else in three days?" Dad asks. After some talk among themselves, they agree but ask that we come back in exactly one week. Apparently, they have a hunting trip planned, which at the moment is much more important than an end-time Bible study.

Dad surprises me when he reaches into both of our backpacks and gives them every food item we have. At that moment, I notice how gaunt they all look compared to us. They are clearly malnourished. His gesture elicits the first smiles I've seen from any of them since we met an hour earlier. We agree to meet at nine o'clock in the morning one week from today at the clearing. The older man gives dad a long handshake as we get ready to leave. I shake Jason's hand and smile at everyone else, and we head back toward Alyssa.

As we approach her, she is almost crying as she says "I'm so sorry! Please forgive me! I totally blew it! I saw that guy approaching you from behind the building, and my mind went blank! I couldn't figure out how to signal you, and by the time I did, you were already talking to him! You could have been killed! I'm such an idiot!"

I hug Alyssa and let her know that, far from being in danger, we made some new friends! We tell her the whole story, then pack up and head for the cabin. Before we leave, Dad calls home on the walkie-talkie to let everyone know we're safe and heading home.

CHAPTER TWENTY-TWO

A CLOSE CALL

We stay inside the tree line as we head home. As we leave the main road and turn onto the dirt road that leads to our cabin, Dad stops abruptly and holds up his hand. We all crouch down. Dad points to the dirt road. Alyssa and I both see what he sees, tire tracks. There haven't been tire tracks on our road in two years. It must be the Zone Police trucks we saw in town!

"Dad, you told everyone to go to the bunker, right."

"Yes, I did. I just hope they did it right when I told them to," Dad says. We move a little deeper into the tree line for the last leg of the walk to the cabin. As we get close, we move very slowly and approach from the woods rather than our dirt driveway. We stop once we have a clear line of sight to the cabin. Dad pulls out his binoculars.

"I don't see any vehicles or people," Dad says. "It looks like something is painted on the front door of our cabin. It looks like a letter or numbers. It looks like Z1."

"Dad, that's what Jason said the Zone is putting on the back of people's hands who are cleared," I say. "Maybe it's a message to any other Zone police officers who come by that our cabin has been checked out already."

"Let's hope it's some kind of all clear message," Dad says. "It's too risky to go to the cabin. Let's head to the bunker."

In twenty minutes, we arrive at the bunker. We're all thinking the same thing. Did everyone make it here safely? Dad gives four knocks on the door, two quick knocks followed by two slow knocks. This is our signal that everything is okay. We hear the latch open and are relieved to see Uncle Mark's face appear.

"Please, come in quickly," says Uncle Mark.

The three of us descend into the bunker, and Dad closes the door. Mom hugs the three of us.

"We had a really close call," Uncle Mark begins. "When you told us over the walkie-talkie to head here, we packed up pretty quickly. Just as we were leaving the cabin, we heard the alarm go off, the one from the trip wire on the road. We knew we only had a few minutes to get away from the property. We ran as fast as we could. From a distance, we heard what sounded like large trucks pulling up to the cabin."

Uncle Mark continues. "We heard shouts and doors slamming. We didn't look back and pretty much ran the entire way here to the bunker. It was really close. If we hadn't already been on the way out, they might have seen us!"

"They painted some kind of mark on the front door," Dad says. "It looks like Z1. Maybe it's their way of marking properties they have checked out. We found out in town that the Zone police are putting a Z1 mark on the back of people's hands who are cleared, people they think are low risk. I think we can probably all agree that the bunker is our home now. With only a few months until the midpoint of the Tribulation, my guess is we're within one year of the Rapture. Let's wait a day or two before we go back to the cabin to pick up any supplies the Zone didn't take when they searched it." We all agree. This hole in the ground is now our home.

Two days later, Dad and Uncle Mark return to the cabin. The place is torn apart, but amazingly they didn't take any of our food. Dad thinks they were searching for weapons. Thankfully, Uncle Mark moved all of our guns and ammunition to the bunker more than a month ago. A few days later and one week after our encounter in town, Dad, Alyssa, and I return to the clearing. Dad decides to bring some extra food to give away. The group we meet with the second time is about three times as large. The word must have gotten out. Through the summer and into the fall, we meet with the group weekly, and it grows to over one hundred people. Most of them are eager to hear about what the Bible says about the Tribulation. Most of them make a commitment to Jesus, including Jason.

CHAPTER TWENTY-THREE

THE RESCUE

When we are two weeks away from the mid-point of the Tribulation, Dad decides that all of us, including Mom, Hannah, and Uncle Mark should attend the next meeting. We all gather right on schedule at nine in the morning at the clearing. After some quick introductions for Mom, Hannah, and Uncle Mark, Dad gets down to business.

"You all know from what we've covered in the past couple of months that we are now fifteen days away from the midpoint of the Tribulation. Salam will travel to Jerusalem soon, and at exactly the three-and-a-half-year mark, he will go into the Temple there and declare that he is God. He will require everyone in the world to receive a mark on their right hand or their forehead. Those who receive the mark are basically agreeing with him that he is God. The mark could be his name or the number 666. No one in the world will be able to buy or sell without the mark.

"Also, he will erect images of himself throughout the world. I think each image will be possessed in some way by a demon, because the images will be able to speak. Anyone who comes near one of the images and refuses to bow down and worship it will be killed by fire that will fall from the sky. I know some of you might be wondering how Satan could have this kind of power. Well, unfortunately, he does. In the Old Testament Book of Job, Satan causes fire to come down from the sky that destroys Job's property and servants."

"Do you think they'll put one of those images in our town?" someone asks.

"I personally don't think so," says Dad. "The town is pretty much deserted. I don't think they would waste their time on small towns. I have no doubt that they will put one in every major city in the world, though. Once this begins, my guess is that Christians who are still alive in the major cities in the United States will flee to remote places like here. We could see thousands of Christians in the next few months in our area. We need to consider what we should do if that happens."

I hadn't considered this. My first thought is that we barely have enough food to make it another year. Dad has already given away at least six months of our own food to our new church family here in the clearing. We have been able to hunt occasionally, but game has gotten a lot more scarce in the past year. This last spring, we didn't see any fawns. Uncle Mark thinks that it's due to radiation carried east on the jet stream from the west coast. He thinks the radiation is preventing most animals from reproducing. With so many people hunting wild game and no new animals being born, it's just a matter of time until there's nothing left to shoot.

We have a long discussion on what we should do if Christians start showing up in our area. Some people think we should have them join our group. Others are concerned that if we do, we'll all run out of food in a matter of weeks or months. The one question on everyone's mind is how long we will have to survive between the three-and-half-year point and the Rapture. Dad and Uncle Mark both think it will be less than one year. That would leave roughly two and a-half years for God to pour out *his* wrath on those that are left behind after the Rapture. We all agree to meet again in fifteen days to pray.

As the six of us begin the hike back to the bunker, it occurs to me just how amazing it is that we are all still alive. Most Americans who are still alive are hanging by a thread. We are all healthy, and we have enough food to make it almost one more year. We might all make it to the Rapture, but the question I keep pondering is, "Should we?" I'm glad that we are no longer just hiding out in the woods. We've started this little church in the clearing. People have gotten saved and now have real hope, but is there something more we should be doing? I bring it up for conversation as we walk.

"Have any of you thought about what else we could be doing in this final year or so that we have left?" I ask.

"What do you mean," asks Mom. "Do you mean with our new church family?"

"No, I mean apart from that. Should we be going into a larger city? Should we go into a large city to the south before Salam declares that he is God and warn people?" I ask.

"What would you tell them to do?" asks Mom.

"I don't know for sure," I say. "Maybe I would just tell them to get out of the city. I think so many people will be caught by surprise. Maybe if we warn them, they can have a chance of making it to the Rapture like us."

Uncle Mark joins the conversation. "We don't know what it's like in the bigger cities," he says. "We've learned a little from our church group, from those who came north from Denver. The Central Zone seems to be in complete control. Within forty-eight hours, my guess is that you'd be arrested by the

Zone Police. You saw what they did in town, the firepower they have. How would you know who is safe to talk to? And none of us have that Zone tattoo, the Z1, on our hands. I'm not trying to shoot down your idea; I just think it's probably a one-way ticket."

"A one-way ticket to Heaven," I respond before thinking.

"Well actually," continues Uncle Mark, "we all have a round-trip ticket. Remember, once we're in Heaven, we all get to come back here in two or three years. And there'll be a little more to eat of course."

We all laugh.

"You're right Uncle Mark," I say. "We do all have a round-trip ticket, but some of us might have a different flight path on the first leg of the trip," I say with just a hint of humor in my voice.

"Are you saying you want to be a martyr?" asks Mom. I sense that familiar sadness in her voice. It's the same tone she uses when she talks about Jackson.

"I'm not saying I want to go that way; I'm just saying that if God wants me to do something more then he will decide which way I get there. I'm honestly good with either path." Everyone is quiet the rest of the way back to the bunker.

I feel bad that I'm always pushing back against the status quo, but we now have a church family because of this. If we had just stayed in the bunker, none of these people would have been told the truth, at least not by us. I'm sure God would have sent someone else to them. He's not going to be thwarted by our inaction, but I just can't shake the feeling that we should be playing offense more often. We continue the conversation in the bunker after dinner. Uncle Mark pulls out a map of the United States, and we discuss logistics.

"This is where we are now," he says, as he points to a spot on the south end of Kootenai National Forrest.

"The closest large city is Spokane, Washington," he continues, pulling out a ruler. "It looks like the best highway route is the 2 to the 95 to the 90. It looks to be about one hundred and fifty miles. Assuming we could keep up a pace of three miles per hour and walk for ten hours per day, it would take us five days to get to Spokane."

Mom perks up. "We have family in Spokane," she says. "My brother, his wife, and their two kids live there. Do you think they got hit, by the nukes I mean?"

"There's no way of knowing for sure," says Uncle Mark. "We haven't met anyone from that far west, so it's not a good sign. However, most Americans in that part of the country probably headed straight for Canada after the war, so maybe that's why we haven't run into anyone from there. And besides, we rarely venture out, so for all we know, thousands of people from Spokane could have passed through our area in the last two years."

"If they didn't get hit directly, do you think they could still be alive?" Mom asks. I detect a glimmer of hope in Mom's voice that I haven't heard in a very long time.

"Maybe," he responds. "That part of the country has a lot of game and fresh water. Does your brother own a gun?"

"I'm not sure," says Mom. "He is retired from the Air Force, so it's possible." I find myself getting excited about this potential adventure.

"So what about the logistics?" I ask. "If it's a ten-day round trip, we could carry enough food and water, right?"

"Yes, we could," says Uncle Mark.

He looks at Mom and says, "But if this is going to be a rescue mission, then we would need to carry quite a bit of extra food and water."

I'm convinced this is what we're supposed to do. I look over at Dad and say, "Can we rescue them, Dad?"

"We can try, or die trying," says Dad.

Mom immediately starts crying. Alyssa and I join in the waterworks.

We spend the rest of the evening working out the logistics. We decide that Mom, Uncle Mark, and I will make the trip. Dad, Alyssa, and Hannah will join our church in the clearing as planned in fifteen days to pray. If we get back from Spokane in time, we'll join them. We pack enough food for two weeks, plus food for another four people. The packs are really heavy. I'm not sure Mom and I can maintain a three-miles-per-hour pace for ten hours each day carrying this much weight, but we'll have to try. We have a map of Washington State, so we highlight the path from the freeway to Mom's brother's house. We pick a path that keeps us on the edge of the city for as long as possible. This trip feels scarier than anything we've done so far. Our walkie-talkies only transmit twenty miles, so seven hours after we leave, we won't be able to communicate with anyone at the bunker.

We are up early the next morning, before sunrise. The three of us adjust our backpacks and make sure we have the right amount of water. The clock is ticking. In just fourteen days, Salam will begin murdering Christians in large numbers. If all goes well, we will arrive in Spokane in five days. That will give us a day or two to find them and get out of town before the chaos begins. With luck, we could even make it back right at the three-and-a-half-year mark, maybe even in time to head to the clearing. As we all hug goodbye, there is a sense that this could be the last time we see each other until after the Rapture. The thought of never seeing Dad again hits me as I hug him good-bye. I lose it again, which of course triggers a group-wide waterworks episode. Dad prays over all of us, and the three of us head down our dirt road toward the main highway. We will hike northwest for just over one day, then southwest for almost four days.

It takes us almost two hours to get to the main highway. Uncle Mark stops to check in with the bunker. Everything is good back home. Uncle Mark says he will check in every hour since he has never tested the true range for the walkie-talkies. He tells them that, by sunset, we will be out of range. As we survey the main highway, we see dozens of rusting cars in both directions. It's like a graveyard. I can't imagine the confusion and eventually the chaos that must have occurred when the EMP hit. I wonder how quickly they discovered what happened. Where did they all go? I'm sure that most were not prepared to walk for several days to the nearest town. They must have been terrified as the realization sunk in. I try not to think about it.

Normally we would walk in the tree line, but we have to walk on the highway if we have any hope of making it to Spokane in five days. I know Uncle Mark is carrying a gun under his shirt and that gives me some comfort. After two hours, we take a food-and-water break inside the tree line. Uncle Mark is still able to reach the bunker with his walkie-talkie, but the signal is weak. As Mom and Uncle Mark are taking turns telling everyone back home what we've seen so far, I venture out onto the highway to examine a few cars. As I approach a four-door sedan, I let out a scream! Inside are the skeletal remains of two people! I run back toward Mom and Uncle Mark, and I see that he has pulled out his handgun.

"What is it?" Mom asks as she embraces me.

"There are dead people in that blue car, Mom!"

Uncle Mark puts his gun away. We had heard about this from the Christians we met on the road to town, the ones who spent the night with us. They had warned us not to sleep in the abandoned cars at night.

After a few minutes, I calm down enough to continue our trip. I make a deliberate effort to avoid looking at any of the cars. Uncle Mark does the opposite; keeping a close eye on each one we pass by. We finally lose contact with home toward the end of the first day. We make a camp inside the tree line. Surprisingly, we don't see any people or animals the entire first day. In the middle of day two, we begin heading southwest toward the next highway. Although Uncle Mark doesn't talk about it, I can tell that he sees more bodies in some of the cars.

Uncle Mark uses the highway mile markers to track our progress. We are actually a little ahead of schedule, so by day four, we are only about ten miles from Spokane. The morning of day five, we start to see houses and businesses on the outskirts of town. All of them are deserted, or at least we think they are. We don't venture too close to any of them, for fear of getting shot at. From the map, we see that it will be impossible to avoid large sections of the city on the way to their house. Uncle Mark chooses a path that will take us through mainly residential neighborhoods. For a city this big, there should be Zone Police activity, but we don't see anyone. All of the neighborhoods are overgrown. It looks like something out of a zombie apocalypse movie. In some houses, I think I see shadows moving around, but maybe it's just my mind playing tricks on me. I think if I saw someone, I might actually jump out of my skin.

"This is starting to look familiar," Mom says, as we get close to her brother's neighborhood. I was really young the last time we came up here, but as we get close, I, too, start to remember the area.

"Their street is just up ahead," Mom says. I sense excitement in her voice for the first time in months.

"That's it," she says, barely above a whisper, as if she's afraid someone will hear her. "That's their cul-de-sac!"

Our hearts sink as we appoach. It looks abandoned. It seems like a strange thing to do, but Mom knocks gently on the front door. There's no response. She reaches for the door knob. It's unlocked. She pushes it open, and we walk in slowly, cautiously. We move together from room to room with Mom in the lead. I begin to remember more of my visits here. After searching every corner of the house, including the basement, we meet in the kitchen. Mom's eyes begin to tear up.

"Maybe they escaped into the woods like us," says Uncle Mark, trying to offer her a glimmer of hope.

"The cabin," Mom says excitedly. "Of course! They wouldn't have stayed here! They have a cabin on the Pend Oreille River. It's north of here. In a car, it takes about an hour and a half."

"That's where they would have gone," she says excitedly. "I don't know why I didn't think of it. We should have gone there first."

"Do you know the address or how to get there?" asks Uncle Mark.

"I don't have the address, but there must be some paperwork somewhere in the house with the address," Mom says.

"Well, let's tear this place apart and find it," says Uncle Mark.

Mom starts in the office, Uncle Mark takes the kitchen, and they send me to the master bedroom. Ten minutes later, I hear Uncle Mark yell, "I think I've got it!"

We pull out our map of Washington State, and Uncle Mark uses the grid to find the address.

Mom looks carefully at the route for a minute, and then says, "That's it! I remember! How long will it take to get there?"

Uncle Mark uses a piece of string to estimate the number of miles. "Two days," he says.

"So we'll get there seven days before Salam starts his war on Jews and Christians," I add.

"That's about right," says Uncle Mark.

"Well, we'd better get moving, then," says Mom.

It's the most motivated I've seen her in years. It takes us just over two days to get to the cabin, just as Uncle Mark thought. The last stretch is a dirt road. Because there hasn't been any maintenance on any roads in two years, it is almost completely overgrown. It's more of a trail than a road. Finding the entrance to their cabin is hard, but Mom spots it.

"There, that has to be it," she says. We dig into the foliage to find the mailbox. It's the right address. The small path from the dirt road to the cabin is barely visible due to the overgrowth.

Mom asks us to let her go first. We agree. It's only about a fifty-yard walk to the cabin. As we get close, Mom starts to call out softly to her brother. "Ken? It's Cathy. Are you there? Ken?"

"Cathy!" a voice shouts from just inside the cabin. The back door of the cabin swings open, and I see my Uncle Ken run toward Mom. As they embrace, Mom begins to sob uncontrollably.

"I can't believe you're alive!" says Mom.

"I can't believe you're here!" says Uncle Ken.

"How did you get here all the way from Dallas?" he asks in astonishment.

"It's a long story," Mom says. "Where are Beth and the girls?"

The expression on Uncle Ken's face changes.

"The girls are down by the river, checking our fishing lines. Beth didn't make it. She got sick a year ago. There was nothing we could do to save her."

This time, all of us start crying.

"What about Ray, Jackson, and Hannah?" Uncle Ken asks. "Ray and Hannah are fine" Mom says. "I'll explain it all to you." Mom introduces Uncle Mark to her brother.

Uncle Ken asks us to stay in the cabin while he gets the girls. In just a few minutes, he is back with them, and we all embrace. We introduce them to Uncle Mark. For the next hour, Uncle Ken describes how they managed to survive at the cabin by fishing, hunting, and collecting wild berries. Mom explains how we escaped to Montana just before the war started.

"I'm sorry I didn't tell you about our plans," Mom says to Uncle Ken. "We didn't think it was safe to talk about it with anyone. We didn't tell Jackson. He didn't come with us. I don't know if he's still alive."

Uncle Ken and my two nieces look so skinny. Their eyes light up when we all begin sharing our food with them.

"Ken, we figured this all out before it started," Mom says. "Salam is the Antichrist, and, in seven days, he will go into the Temple in Jerusalem and declare himself to be God. He will then kill two-thirds of the Jews and many Christians. As bad as things are now they are going to get much worse in just a few days. We want to take you and the girls back to our bunker in Montana. It's a five-day walk from here. Please say you'll come."

"Well your timing is perfect," says Uncle Ken. "We haven't been able to find any game for weeks now, and even the fishing is getting difficult. If we had to stay here, I don't think we would survive the winter. So yes, we're in!"

Mom and Uncle Ken embrace, and Mom starts crying again. I look over at my nieces, and they have a profound look of relief on their faces. We all decide to leave at first light in the morning.

The trip back to the cabin takes a day longer than our trip to Spokane. Uncle Ken and the girls are in bad shape physically and are not able to walk as fast as the rest of us. When we are a few hours away from the cabin, Uncle Mark uses our walkie-talkie to call the bunker with the good news. We make it home one day before the three-and-a-half-year mark. We are all thoroughly exhausted but agree to keep our promise to meet with our church in the morning.

CHAPTER TWENTY-FOUR

THE ABOMINATION

The nine of us arrive at the clearing the next day just before noon. Given the time difference between Montana and the Middle East, we're pretty certain that Salam has already declared himself to be God. We spend several hours praying for the Jews and for the Christians, who will now be hunted down by the Central Zone. It is one of the most moving prayer meetings I've ever attended.

After the prayer meeting, there is talk of what we might see in the coming weeks. Everyone agrees that we might see a significant number of Christians moving through our area and away from the major cities. Most people agree that we should let them join us, as long as they don't have the Z1 mark or what will now be some new Salam mark on their right hands or foreheads. The question of food is discussed. The newcomers will have to do their own hunting and fishing. There is also talk of the risks of letting a large number of people join our church. We agree to all meet again in one week.

Dad and I decide to camp out for a few days in the woods near the intersection of our dirt road and the main highway to watch for people fleeing the cities. It's nice to get away from the bunker for a while. With nine people now, you can hardly breathe in there. Also, it gives me a chance to talk to Dad privately. As we sit inside the tree line near our tent, I decide to talk about Jackson. We haven't mentioned him in months, but I know we're all still thinking about him.

"Dad, if Jackson is still alive, do you think he'll take the mark?" I ask.

"It's funny you should ask, Chloe," Dad says. "I've been thinking about that lately. Not just for him, but for all the people we know back in Dallas who might still be alive. My gut tells me he probably will. I hate to say that, but it's how I feel. I think there is an invisible line people can cross, and once they do that, it's not possible to turn back. Mom and I always told him the truth about God; we didn't hold anything back, and yet he made a deliberate decision to reject the truth. The Bible says that this group of people during the Tribulation will be sent a strong delusion to believe the lie. The lie they will believe is that Salam is some kind of God who is worthy of their worship."

"If that's true and he ever finds us, he will have us all put to death," I say. "It's so hard for me to imagine this, Dad. I know I've said this before, but how can someone whom I grew up with, who was my best friend when I was young, have me executed? It's so difficult for me to understand."

"I know, Chloe," Dad says. "I agree it's just crazy to imagine this, but it's happening right now all over the world. Family members are turning in other family members who refuse to take Salam's mark. Mothers are having their children put to death. Fathers are having their daughters beheaded right in front of them. How is this possible? You're the student of history, Chloe. It's been this way since Cain killed his brother Abel. The heart of man is desperately wicked. Sorry to depress you, but I don't have any other explanation for you, but there's hope. In just under three and a-half years, Jesus is going to return physically to the Earth and fix this big mess."

Before I can respond, movement on the main highway catches my eye.

"Dad, look! Do you see them?"

We both take turns with the binoculars. They must be more than a mile away, and they are coming from the north. We had been expecting to see people coming from the south.

"I see them," Dad says. "It looks like a big group. Maybe twenty people."

"Do you think we should try to talk to them?" I ask.

"Let's wait until they are closer so we can get a better look at them." Dad's right. This could be one of the gangs that kill people along the highway. We stay low in the tree line. We are high enough to where it will be difficult for them to see us as they approach.

As they get closer, we notice that there are a few children in the group. It looks like it could be a group of extended family members.

"Dad, they look pretty safe" I whisper. "What do you think? Maybe they came down from Canada."

Dad doesn't respond at first. When they are fifty yards from us, Dad whispers, "I think we should make contact with them." I nod in agreement.

"Follow close behind me," he says. Dad stands up and starts moving down the embankment toward the highway. I follow close behind. The group spots us immediately, and they freeze. They all move closer together in a kind of huddle. Dad waves toward them. They don't respond. We walk toward them slowly. I walk to the right of Dad as we approach them. We stop about forty feet from them.

"My name is Ray," Dad says. "This is my daughter, Chloe. We were hoping to get some information from you."

None of them say a word.

"Our hands," I whisper to Dad. "We need to show them our right hands, so they know we're not with Salam." We both lift our right hands to our chests with the backs of our hands facing the group. A few in the front of the group look at each other, then do the same. No marks. One of the men in the group approaches us, and Dad shakes his hand.

"I'm Mike," he says.

"Where are you coming from?" asks Dad.

"Just over the border in Canada," the man says.

"Are you all Canadians?" asks dad.

"No," he says. "We're originally from Wyoming. We headed to Canada about a month after the power went out. We had heard that the power was on in Canada."

"Was it true?" I ask.

"Yes, at least in the part of Canada where we were staying," he says.

"Why are you on the move again?" asks Dad. We both know the answer but decide to play dumb.

The man looks back at the group for a second; then he looks back at us. I think he's trying to decide how much he should tell us. "A few days ago," he says, "there was a worldwide broadcast from Salam, the world Zone President. He was in the new Jewish Temple in Jerusalem during the broadcast. What he said was shocking. He claimed that he is God and declared that, effective immediately, every person in the world was required to worship him. He stated that, within a few days, loyalty-processing centers would be active in every major city in the world. In order to buy or sell, every person must receive an implant in their right hands or in their foreheads. By accepting the mark, people agree that he is their God. He also said that images of himself would be erected in cities around the world. When a person approaches his image, they are required to bow to the ground and worship the image. Those who refuse will be put to death." The man seems shocked by his own words, almost as though he doesn't believe what he's saying.

"We have been able to survive in Canada, but there is no way we are going to worship Salam. Lots of people like us are leaving the bigger cities and heading south. We would rather die free back in the United States than be executed for not worshiping Salam. What about you and your daughter? What's your story?" he asks.

"We're from Dallas originally," Dad says. "We got up here to Montana just before the war started. Actually, just in time. We've been living in this area for a couple of years now. There are others who live around here. We survive by hunting and fishing."

"What about the radiation?" the man asks. Dad and I look at each other.

"What radiation?" I ask.

"We've heard that the fallout in this part of the country is very dangerous. You know, from the nukes that hit Seattle.

"We hadn't heard that," Dad says.

"Well that isn't exactly a big concern now," the man continues. "We wouldn't last long in Canada if we had stayed."

"Good point," I say.

"Is it safe to stay in any of the small towns?" the man asks.

"I wouldn't suggest it. The Zone Police were here just a few weeks ago and searched the local town. You probably saw the town about ten miles back, just off the main highway," dad says.

"We did," the man says. "It looked deserted."

"You might try to find an abandoned home or farm out in a remote area. That would be safer," Dad suggests. "Also, don't sleep in the abandoned cars on the highway. It's not safe. At night, sleep at least thirty yards into the tree line." We talk for a few more minutes; then the group continues south. We wish them luck. They look healthier than our relatives from Spokane, but they won't last long unless they can find game, and with winter coming, they'll need to find shelter. Dad and I wave to them as they continue down the highway.

"Dad, do you think that's why Aunt Beth died? Could it have been the radiation?" I ask.

"Maybe," he says. "Spokane is much closer to Seattle, but that's the least of our worries now, Chloe. Here in Montana, it could take several years for the radiation to kill us. We'll be long gone before that happens."

"Why, are you worried about losing your hair?" he asks with a hint of humor in his voice.

"Actually, I'm surprised it hasn't fallen out already, given I only wash it a couple of times a month!" I say.

"Maybe you should consider dreadlocks. That seems like a low-maintenance solution," Dad jokes.

"You first, Dad!"

We have a good laugh and decide to head back to the bunker and let the others know what we learned.

Everyone is eager to hear what's happening in Canada. No one is surprised by the news. We didn't ask the group we met if they were Christians. We speculate that they probably were, but we think that even some atheists will be on the run.

After all, they don't believe in the existence of any god, so why would they worship Salam? That would be a gross violation of their non-religion. Some will probably just make a show of it in order to stay alive. We speculate whether the Central Zone will set up an image of Salam in our local town. It doesn't make sense that they would since no one is living there. However, with all the people heading south, the town might fill up again. I ask Dad if the two of us can do some recon on the town. He agrees but suggests we wait a couple of weeks. He wants to see what we can learn from our church group.

At the next meeting, we hear a mountain of updates from our church in the clearing. They have all run into people leaving Canada. Some are moving into the town. Some are trying to get as far south as possible before winter. There is a mix of Christians and non-Christians. Some have the Z1 mark but aren't willing to worship Salam. Our church members agree that it's not safe to move back into the town, even during the winter.

CHAPTER TWENTY-FIVE

THE IMAGE

Dad and I decide to camp out above town for a few days just to see what's happening. We arrive at our camping spot around noon on a Monday. We set up camp, and then take turns with the binoculars. Dad spots something toward the south end of town. Some type of statue.

"Chloe, take a look over to the right end of town," he says. "Tell me what you see. My eyesight isn't the greatest anymore."

He hands me the binoculars, and I take a look.

"Dad, it's something new. That wasn't there before. It's some type of statue. I can't tell from this distance, but it has to be a statue of Salam. I can't believe they would put one way out here!"

My breathing is heavy, and my hands are shaking. Dad senses my fear.

"Chloe, don't panic. There's no way anyone or anything in town can see us way up here," he says reassuringly.

"And I agree" he continues. "Why would they put one in such a small town like this one?"

"It's just really creepy, Dad," I say. "I mean, there are going to be demons in every one of those statues all over the world. That has to be how it's able to talk and kill people who don't bow down to it. It's so creepy to think that there is a real demon right down there. I don't want to look at it. I'm afraid it will see me," I say, still breathing heavily. Dad takes another look at the statue.

"Someone is approaching it, Chloe," Dad says. I almost come out of my skin! I refuse to look.

"A man is walking toward it from the tree line," he says.

I feel like I'm going to pass out! I curl up in a ball, trying to make myself as small as possible.

"It looks like he's talking to it," Dad says. "He's waving his hands at it. He just gave it the finger! He's on fire, Chloe!"

I start to cry. My whole body is shaking!

"Dad, let's get out of here!" I say through my tears. "Please take me home!"

We run almost the entire distance back to the bunker, and are both out of breath by the time we get back. When Uncle Mark opens the hatch, he says to me, "Chloe, you're as white as a sheet of paper! What happened?"

I don't say a word. I climb down and find Mom and just hug her.

"It's here," Dad says. "The Central Zone put an image of Salam in our local town. I watched through the binoculars as some guy approached it. He was talking to it, arguing with it. One second after he flipped it off, his whole body was on fire. It was awful. He tried to roll on the ground, but the flames wouldn't go out, no matter what he did. It took him more than a minute to die. We both felt like throwing up afterward. We made record time getting back here to the bunker. We pretty much ran the whole way."

"I think everyone would agree that going near town is out of the question now," says Uncle Mark.

"If they would put that thing in our small town, then they are probably putting them everywhere," he continues. "And that means we will start to see a lot of people on the move, especially Christians. There is something I didn't tell any of you about this area. There are several large caves in the area. I always imagined the cabin as our Plan A and the bunker as our Plan B. Well, the caves were always a type of Plan C. I don't think we will need to move to one of the caves, but we might consider taking Christians there."

"How safe are they?" Dad asks.

"I've only thoroughly explored the one closest to our bunker, and it's very safe," says Uncle Mark.

"How many people can they hold," dad asks.

"The one I just mentioned could hold more than one hundred people. It's enormous. Of course, the challenge is food. They would have to find a way to hunt, and game is getting really scarce. Also, they would need a way to stay warm. There might be supplies in town, but with that statue, it won't be safe to go there anymore."

"This has worked in the past," I say. Everyone looks at me.

"What do you mean," asks Mom.

"During World War II, there were Jews in Ukraine who hid in caves and holes in the ground to avoid being captured by the Nazis. Some of them survived for several years. Some made it all the way to the end of the war. If it worked for the Jews, I'm sure it will work for Christians. Couldn't we use stuff from our cabin or abandoned homes in the rural areas to make the cave you mentioned livable, Uncle Mark?" I ask.

"We could certainly give it a try. There's still lots of stuff in the cabin" he says. "It would be a lot of work to get it up to the cave, but we certainly have the time. We would need to get started right away before the weather changes."

This new mission takes my mind off the horrors of what just happened in town. We spend the next few days moving everything that is usable from our cabin to the cave. The cave is even bigger than I had expected. The entrance is fairly small, but after thirty feet, it opens up into a wide chamber. Just enough light reaches the main chamber, so you can sort of see your way around. The entrance is small enough so that we can cover it up with dead trees and branches. Uncle Mark knows of several other cabins within a one-hour walk from our bunker, so we go looking for other supplies. After a week, we have enough bedding and supplies in the cave for about thirty people.

One evening after dinner, we begin to discuss how we will find and direct Christians to the cave.

"It's been almost three weeks since Salam declared that he is God," says Uncle Mark. "My guess is that, by now, there are lots of Christians on the move. Some will be coming south from Canada. Some will be heading north from larger cities in Wyoming and Colorado. I don't think we'll have any difficulty filling up the cave, but we need to think through how we will approach people."

We spend some time debating the best approach. We also spend a good amount of time praying. There are huge risks in approaching people we don't know, given how desperate people have become. Mom's brother and his two daughters from Spokane were close to starvation when we found them. We could be killed if people think we have food.

Given how dangerous it will be, it's decided that only Dad and Uncle Mark will solicit people to move into the cave. Both will carry guns when they go out, and Dad will bring one of the walkie-talkies. They decide to camp out at the intersection of our dirt road and the main highway and only approach people if they feel it's safe. They pack enough food and water for several days but promise to return in two days. As they prepare to leave, I have knots in my stomach. The thought of losing Dad is too much for me.

"Dad, please promise me you'll be careful and that you'll come back in two days," I say.

"I promise to be careful, Chloe," he says. "Be sure you have everyone pray for the two of us while we're gone."

"Of course we will!" I respond.

They leave the bunker at first light and promise to call in, using the walkie-talkie once every hour. The rest of us huddle together on one end of the bunker and pray. It seems like an eternity, but we finally hear Dad's voice.

"We're about halfway there," he says. "We haven't seen anyone, so far."

Mom reminds him to be careful and to call back in one hour. An hour later, I catch myself staring intently at the walkie-talkie. I start to memorize all of its buttons and labels. It has now been an hour and fifteen minutes, and there is no call. Mom checks the walkie-talkie to make sure it's still working. It is. The minutes drag by like hours.

"Hello base." It's Dad!

"Yes, this is base," says Mom.

"We found a family just as we got to the highway. There are four of them. They've been walking for a week and are in pretty bad shape. They're Christians! We told them about the cave, and they're all for it. We are going to take them there now. Chloe, can you and Alyssa bring our medical kit to the cave?"

I take the walkie-talkie from mom and say, "Absolutely."

"Should I meet you all there in about two hours?" I ask.

"Let's make it three hours," Dad says. "They aren't going to be able to move very fast."

"Okay" I say. "Alyssa and I will meet you there in three hours."

Since the cave is about thirty minutes from our bunker, we wait a couple of hours before we leave. When we get to the cave, Dad isn't there yet, so we hang out inside. Alyssa and I try to organize the stuff to try to make it feel more like a home. After about thirty minutes, I hear footsteps at the entrance. I see several figures coming toward us slowly. It looks like Dad is helping a woman walk.

"Dad!" I say, as I move to him as quickly as I can, being careful not to trip on something in the darkness. I side-hug him, since he is still helping the woman walk.

"Chloe, Alyssa, this is the Johnson family," Dad says. We can't see their faces very clearly, but Alyssa and I introduce ourselves to the two parents and their son and daughter. The kids look to be around ten or eleven. The four of them look very skinny.

"Do you have the medical pack?" asks Uncle Mark.

"Yes, it's right here," I say.

The woman lies down on one of the beds, and Uncle Mark turns on one of the propane lanterns. The cave fills with light. I look immediately at the woman's face and almost pass out. Alyssa screams.

"Girls, if you need to go outside, please do," says Uncle Mark.

I feel so embarrassed. "I'm sorry," I say, as I try to compose myself.

"How did this happen?" I ask before thinking.

"Chloe," Dad says sternly.

"It's okay," the man says. "She has a right to know, especially given all the kindness you have shown us. We have been living in a larger city in northern Wyoming. For the past couple of years, the Zone police would come through occasionally and search for weapons. We don't own any, so they mostly left us alone. Everything changed after they put up that statue of Salam.

"A man who we've known for many years told us that everyone was required to bow down to it. He said the mouth would move, and it would look at you and talk to you. He was afraid, so he bowed down. After he had done this, the image told him to approach the statue and extend his right hand. The statue then asked him if he agreed that Salam was God. He was so afraid that he said yes. The statue then asked if he would prove his faithfulness to Salam by receiving his mark on the back of his right hand. He said yes. A mark then appeared out of nowhere on his hand. He showed it to us. It had Salam's name and some type of circular design, as well. I asked him if he understood what he had done by taking this mark. He said it means he gets to stay alive. He told us where the statue was located and encouraged us to get the mark. He said that if we didn't, we might starve to death. He seemed genuinely concerned for us.

"We thanked him for telling us and said we would give it some thought. We didn't tell him the truth, that Salam was the Antichrist and that because he received his mark, he had sealed his fate forever. What would be the point of telling him, it was too late? So after he left, we knew we had to get as far away from civilization as possible, and fast. When we were almost out of town, a gang of boys chased us down. They started shouting, 'Show us your marks!' Our two children were able to make it into the woods, but my wife and I couldn't outrun them. They knocked me out cold. When I came to, I saw Kaitlyn on the ground next to me. They almost beat her to death. I won't tell you the other things they did to her. I bandaged her up as best I could and went looking for the kids. Once we were all back together, we headed north. That's when your dad found us."

Tears fill my eyes. I walk over to the woman and hold one of her hands. She feels cold. I ask Dad if we can all pray for her. We huddle around her and pray. She asks for her two children to come close to her side. Tears fill their eyes.

"I love you both so much," she says softly. Her voice is like a whisper. She pulls them down to her one at a time and hugs them.

"Jesus is here for me now," she says. "I have to go with him. His eyes are so beautiful. I know you're sad, but, in just a little while, we'll all be together in Heaven. Help your dad. I'll see you both soon." Her eyes look up, and her arms go limp. All of us, including Dad and Uncle Mark, are now crying. A woman I've only known for only five minutes, but who I will know for all eternity, is gone.

CHAPTER TWENTY-SIX

RESCUED!

In the next few weeks, Dad and Uncle Mark have no difficulty filling the cave with more than thirty Christians who are on the run. Some are from Canada, and others are from the United States. Because the Canadians never lost power, they provide updates on what is happening in other parts of the world. Public executions are taking place in all major cities around the world. Most are beheaded, but others have died in even more horrific ways. Some cities are feeding them to wild animals. Millions of Jews have also been killed, mostly in Israel. Although the official Zone news agencies won't admit it, more than one million Jews have escaped to the rock city of Petra in southern Jordan.

As we expected, no one is able to buy or sell in any Zone unless they have Salam's mark on their right hand or forehead. There are rumors that some people without his mark have been able to buy food on the many black markets that have sprung up all over the world. The Canadians told us there is one in their city in Canada, but they also said that the Zone uses these as traps to catch those who haven't taken the mark. Several of their friends tried to use gold to purchase food on one of the black markets, which got them arrested. They assume they were executed.

My thoughts drift back to Dallas and Jackson. What will he do? Will he take Salam's mark? Why wouldn't he? He never had anything bad to say about the Zones, and the only time he would talk about Christianity was to make fun of it. Would he turn all of us in if he was with us now? Probably. What about our small group of Christian girls from Hebron High? I can't imagine any of them taking the mark. Have they already been executed? I find myself thinking about Mr. Bradly. I have very little doubt that he would have been one of the first one killed after Salam declared himself to be God. It's so sad thinking that he's probably gone, but I'm guessing it won't be very long until I see him again! Maybe even in just a few months.

As the weeks turn into months, food begins to become an issue, both in the bunker and at the cave. It has now been just over four years since the start of the Tribulation. We had collected enough food to last just over five years, but we hadn't factored in Alyssa or Mom's family from Spokane. Also, we've given away a lot of food to our church friends and the Christians in the cave. I decide to wait until I am alone with Dad on one of our hunting trips near the bunker to bring it up with him.

"Dad, how is our food supply looking?" I ask.

"Not great," he says.

"How bad is it?" I continue.

"Well, the only way to accurately answer that question is if we know the exact date of the Rapture, which, of course, we don't," he says.

"Well, how much longer can we make it?" I ask.

Dad is quiet for a minute. I'm sure he's doing the math in his head.

"Well, with nine of us continuing on half rations, I'd say three more months, maybe a little longer if hunting improves," he says. We both know it won't.

"So what happens when the food runs out, Dad?" I ask.

"Let's not dwell on that, Chloe," he says. "God has sustained us for more than four years. We made it to the cabin just in time, we've avoided the Zone police, and we're all relatively healthy. With all the radiation in the air, one of us could have died of cancer by now, but we haven't. I don't think God would go to all the trouble of keeping us alive this long just to have us starve to death, do you?"

"You're right," I say.

"Hey, Dad, can we drop by the cabin on the way back?" I ask. "I want to see if there's anything we missed that they could use up at the cave." Dad agrees.

It takes us a bit longer than usual to hike back to the cabin. We move more slowly and move through cover rather than use game trails, knowing how dangerous it is now for Christians. We approach the cabin cautiously. As always, whenever we approach any structure, we have a twenty-minute rule. We watch the structure for twenty minutes to make sure there is no one inside before we approach. We settle down behind a large fallen tree about fifty yards from the cabin. I take the first watch.

"Dad, it's so strange to think that we'll be back here in just over two years," I say. "The entire planet will be a mess. Every tree and all of the grass will be burned up. All of the fish in the sea will be dead. Do you think we'll get to see the Battle of Armageddon?" I ask.

"I think we will, Chloe," he says. "I'm not sure if we actually fight in it with Jesus. But I'm pretty sure we'll see the battle.

After it's over, we'll watch as the angels separate the people who are still alive into two groups."

"That's the whole sheep-and-goat thing, right?" I ask. "Where those with Salam's mark get sent to Hell, and the others get to live here on the new Earth?"

"Exactly," Dad says.

"So, Dad, it's going to be really weird if Jackson makes it to the end, assuming he's not dead already. We might see him. I don't know what I'll say to him. I guess it depends on if he took the mark. Dad, if he did take the mark, I'll be so incredibly sad. I thought there wouldn't be any more sadness once we go to Heaven."

"I'm not sure if we'll see him, Chloe," Dad says. "And if we do, I'm not sure how we'll feel. We won't think the same as we do now once we get to Heaven. We'll fully understand God's justice and his fairness once we're in Heaven. My guess is that if seeing him with the mark will make us sad, then God will make sure we don't run into him when we come back. I don't know. It's just a guess."

Suddenly, my eye catches movement in the cabin.

"Dad, I saw something move in the cabin!"

Dad swings his rifle around and points it toward the back of the cabin.

"Maybe an animal has moved in," he says. "You were worried about our food supply. Maybe dinner's walking around inside our old cabin!"

Dad steadies the rifle on top of the log we are hiding behind. Our breathing is fast now. A shadow moves through the kitchen and toward the back door.

"Dad, it's a person" I whisper. "Don't shoot."

My heart is pounding now. The person steps out onto the back porch.

"It's Jackson!" I say much too loudly.

Just as I say these words, Jackson looks over in our direction. Without thinking, I jump to my feet and run toward him, stopping just a few feet in front of him. Jackson is so skinny that I hardly recognize him. Instinctively, I glance down at his hands to see if he has the mark, but he's wearing gloves. Our eyes meet. My whole body is shaking. Just as I'm about to speak, I hear the most beautiful sound, a trumpet! I'm immediately surrounded by the whitest light I've ever seen!

I'm in Heaven!

CPSIA information can be obtained
at www.ICGtesting.com
Printed in the USA
LVOW03s1212260417
532259LV00001B/98/P